SUNRISE NIGHTS

JEFF ZENTNER
and
BRITTANY CAVALLARO

SUNRISE NIGHTS

Quill Tree Books
An Imprint of HarperCollinsPublishers

Quill Tree Books is an imprint of HarperCollins Publishers.

Sunrise Nights

Library of Congress Control Number: 2023943580
ISBN 978-0-06-332453-4

Typography by Laura Mock
24 25 26 27 28 LBC 5 4 3 2 1
First Edition

For Tennessee Luke Zentner.
May you find who you can't be without.
—J.Z.

For Andrew.
But you knew that already, didn't you.
—B.C.

NIGHT
ONE

JUDE
HOLINESS

Here's a truth about me: left to its own devices
my mind treats me badly. Sometimes

(okay, a lot of times) a thought gets stuck
like a twig in a river eddy, never quite making it
to freedom or even ruin, which I'd prefer
to the chaotic spinning.

Sometimes it's a shapeless feeling that looms
over me like constantly dwelling
in the terrible space between knowing
you're falling

and then falling. I think: *What if I'm never*
enough? What if I'm wasting my life?
What if no one loves me? What if
I'm not good? What if this is
all there is? You know. The normal stuff,
being the architect
of my own undoing. But then

I pick up my camera and the vortex
stops. And so does the sense of falling.
And for a moment, everything
is still and I can hear the world speaking
to me over me.

FLORENCE
THAT JUNE

I was good. I was better than good,
I moved in a way to make water
jealous. I had strong hips. I could crack open

walnuts between my calves if I wanted.
I did want to. I wanted someone
to dare me. I wanted to eat it all up,

the hot lights, the marley floor, someone
lofting me like a hawk on a glove,
and when the advanced class wasn't enough

I took private lessons. My parents paid,
we had the money, and anyway
a few years from now I'd be benched forever.

Why not? I wanted to burn through the sky
like something to make your eyes hurt
from looking at it too close, like something

that was born to disappear. I wanted
hard-ass teachers, the meanest competition,
and when I came to Harbor Arts that June

I wanted someone to look my tendu up and down

day one and say, *not nearly good enough.*
I wanted my feet to bleed. Fine, it was camp,

but I didn't want bonfires or sing-alongs
or bunkmate truth-or-dare. I didn't want
friendship, or pity about my failing vision,

or the other dancers to think I wasn't
their top competition. Because I would be
until the bitter end. I wanted the truth

about my body, the limits of what I could
make it do. I wanted the solo
in the Imogen Heap piece, and when

I got it I wanted to dance it to make
people cry, and when I got that
it was the night before the last night of camp and

sweating delicately on that stage I looked up
and saw that the standing ovation came
from four hundred people who owed me nothing.

JUDE
THE GOOD FIGHT

I read once that ancient people sometimes died
of fear during a solar eclipse, thinking
that some Great Devourer, too vast

to see, the size of heaven itself, was consuming
light itself into its belly. My photography teacher
at Harbor Arts Camp talked about these people,
how they painted on the walls of caves, trying to capture

the fleeting image of what they held dearest, frozen
like an insect in amber. *They'd be so jealous,*
she said, *of what we have.* How we can point a lens,
press a button, and capture a congregation

of birds, black as inkblots in the soaring white
of the sky, exactly as they appear on
our retinas, and if you're lucky

even better. If you're lucky, the way
your brain turns them into memory. Safe
from the Great Devourer.

I'm alone in Chapman Hall,
my fellow HACkers (Harbor Arts Campers; we have fun here)
gone to Bonfire, the orange glow already illuminating

the late June Michigan Upper Peninsula dusk,
and I'll join them soon
enough, even though I'd really rather stay

here, letting my ears lap up the quiet,
the photos of my thesis exhibition arrayed before me
like ranks of unspeaking soldiers, and I, their general,
thanking them for their victory over me.

FLORENCE
GOODBYES AND WHATEVER

Two curtain calls, then a third. Dr. Rojas ushers
me forward, center stage, and as I dip into a curtsy
I can feel the scrape of the other girls' eyes

behind me. None of them would want my place
if they knew. Good thing they don't. In the hall
outside the dressing room Rojas purses her lips,

pulls me aside. *Juilliard scouts tonight*, she says,
BoCo, ABT, and I say, *don't you remember
that I'm a sophomore?* Which is easier

than *this here's my last rodeo, partner.* Second
to last? Well, nystagmus doesn't get worse
on any set schedule—plus if I've learned anything

these last few years it's that teachers don't read
our health forms. Back in warm-ups but I leave
my arms bare in my unitard, and I'm out

the stage door before I'm reminded that no one's
waiting for me with flowers. Bonfire tonight.
Capital B. Camp tradition, or so say

my bunkmates. They're not dancers, so they don't

hate me. I asked why it was special and Makayla said,
dude, we roast marshmallows and pick out someone

for Sunrise Night, another tradition that needed
explaining. Sammy made some really amazing
disgusting hand motions to illustrate. They said,

find us at Bonfire, and so I'm taking the path
through the woods, watching my feet
as always. I couldn't tell you the kind of trees

in this forest, the insect things singing high-pitched
around me. I like it all fine, but it's ephemera.
It's additives. It's irrelevant for what's coming

for me, just like the rest of the world is. Like,
I like it all fine, but none of it knows my name.

JUDE
BONFIRE

My heart crackles, on fire,
as I approach the crowd milling around
Bonfire, and not in the way
your heart sometimes glows
in joyous anticipation of something
that will nourish it. More in the way

of something being consumed
by a force that does
what it will, that resists
your control, that makes less
what it touches. There's probably something

you can take to dull
the edge of this feeling, but I'm scared
of dulling other edges

that I need sharp, that let me cut
a path through this world.
The funny thing is that I love
people. In fact, I think I love them more

than is normal—in fact, I'm afraid
sometimes of how much I love
them and then that's one more thing
to worry about. At Bonfire,

the older HACkers assemble
in their cliques, reliving years past
with raucous laughter,
while the younger HACkers like me, unmoored
from history, drift aimlessly, looking

for some salvation in a familiar face.
I make small talk with a couple kids
from my photography cohort.
We weren't close. Photography isn't a team
sport. Also I hate small talk.

Then I see her, alone and silhouetted
against orange, like she's the dark
part of the flame. One of my favorite things

to photograph is people intentionally doing
what others do only by accident
and the clear determination
of her aloneness makes my hands itch

for my camera, which I didn't bring
because I was afraid
it would be like wearing the band's T-shirt
to the concert.

Obviously I have my phone, which takes
decent enough photos, but then there are still the complicated
ethics of taking a stranger's picture without their permission

(which I learned about two days ago)
and then there's—
and also there's—
and of course there's—

but it's perfect.

I take the photo.

JUDE
THE GIRL

The image: she sits close to the fire (maybe too close)
holding a marshmallow roasting stick like a sword.
Her face is shadowed in the light.
A shower of sparks rises behind her
head like she's shaken them from her hair.

She's the only thing in focus
and everything is blurry and dark behind her.

There's something in her gaze;
she looks at the fire like she wants
to be it.

JUDE
BONFIRE, 8:17 P.M.

"Hey, sorry," I say. "Not to be a weirdo, but—"

"*Not to be a weirdo* is always a promising start," the girl says, but smiling.

"Yeah. I know. I—"

"Go ahead. Be a weirdo."

"So I'm a photographer and I took a photo of you a minute ago and I wanted to make sure it was cool. If not, I'll totally delete."

"That's somewhat less creepy than I was expecting."

"I don't even wanna know. I can show you."

"I'm good."

"You sure?"

"I mean, maybe don't do weirdo stuff with it."

"I won't do— Hey, marshmallow's burning," I say.

"Oh yeah?" the girl says. "How'd you know?"

"It was the fact that it was on fire that clued me in."

"Good eye," the girl says, with a glint like she's remembering a dirty joke.

"Now your line is: *I prefer burnt marshmallows.*"

"I do."

"That's what people who burn marshmallows say to hide their shame."

"I like what I like."

"You'd prefer a nice, golden-brown one."

"You don't know me."

"I don't, yeah. But. May I? No, I have a stick. Here. Now you're just gonna—"

"Okay, you're gonna burn it too."

"No, I'm not, watch."

"I'm watching," the girl says.

"Sorry, I'm not meaning to marshmallowsplain or whatever."

"I still think you're gonna burn it."

"You sound awfully worried for someone who claims to prefer burnt marshmallows. Promise I'm not. I used to spend summers at scout camp instead of HAC."

"You earn your marshmallow roasting badge or whatever?"

"Wait until you taste this. Just a little longer on this side. Okay. Now hold on. Give it a sec."

"Okay, I'm gonna—"

"Don't eat it yet. You'll burn yourself."

"No I won't."

"Lemme guess: you like burning yourself too."

"I'm a dancer. Pain is, like, my life." She bites into the marshmallow and gasps. "*Shit.*"

"Warned you."

"No, the temperature's fine. I just don't want marshmallow all over my chin. Like I hooked up with the Stay Puft guy from *Ghostbusters.*"

"I watched that with my dad for the first time just last year."

"So if I'd made this joke a year earlier—"

"Completely lost on me."

"Nice timing, huh?"

"Great."

"So, this is good," the girl says, and bites into the marshmallow again.

"What'd I say? Better than burnt?" I cup a hand to my ear.

"What? What's that? Come again? I can't hear you."

"I very audibly said *yes*," the girl says. "Fine. You win, Marshmallow Expert Guy."

"Aka Jude Wheeler. I never caught your name," I say.

FLORENCE
FIRST IMPRESSIONS

It's probably the first thing you want me to tell you
since he's a boy and I'm (as far as I know)
straight. So I don't know, sort of Timothée Chalamet?

(I reserve the right to change that comparison
if Chalamet ever turns out to be gross.) He has
that longish nineties hair, but so do lots of boys here

and most of them can't pull it off. Maybe this one
does, but I'm not sure yet. Firelight
can lie, dress everyone up in shadow, darken

up the edges like film. I don't want to see the picture
he's taken of me. My eyes don't line up—you can only see it
when I'm still—and also then I'd have to admit

that I care about that. That I care that he's flopped down
next to me on this log, roasting me another marshmallow
like a dare. Dancers don't eat marshmallows, but how long

am I a dancer for?

It's these anxious thoughts that make me
alone. It's the fear that I don't want to be. Jude asks me

all casual, *hey, so what is there to do in Harbor City*
on something like a Sunrise Night? and across the fire
Makayla has lifted her eyebrows straight up into her hair,

and I take all three marshmallows off the end
of the stick and say, *I don't know, everything.*

JUDE
EVERYTHING TO DO

She says her name is Florence.
It's one of those names where you wonder
for a second if someone is messing with you
because it seems like only British celebs are named
that, so you study
her face for a second or two
longer than you otherwise would, searching

for some hint of a joke. She doesn't meet my eyes.
I blessedly resist the urge to ask, *the Machine*
couldn't make it tonight? Something tells me
she's heard it before and besides I think it's healthy
to suppress my inclination to make dumb
jokes when I'm nervous. Instead I think

of the Italian city of Florence
which I've never seen. That's not to say that I haven't
been there. I have. But I'm told I only saw
a whole lot of the inside

of my mom's uterus. This was, of course,
when things were better between my parents
and they did things together like go
to the Italian city of Florence and become
pregnant with a son.

It's gotten me thinking about cities
and actually seeing cities instead of staring at the wall
of a uterus—and an alien, marshmallow-drunken boldness
passes over me, the same feeling of impending opportunity

as when I see a chance for a good photo
and so I ask: *hey, so what is there to do*
in Harbor City on something like a Sunrise Night?
I hope she takes the *something like a Sunrise Night*
to be a knowing mockery
of a clumsy attempt
at self-conscious casualness
when in fact it's precisely such an attempt
and part of me hopes she won't take the bait,

so I'm a little glad when she responds
with a noncommittal *I don't know, everything,*
and then eats three marshmallows like she's beyond
caring about whether it looks like she hooked up
with the Stay Puft guy and instead
wants to look like she hooked up with him, regretted it,
then immediately did it again.

And now I hope she does
take the bait. Because there's something I admire
about such naked hunger.

And also because I bet two people
who each love to be alone can have
a great time together.

JUDE
BONFIRE, 8:34 P.M.

"Are you—" I start to ask, but Florence speaks simultaneously.

"Sorry," I say. "Go ahead."

"No, you go," she says.

"Were you gonna—"

"No, it's fine, go."

"Are you hanging here tonight?"

"I dunno."

"Because if we're both just—"

"Big losers who no one likes?" she asks.

"I was gonna say *hanging out alone.*"

"Because we're big losers who no one likes so we're hanging out alone?"

"You're saying it, not me," I tell her.

"I'm messing with you."

"You've been so busy messing with me that you never answered my question."

"Which was?"

"You wanna hang out?"

"I'd remember if you asked that."

"I'm asking now," I say.

FLORENCE
PLANS

Sunrise Night: when they uncollar us and let us roam
out into the world until dawn, when the cars pull up
to take us home. Harbor City's not much of a city

but for one night it's ours. I was just going to lock myself
in the studio, do some stretching, but this boy is looking at me
like a dare—like he's daring himself or maybe me

and what are the terms anyway? *There's a barcade,*
he says, *not that I drink. Not that they'd let me
drink. But there's an arcade and I heard they have*

that zombie-killing game—
               I kill, I tell him,
at the zombie-killing game. And now we're off

to the races. We put together hearsay with what we can find
on our phones. Jude says, *well, there's a swimming hole*
in the voice of someone who's a connoisseur

of swimming holes and I think about a little pond, mist
edging it, me in a swimsuit. Romantic. Too bad
I don't want romantic. I say, *Target, there's*

a Target, just to see if he calls me basic, but he smiles

a little and says, *I love Target. I'm not a monster.* Game on.
Scrolling my phone, I say, *pizzeria.* He says,

*there's an anarchist coffeehouse where we could play
chess,* and I say, *we?* because I can't help it,
because I challenge everyone always and it's good

if he knows that up front—and since when
are *we* spending Sunrise Night together? But then he says
with a sense of real gravity, with a look

in his eyes I can only call haunted, *I hear
there's an all-night donut shop,* and I can't help it
(I never can), when I start laughing

it bursts out of me, and just like that it's checkmate.

JUDE
WHAT YOU EXPECT

This is the sort of thing that only happens
in movies, I think
as the din and heat of Bonfire subsides at our backs,

as we walk into the summer-cool night
of possibility; *two strangers meeting*
and embarking on some grand adventure

with the ease of two eleven-year-olds becoming
friends instantly over a shared love
of Spider-Man and pizza. I told myself

I wanted to be alone
tonight but only now I'm realizing
I wanted nothing less. Maybe

our bodies produce a chemical
that only allows us to feel the full extent
of loneliness in retrospect, like gazing

at a sad photograph. I look
at Florence for some hint
of how she's feeling about all this

and our eyes meet and we both smile

like we're pulling a prank,
which I guess we are, but on ourselves.

Isn't a prank just a violation of what you expect?
Ring the doorbell; there's no one there.
Wake up; your yard is adorned

in toilet paper. That flaming bag
on your front porch that you frantically stomp
out? Surprise! It's full of poop!

We arrive
at the hill that bottoms out
in the road that runs past campus

and as we start
to descend, Florence grips my arm—
not necessarily in a romantic way—

more like she's trying
to keep from drowning.
But lots of times you can't
tell the difference.

JUDE
WALKING GINGERLY DOWN A LARGE HILL IN THE GATHERING DARK, 8:44 P.M.

"Uh so," I say.

"Calm down, dude," Florence says. "I'm not trying to hook up with you."

"I didn't think—"

"You tensed up."

"I just, you know—have a girlfriend." I say it in a way where the only possible response is an overly long, awkward pause, which is exactly what happens.

"And I applaud you for it. The fact that there's a girl who can stand you bodes well."

"Who said she could stand me."

"Fair enough. You gonna be weird about hanging out?"

"No."

"Is your girlfriend—what's her name?"

"Marley."

"As in the floor."

"Huh?" I eye Florence quizzically.

"Marley floors are a type of vinyl floor in dance studios. Kinda springy."

"Okay, so that would be the very first time in my life I've ever heard of a marley floor and also the first time in my life someone's gone with something other than *as in Bob* when I've told them my girlfriend's name."

"What I hear you saying is that you're already having an

extremely exciting and rewarding Sunrise Night," Florence says.

"Yep."

"Is Marley gonna be weird about it? I don't wanna get you in trouble."

"She knows I hang out with friends at camp. Who are sometimes girls."

"But you don't, actually," Florence says. "From the look of it."

"Theoretically. But yeah no. Not really. What about you? Boyfriend?"

"Huge. MMA fighter. He finds out we're hanging out tonight, you're dead."

I laugh nervously.

"What?" she says.

"Wait, you serious?"

"He's gonna pull off one of your femurs and beat you senseless with it while you try to balance on one leg."

I continue scrutinizing Florence's face for some hint of jest. She's stone-faced.

"No, I'm not serious," she says. "Or . . . *am I?* No. Yes?!"

"I'm gonna make you sign something. Like making you responsible if I'm murdered by fist."

"No boyfriend. You won't die that way. Or at least not at the hands of my nonexistent boyfriend."

"You're a good liar."

"Thanks. So, bear with me, I have a spiel to give you."

FLORENCE
THINGS YOU DON'T TALK ABOUT

That's the title of my memoir. *Florence Bankhead:*
Kind of Surly. I wasn't always
this way. Nobody is, really. You aren't born

with your lip buttoned shut. You have to be made
like that. It doesn't have to be trauma
or whatever—it can just be you learning

the way your world needs you to be. Mine needs me
to be tough. If it wanted me gentle, it would've given me
20/20 vision and a mom who doesn't get choked up

every time she watches me take out the trash. Because
someday soon maybe I won't be able to do it.
Like my life to her is a series of warning signs,

some music cue shivering in the soundtrack
every time I reach for a doorknob and
miss. An ending buried in everything I do.

It could make you lose your mind
or it can make you kind of a bitch.
I can track it back: me, age twelve,

dumping Jacob Olsen on the blacktop after I watched him

raise his foot and squish a spider (like really casually,
like a killer in training), and then in retaliation

his best friend Kaden told everyone I was a freak
because I had zombie eyes. *They're, like, dead,
they don't work, but they move on their own—*

cue people looking at my nose when they talked
to me. So yeah, you bet I ordered a shirt that said
"My Eyes Are Up Here, Asshole"

and wore it over my flat chest. Or, I don't know,
third grade, January, me home for weeks
wearing sunglasses inside, and behind them

the whites of both my eyes were bright red
from another surgery. Talk about
the walking dead. The way my mom watched me,

it was like I was a reminder of some failure
of hers, not a mostly normal blond girl
with two pairs of ballet shoes, watching videos

of Misty Copeland on the couch. Not a ten-year-old
who loved her cockapoo Lucky and playing soccer
with her dad in the yard, who had a freckle

on her big toe and double-jointed elbows

and also a weird thing where her eyes shook uncontrollably
when she was tired or stressed or alone.

Who sometimes saw haloes around lights
when there weren't any angels around. Who looked
down a flight of stairs and saw a drawing

of a flight of stairs, who looked at a hill in the dark
and felt vertigo. Who looked at a spotlight
on a stage and decided to grand jeté into it

anyway. Who was brave enough six years later
to take a boy's arm on a warm night in June
and tell him everything, except maybe the part

where she was surprised at how good it felt
to press up against him for a few moments
in a dark so complete she couldn't see anything.

FLORENCE
QUICK CONFESSIONS ON THE WAY INTO HARBOR CITY, 8:48 P.M.

"So," I say. "I have issues."

"Issues?"

"Not, like, serial killer issues. I don't kill spiders for fun."

"Spiders are very helpful. They keep your house bug-free."

"*Thank you.* Anyway, no, it's like—okay, I have depth-perception issues."

"Okay."

"Okay?"

"That's not a big thing, is it?"

"I mean it's not. On its own. But that's why I grabbed your arm. I have . . . a smorgasbord of eye issues."

"That's kind of a gross visual."

"Right? Like, sandwiches made of eyes?"

"Between little slices of bread."

"I'm trying to tell you something," I say. "I'm not doing it super well. Basically, I have nystagmus—my eyes shake uncontrollably sometimes. More often now. I have a bunch of other things. But sometimes I just . . ."

"Need an arm?"

"Yeah. And I need to not talk about it a bunch because it's a total bummer. My dance friends don't even know, but I wanted to tell you I wasn't, like—hitting on you."

"Your dance friends don't know?"

"Yeah. I don't like to show my belly like that."

"So in this metaphor you're a dog."

"Yep."

"A dancing dog."

"Jude," I say, laughing. "Thank you, yes, a dancing dog."

"See? I can take direction. No bummer eyesight talk. Just dog talk."

"Cool."

"Cool. So, is that it? Not that it's not a big deal, but are there other things I should know?"

"No," I lie. "Nothing. That's the whole story."

JUDE
THE COLD AND DARK

Of course I want to know
more. I have a perverse impulse
to confront the things
that terrify me.

When I was little, my parents gave me a book
with a richly detailed illustration (almost photo-real)
of a squid, the outraged crimson of a wound, fighting
a midnight-colored whale, deep in the ocean—
a clash no human has ever seen. And the specter
of battling for life with some boneless, alien,
tentacled monster with wide, unseeing eyes
in the cold and dark made my blood
run cold and dark. I hid

the book under my mattress, so I wouldn't
be tempted, but I wanted to stare
into the sun.

The less I tried
to think about it the more
I did.

Photography is all I have,
the only time I feel
completely in control.

Just the thought of losing it, of going
to look through a lens and having to wait
for my eye to stop involuntarily trembling,
wondering if this would be the time
it never stopped.

And so now my brain is, naturally,
willfully descending into the abyss,
to wrestle the many-armed beast, the one
always trying to pull me
deeper.

JUDE
ENTERING THE HUMMING METROPOLIS OF HARBOR CITY, MICHIGAN, POP. 15,368, 9:01 P.M.

"You okay?" Florence asks.

"Yeah," I say. "Just remembering something. Where to first?"

"Lead on," Florence says. "I haven't been to Harbor City."

"At all?"

"I mean, driving through to get to HAC, but."

"Your program—by the way, what is your program?"

"Dance. Modern, specifically."

"That's why you go to *marley floor* before *Bob Marley*."

"Bingo."

"Also why Bonfire was the first time I ever saw you at camp."

"Yeah, dance is its own thing. It's intense. Lots of practice, and then the warm-up and the cool-down time. They keep us pretty separate from the other tracks at HAC."

"You seem like a dancer."

"People say that. I think it's because they don't know what else to say. I never know what they mean."

"I just meant you move sorta . . . gracefully? You walk like a cat." She laughs. "A cat?!"

"That's a compliment, right? People wanna have catlike reflexes and stuff. That's a thing."

"That *is* a thing. People wanting catlike reflexes."

"If someone offered to give you catlike reflexes, you wouldn't say no."

"I would not say no to some catlike reflexes, you're right."

"So yeah. I'm not saying you bathe by licking yourself or poop in a box."

"You don't *know* that I *don't* do those things," Florence says.

"There I go assuming. So, I was saying, before we got off on this tangent—"

"This wasn't the point? To discuss the desire for catlike reflexes?"

"No, I was gonna say, didn't your program come into town for stuff?"

"Like what? So we could dance on the courthouse steps?"

"Or even just to, like, eat. I dunno."

"You ever been in a dance program?"

"Why, do I move like a cat?"

"Well, eating isn't a huge part of it, unfortunately."

"You hungry now?" I ask.

"Always," Florence says.

"Should we go eat first?"

"I'm into that. Let's see what's around here." Florence looks at her phone. "You vegetarian or vegan or anything?"

"No. Nothing against vegetarians or vegans if you are."

"Nope. Marshmallows have gelatin or something vegans can't eat."

"You definitely eat marshmallows."

"My point exactly," Florence says. "So Google Maps is telling me there's this pizza place like .3 miles from here. Pietown, it's called."

"It stresses me out when people call pizzas *pies*."

"Oh same. But this place gets good reviews."

"Like?"

"Says it's popular with college students. Okay, here's *Best place* to go in Harbor City after smoking a late-night bowl. Here's *You have to try the tavern-style pizza.*"

"What's tavern-style pizza?" I ask.

"It's good. It's a Chicago thing."

"Like deep dish?"

"No, that's tourist garbage."

"I think pizza's pretty hard to screw up. Even bad pizza is good."

"Well."

"Okay, fair. I guess I've had bad pizza. You from Chicago?"

"Madison, Wisconsin," Florence says. "But I've spent a lot of time there."

"Never been."

"It's amazing. It's like a slightly smaller and friendlier New York City."

"Never been there either."

"Where *have* you been?"

"Atlanta. Louisville. Orlando. Nashville a bunch of times. I live right outside Nashville, in Dickson, Tennessee."

"Never heard of it."

"No reason for you to."

"You don't really have a Southern accent," Florence says.

"It comes out when I'm back home. I hide it a little here. You don't have an accent either."

"Not so much. I pretty consciously try to keep it from creeping in. I don't love the Wisconsin accent, honestly. GPS is telling me . . . we go—hang on—no, this way."

We start walking.

"So you never said what program you're in. But I think I can guess."

"Let's hear it," I say.

"Photography."

"Excellent guess."

"As in I nailed it?"

"Nailed it."

"Eh, wasn't hard," Florence says.

"No."

"What's it like being a photographer?"

"You know. It's cool. I get to eat."

"It's cool and you get to eat."

"Yeah, I mean, there's more to it than that. We get to come into town on little field trips to photograph stuff. We learn how to use a darkroom and film. We—"

Florence cuts me off. "Tell me why you love it. Why you spend a month out of the summer that you could be gaming with your friends to come to HAC."

I think for a while. I'm ready to share pizza with her but maybe not to share the ways I'm broken.

"Hmm. When I was little my parents gave me my dad's old Android phone. It had a crap camera, but that was my favorite part about it. I played some games on it, but mostly I'd go around taking pictures of stuff. I'd try to set up my Lego guys in little scenes. Then I moved on to nature photography. When I was twelve my parents got me a decent DSLR camera. I kept taking photos. Started getting into portraits. They're actually still my favorite to do. I like photographing people in nature. Just . . . being joyous or whatever. I sound dumb. I'm not used to talking about it. No one's ever asked like you did."

"Show me."

"My photos?"

"Yeah."

"Okay," I murmur as I pull up a gallery on my phone. I hold it up to her.

"Can I?" she asks, and takes my phone. "If I scroll I'm not gonna hit any dick pics, am I?"

"No."

"No topless Marley?"

"No . . . she's pretty Christian. She's at church camp now."

"Otherwise?"

"Otherwise what?"

"Would you have nudes?"

"Still no. Not my thing."

"You're not always trying to take naked pics of her?"

"Like I said. Not what I'm about."

"Lots of photographers are pervs."

"I know. Not me."

"Good," Florence says. "Hang on, we gotta stop walking while I—"

JUDE
IN A NEW LIGHT

She scrolls through my photos, holding
the phone at a tilt, adjusting the angle
every so often like she's trying
to signal with a mirror.

Sometimes she makes
a small noise—a sort of murmur—at seeing
one. She finishes and hands me back
my phone and looks me straight
in the eyes for the first time
since we met. *These are good,*
she says. *Really good.*

I like the forthright surprise in her voice because
it tells me she isn't lying.

I don't know how to explain it. It just makes me
feel less hungry somehow. I don't know
if that makes sense.

Yeah, she says. *It does. And speaking of, let's walk.*

I keep in my mind a chronicle
of light and there's none
I love like the new light.

FLORENCE
THE PRESENT

I do this thing where I'm not really
where I am. There's a psych term for it,
I know—there's one for everything—

but while my mouth is telling
my mom about geometry class or
while I'm asking Alma, the dance studio

receptionist, if she crocheted
her new scarf herself (she always has
but I pretend to forget; she's

sixty-eight, I humor her, sue me)—
the rest of me is in the future. Not like
five years from now, my possible

guide-dog future, slipping
a tin can lid into a pot of water
so I can hear when it's come to a boil,

but like next week. I like the plan
more than the execution
of the plan. I like the thought

of the pizza more than the pizza

itself. Like, what's the story of this night
gonna be when my stories change

completely? I want to have good ones.
I want to be able to say, look,
I went out there and did that, I took

a strange boy to Pietown and told him
at least some of my secrets. To say,
we got a medium pepperoni

tavern *pie* (shudder) and I put
all the little triangle slices, *one two three
four five six seven eight,* into a tower

on the table and then ate them
like a huge disgusting sandwich. That
I didn't let him have a single one, but he still

laughed helplessly with his hand over his eyes
in the booth across from me, he knocked
the parmesan shaker sideways onto the table

and the waitress gave us both a *screw you*
stink eye and I didn't know where
we were going next, I didn't care. I was

here I was here I was here.

JUDE
PIZZA TRIPTYCH

Panel I
My parents took me to a pizza place like
this one and there they announced,
in faltering words, that most things end
even if they were beautiful at their beginning

and so it was with their marriage,
thankfully sparing me
the part where it wasn't my fault,
which wouldn't have even occurred to me unless
they had absolved me without my requesting it.

This was late this spring and the streets
in downtown Dickson were damp
from new rain, the air humid
with the perfume of new blossoms,
making part of me wonder if
they appreciated the irony
of their announcing a death
during the season of birth

because I sure didn't.
I took in the news while I stared
into my red plastic cup,
(where do pizza places get those cups and why

is no one else allowed to own them?)
at the Dr Pepper bubbles, clinging
to the sides, trying desperately
to keep from falling upward
to their doom, and I thought, *I get it.*

Panel II

Sitting with Marley, at the same pizza place
(it's Dickson, there aren't that many choices),
and she abruptly asks me, out of the clear blue, if I've accepted
Jesus in my heart as my Lord and Savior
        (it's Tennessee, it's a more normal question
over sausage and Canadian bacon pizza than you'd expect)
I guess she'd been taking for granted all this time
that I had. And I laugh because the only honest answer
coming to mind is *I haven't* not *accepted Jesus
as my Lord and Savior* and I envision offering
that to the keeper of the gates of Heaven.

And she gives me that *look*, the one
that makes me wish our relationship
was a little bit (by which, I mean a lot) easier, and says,
not everyone would laugh at that question. Which really means
Peyton wouldn't have laughed. Peyton being,
of course, the absolute worst, two years older than us,
handsome like a newly waxed Range Rover, a cool-youth-
pastor-in-embryo who has a YouTube channel
on which he does "Christian social experiments"

which suck even worse than you think.

(SPOILER ALERT: they *never* involve acts of generosity
or compassion.)

So get with that hypothetical person or persons, I say, not really
meaning it but wanting to see how she responds,
and she says, *I love you, that's why I'm worried
about your soul.* But all I hear is *I love you.*

Panel III
I look across the table at Florence, who's laughing
at something I just said, her shaggy blond hair
covering her eyes, making me wonder
if she wears it like that on purpose.
Who do you look like? I ask.
 She tells me her mom's friend Grace
(which she says as though I'll be like, *oh sure, classic Grace*)
always says she looks like young Stevie Nicks,
who I have to Google on the spot and in so doing
learn that this is a great person to resemble. *Do you
agree?* I ask. *I don't look like anyone
famous*, she says with quiet finality.
Well, I agree with Grace, I say,
and Florence smiles.
I mean, when has Grace ever been wrong? I say,
and Florence smiles wider. *Plenty.*
But all I can think about is how much more fun
I'm having this time, watching the bubbles

of my Dr Pepper through the side
of the clear red plastic cup, rising
as if to freedom, bursting
as if with joy.

FLORENCE
SEVENTEEN DOLLARS AND FOUR DR PEPPERS LATER, ON THE STREET WITH THREE NOVELTY T-SHIRT STORES, 10:17 P.M.

"You're bouncing a little."

"I don't think I've ever been this caffeinated," he says. "Like I'm pretty sure I can hear colors right now."

"What does red sound like?"

He smiles, caught out. "Like static, maybe."

"I'd think it would sound like a scream."

"See, you're doing the whole *red equals angry* thing. Don't know if I buy that. Maybe it sounds like a heartbeat."

"Because hearts are red?"

"And ugly. Have you ever seen one beating? Like a video from doctors doing surgery? It looks like a weird wet pit."

"You're really selling me on the idea of love."

"Love isn't in the heart," he says, with confidence. "It's in your chest, maybe. In your gut. But your heart just keeps time as you walk around."

"That, and it moves your blood," I say. "It lets you think."

"You've had too much Dr Pepper too."

"I mean, the pizza was salty. The soda was sweet. All of it was, like, endless empty calories, and if I tried to dance now I'd just, like, burp and fall over. I'm made of gas. I'm a gas planet."

"What does a gas planet sound like?"

"Like a fart, probably."

"Try it," he says, stopping. "I don't know where we're walking to anyway. Do a—"

"*Fart?*"

"No! A dance!"

"A dance? You want me to do a dance for you?"

"All the words are French! I take Spanish."

I look around and then I do a quick fouetté.

Jude applauds. "Are you trying not to burp?"

"I'm always trying not to burp," I say, and I'm giddy. "Where are we going? Straight to the donut shop? I don't hate the idea of a donut shop. I can walk to one from my house. Is your town the kind that you can walk around?"

JUDE
WALKING THE STREETS OF DOWNTOWN
HARBOR CITY, HEADING WITH NO PARTICULAR
URGENCY TO AN ALL-NIGHT DONUT SHOP,
10:22 P.M.

"Sure," I say. "But people aren't big on walking. It's the South."

"Do you?"

"Yeah. You have to walk to notice things. You only see the best stuff when you're moving slowly."

"What's the best stuff? Like a plastic bag dancing on the wind? Shadows on a brick wall?" Florence says it flippantly.

I let a few moments pass and look at her. "You mocking me, or—"

"I hit a nerve?"

"No."

"No?"

"I mean, a little. Here I barely know you and you're going in on the thing I love most."

"Hmm. I wonder if the fact that you barely know me also makes you really bad at reading my tone," she says.

"Maybe I wouldn't have to be, like, a fortune teller of tone if you just generally said things that were unambiguously unshitty."

"Maybe you're really fragile."

"Hmm. I wonder if the fact that you barely know me also makes you really bad at knowing who I am," I tell her.

"Just my impression."

"That sucks, you know? Make fun of something important to me and then put it on me."

"Come on," she says.

"Do you not have things that are sacred ground for you? That hurt no matter what?" I almost say, *like your eyes*. I wouldn't have meant it in a mean way but we seem to be misreading each other.

"I told you I wasn't crapping on your art."

"You did?"

"Yep."

"Musta missed it. Can I ask you something?" I say.

"Shoot."

"Why did you wanna hang tonight? Is it because some third-year HACker told you it was your sacred duty or whatever to not spend Sunrise Night alone and when I came up to you, I was an easy target, because I didn't know you?"

Florence laughs a little. "One: there's the word *sacred* again. I'm not big on sacred duties or ground or sacred anything. I think sacred things are a luxury only a few people can afford. So that's something you should know right off the bat. Two: *wow*."

"Look. I didn't mean—"

"That I'm a piece of shit liked by no one who really knows me?"

"That. Yeah."

"Guess what? Wouldn't really care if I were. My *wow* was for your nerve in saying it to my face after knowing me for like two hours."

"I wasn't saying it to your face. Or at all."

"Don't backtrack. It made me respect you more."

I smile. "So at least there's one thing about me you respect."

"You have the worst memory on earth. I told you your photos were good."

"Okay. Fine. Let's just reset, okay? Go back to having fun? I don't wanna spend Sunrise Night fighting with someone I just met."

We walk for a little while longer. "Hey, Jude," Florence says. "Do you hate it when people say that, by the way?"

"Kinda but I'm used to it."

"Don't make it bad."

"Eat a bowl of diarrhea. With milk. And raisins." I smile against my will.

"*Raisins?* Harsh. So when we get to the donut shop, buy you a donut?"

"Won't say no to that."

"The catch is I choose. And you have to eat whatever I pick."

"Fine."

"I'm serious."

"Okay."

We walk some more.

"Hey, Florence?"

"Yeah."

"I still think you're cool."

"Even though I roasted you?"

"Even then," I say. And her face lets slip that she's happy.

FLORENCE
PEACE, LOVE, AND LITTLE DONUTS

I open the donut shop door and the bell jingles
like an apology. Hot sugar in the air, classic rock
on the radio, a case of made-to-order minis

laid out before us like a banquet: Coconut Cream
Pie and Cereal Explosion, Banana Split with two whole
cherries on top and a guy in a tie-dyed shirt easing

some fresh ones into the case. He props up
a little sign that says "Snick Jagger" and "Shaka Pecan." *Groovy*,
I tell him, *two thumbs-up*. He's cute, college-aged,

though his puberty mustache is killing the vibe. Still
he smiles at me, and Jude gives me a look, because
I'm being nice (I guess?) to another guy, because

I haven't said *sorry*, and for the record, I won't.
For the record, I hate this shit. The *I take myself
seriously* shit, the *my art is sacred* shit, I don't have time

to stare at myself in the mirror every midnight, crying
because maybe I won't be canonized. Duh, take
your art seriously—late nights in the studio, up at five a.m.

to read or stretch or do the darkroom thing—but do it

because you love it. Not because it's everything
you are. If I was only a dancer, if it were "holy"

to me, then I better just start hating myself now
before the stress gets to me and the nystagmus cuts
my balance and I'm foreign to myself for good. So my plan B

is my plan A, which is to say, I better love a lot
of other things about myself, and in the meantime
if I can't make a tortured artist joke to a boy

without his ego deflating, then I want
out. And now he's *looking* at me again,
with those eyes like he knows what I'm thinking

and he already forgives me for it, and I hate that pity
more than anything, more than the feeling
like maybe I'm gonna cry, and so I shove ten bucks

at the dork serving donuts and say, *pick your favorites,
I don't care*, and if Jude is mad that I'm storming off
(to go cry in the bathroom) he can just forgive me for that too.

FLORENCE
ON THE FLOOR OF THE ONLY RESTROOM IN THE
HIPPIE DONUT SHOP, WHICH YOU HAVE TO GO
THROUGH THE KITCHEN TO GET TO, 10:42 P.M.

"No," I say when Jude comes in. I try really hard to stop crying but I can't.

"No?"

"No, you don't need to do this, I'll be okay soon and we can just go back to HAC. We have to check in soon anyway and I'm sure there are other people there who are actually able to have fun who you can go back out with. People who aren't like all mean and spiny. *Normal* people, not like me."

"You aren't normal?"

"I'm, like, barely a person. I'm like one of those poisonous spiny-ass fish. Lionfish or whatever. Nobody likes a spiny-ass fish."

"I hear they're delicious."

Both of us hear how that sounds after he says it.

"I mean, ew, not in that way. I meant I'd like to keep one as a pet? No. Oh God no. I take that back too. They're—pretty. Spiny-ass fish are pretty."

"No they're ugly and mean and they're no fun." God I wish I could just stop crying.

"You don't have to be fun. And I can hang out here, if that's cool with you."

He sits on his heels next to the toilet paper. "Here. Take a big wad. It always makes me feel better."

"But what about the little sign?"

"The little sign?"

"The one that says, *only take what you need, these come from trees.* Guess we're both terrible people, killing trees and being fishy and yelling at nice people who tell you to be nice to them."

"Nah, I think that last one is just you."

"Do you know what my mom said to me before I left for HAC? She said, *this might be the last time you do this, so savor it.*"

"She meant camp?"

"Dancing."

"Oh."

"She keeps telling me things like, oh, Florence, it's great that you're smart and because of dance you know all about, like, geometry and stuff, maybe you can be an *astrophysicist.* After I totally lose my depth perception, she means. I won't be able to balance anymore but *hey,* I can balance a proof."

"That's . . . a lot. You're going to, like, dance your way into a geometric proof?"

"Which is then going to blast me into space. Nobody can look at me in the moment, ever. Nobody can say, you're an amazing dancer now, be an amazing dancer, and later we'll just figure it out. Everybody wants me to be playing four-dimensional chess with my own life. And I—" I don't mean to, but I catch Jude's gaze and he holds it fast. "I'm so jealous," I whisper. "I'm sorry. I wish there was something I loved that I could do for my whole life, like you. I wish I could love something that I knew I wasn't going to lose."

"But we lose everything," Jude says. "And that's—"

"Don't you dare tell me that's what makes it beautiful."

". . . That's what makes it beautiful."

"Goddammit, I'm going to cry myself a whole ocean."

"Good thing you can swim, spiny."

JUDE
CRYING BEHIND BATHROOM DOORS

The thing is, I have more experience
than I'd like with people crying
behind bathroom doors, just one

of the myriad perks
of your parents' divorce. The thing is,
we go to bathrooms to cleanse
ourselves of the things that poison us
if we let them build up inside us—

—and the thing about sobs
from behind a bathroom door
is they sound like the call
of a distant flock
of gulls come to feast, only
it's you raising the song
and also you the feast.

I've known Florence long enough
to guess she doesn't cry
easily and I want to hold her hand
and assure her *it's okay. The days will pass
and somehow you'll weather
the season of gloaming and still
you'll see.*

But all I can tell her
without lying
is *it's okay. I won't abandon you*
to pass this night alone.
You'll see.

JUDE
BACK IN THE HIPPIE DONUT SHOP, READY FOR POST-CRY CARBS AND SUGAR, 10:51 P.M.

"Everything cool?" the hippie dude behind the counter asks.

"Yeah, fine," I say.

"Sorry for bringing the bad vibes or whatever," Florence says.

"No worries," the hippie says. "I didn't pick you out my favorites though because I wasn't sure you'd still want them."

"Yeah, donut us," Florence says.

"I believe I agreed to eat any donut of your choosing," I say.

"Oh that's right," Florence says. "Weirdest donut you've got. What is it?"

Hippie dude grins. "As it happens, the weirdest donut we've got is pretty much the weirdest one anyone's got. Maple bar topped with dried crickets. The Jiminy Cricket."

"Didn't burn too much daylight thinking up that name, huh?" says Florence.

"I heard the crickets taste kinda like walnuts," hippie dude says.

"Never tried it?" Florence asks.

"Vegetarian," he replies.

"You gonna chicken out?" Florence asks me. "Actually chickens probably love crickets. You gonna . . . human out on me?"

I swallow hard. "A promise is a promise. If I die, will you tell my parents I loved them?"

"I'll tell them you loved them, but not more than you loved eating cricket donuts. Crick-o-nuts."

"One cricket donut coming up," hippie dude says.

"Make it two," Florence says.

"Hang on. I agreed to one," I say.

"The other one's for me," she says.

"Seriously?"

"If we die, we die together."

We grab our donuts. We raise them to our mouths and pause.

"Count of three?" Florence says. "One, two, three—"

"Mmmm," I say. "Doesn't taste as cricket-y as I expected."

"What would you expect crickets to taste like?"

"I dunno but I'd know it when I tasted it."

"Is it weird for me to say I thought it'd taste minty?"

"I mean. Crickets are green. Aren't they? Mints are green."

"So, what about Marley?"

"She doesn't taste like crickets," I say, my mouth full. "If that's what you're asking."

"You didn't ask me to tell her that you loved her if you croaked from the cricket donut. Just your parents," Florence says.

"Yeah, well."

"Trouble in paradise?"

"I mean, I don't know how comforted she'd be if a pretty girl showed up at her door and said, hey, your boyfriend died hanging out with me and eating a cricket donut I picked out for him."

"Pretty? Aw."

"I'm just saying, you have a nice face."

"And you have a solid restroom therapy game," Florence says.

"Solid restroom therapy game? Aw."

"Does Marley make you practice your therapy skills on her in the bathroom? She a bathroom crier like me?"

"I don't wanna talk about Marley tonight."

"Would Marley eat a cricket donut with you?"

"I'm guessing she'd sooner drink warm milk poured through a sweaty ass crack. Now let's change the subject."

"Okay fine." Florence pauses for a moment. "What's . . . up with . . . Marley?"

"Good one."

"These dried crickets really do taste like walnuts. Know what I've learned?"

"That the really important thing is the friends we make along the way?"

"Close. Any time you see weird stuff on a menu, you should get it."

"You think?"

"Because if it's *actually* gross it would never make it on the menu."

"I had Hot Cheetos ice cream at an ice cream place once," I say.

"And?"

"Yeah, it was weirdly good. Your theory checks out."

We finish our cricket donuts and sit looking out the window, the neon "Open" sign bathing our faces in pink glow.

"We better keep an eye on— I mean, we better keep track of the time," I say. "So we're not late to check-in."

"Did you think you were going to offend me by saying *keep an eye on the time?*" Florence asks.

"Maybe."

"You're sweet. But I'm fine."

"Okay."

"Thank you for caring about my feelings."

We sit quietly for a while.

Florence asks, "Think I'm a drama queen for crying in a donut store restroom?"

"Not at all."

"I can't control when things hurt too much."

"No one can."

FLORENCE
TROUBLE

When we finally hit the street Jude says, *oh shit,*
it's ten minutes to first check-in, and so we run hard
back toward HAC. The night feels complete

around us. I feel complete in it, or maybe just
completely in it, I'm not outside of my body
looking in. Which doesn't happen unless

I'm dancing. A tiny part of my brain tests
that idea, like my tongue on a loose tooth,
while the rest of me banters with Jude—

we're half-running now, he's weirdly graceful
in his dark jeans. Long legs, long strides,
quick back-and-forth about the two of us

being like a relay team, nonsense, really, talk
just to hear ourselves talk, and I tell myself
it's the post-cry glow (I wouldn't know, I never cry

in front of anyone), it's that I went
so hard on that stage tonight, that's why
I'm so loose-limbed, light on my feet,

mile-a-minute wit from Jude that I somehow

serve right back. The HAC sign glows ahead
like a finish line and I lift my hand to Jude

to bump it—*we made it*—and when he does
I want him to touch me again.
Shit. Trouble is

the two inches between me and this boy
electric, charged with particles only I
can feel. Trouble is this boy who thinks

I'm beautiful because he thinks
everything is. Trouble is I want to reach into
his past with both hands and hear it all,

find the hairline cracks, hope the telling
helps them heal a little. Trouble is that tonight
my edges softened too. Trouble is

mostly a girl back home named Marley
and I would never push it. Jude's morality
clings to him like sunlight—besides

I'm no "other girl" and I can get over it,
I know I can, even if every HACker around us
is looking at me and him in the check-in line

snorting about how cricket donuts taste like

Snickers. The trouble is there's so much I'm told
I can't have. I need to get better at not wanting it

after that. The trouble is me. It always is.

JUDE
HOLY WATER, OR, I'VE NEVER SEEN MARLEY CRY

As we wait, sweat pouring clean
and cool down the sides
of our blood-warm faces, I remember

I learned once that desert dwellers consider water
sacred, or maybe I didn't learn
this and my mind conjured it
because it does make a lot
of sense that they would.
Either way, I hold it as truth.

Once I went to a friend's church
and at the entrance there was a basin
of holy water with which to anoint
yourself, and I thought,
isn't all water holy.

If eyes are the window
to the soul, how fitting
that they should act as wellspring
for water salted like blood
in joy, in sorrow, in pain.

Because what's holier
than to feel deeply?

To feel deeply is to be alive
and what's holier than to live
and feel.

I don't think you really know
someone until you've seen them
cry. Until they've placed a basin
of holy water at the entrance
to their heart.

I think this is why we enter
the world crying.

All this is to say:
I've seen Florence cry.
I've never seen Marley cry.

JUDE
CHECKING IN AT FIRST CHECK-IN, DEFINITELY NOT SWEATY AND PANTING LIKE WE'VE JUST BEEN FEVERISHLY DRY HUMPING, 12:02 A.M.

"Jude Wheeler."

"Okay . . . Jude Wheeler. There you are. All the way at the end. You having fun tonight?"

"Yes, ma'am."

"*Ma'am.* Aren't you polite."

"I'm from Tennessee."

"Guess that explains it. And your name?"

"Florence Bankhead."

"All the way back at the front. All right. Got you down, Florence. Have fun, guys."

"Okay," I say to Florence. "Now what?"

"I don't know."

"We could go to the—"

"No."

"You didn't even hear what I had to say."

"I don't think it's a good idea."

"Again, you have no clue what I was going to suggest."

"It doesn't matter. I'm thinking I don't want to head back out."

"Wait, *what?* This is Sunrise Night. You want to pack it in"—I take out my phone and check—"at 12:04?"

She looks off into the distance at nothing in particular. "I don't know. Yeah?"

"Well that sucks."

"Why?" Her face is sad.

"Because we were having fun. I was. Weren't you? You seemed like you were."

"Yeah," she says quietly. She sits cross-legged on the grass and starts plucking at blades.

I sit beside her. "I can tell something's up."

She shrugs.

"You wanna tell me? I'm a good listener."

"I know. I was crying in front of you in a bathroom like an hour ago."

I pluck a blade of flat, coarse grass and hold it taut between my thumbs and blow through them to make a honking, kazoo-like sound.

"That sounds like a goose orgasming," Florence says, giggling.

"You tell me what's up with you and I'll set it to music with my goose-sex flute."

"Do not *ever* say the phrase *goose-sex flute* to me again. I hate it so much."

"You're the one who put the idea in my head. I would have *never* thought of it."

"I don't care."

"Fine, I'll call it a GS flute. Tell me what's wrong."

"Show me how to make a GS flute."

"I will after you tell me what's up."

FLORENCE
WHILE HOLDING GRASS FLUTES OF VISCERALLY REPULSIVE SONIC KINSHIP, 12:05 A.M.

"I have a stomachache," I say. "I think the crickets got me in the end."

Jude claps his hands over his heart. "They done got me, Hoss," he wheezes.

I don't say anything.

"Wasn't the plan for us to go eat more stuff? If that's what you're worried about, we can change our plans," Jude says.

"I don't wanna rain on your eating parade."

"I'm going to have to eat again in, like, eight hours. Then four hours after that. And on and on until I die. I'm pretty sure this parade keeps going till, like, the grave."

I like him so much that I want to explode. Not a pretty explosion. Not like confetti. I mean an explosion of blood and guts and viscera. Like *Zombie House 2*.

"I think I'm gonna be sick," I say, and it's not a lie. "Can we just sit here for a second?"

"Sure."

For the first time in hours, I don't have anything to say.

"Want me to tell you a story or something?" he asks. "To take your mind off your stomach?"

"Sure," I say. "How'd you meet Marley?"

JUDE
LOVE AT FIRST SIGHT

I don't believe in love
at first sight, not after my parents
cited their own love at first sight as the seed
that grew into their blighted union.

But I do believe in seeing someone
for the first time in the honey-toned dusk light
of a new September and thinking
there was no one more beautiful
at the Dickson Cross Point Church back-to-school youth BBQ
to which my friend Noah had dragged me.

After a great leap of faith,
one that required me
to make the calculation that if she loved
Jesus, at least she might be nice
when rejecting me,

we started talking and learned
we both love dipping fries in our Frosties,
watching *Friends*, and videos
of baby goats. In the right light,

you can easily decide
that someone who isn't completely

any of the things you most love
probably also isn't completely

any of the things you most despise,
which is maybe all you have
the right to hope for
in love or anything else.

JUDE
AWAITING THE PASSING OF POTENTIALLY CRICKET-OVERCONSUMPTION-INDUCED NAUSEA, 12:15 A.M.

"So that's how we met," I say.

Florence, now lying on her back on the grass, doesn't look impressed. "So you guys kinda decided you were soulmates because you both like stuff everyone likes."

"Who said I thought we were soulmates?"

"Then what are you?"

"I don't know. We're us. Why does it, like, need a label or whatever."

"I mean, why are you dating if you don't think you might be perfect for each other? If it isn't special?"

"I'll give you baby goats and even *Friends*—fine, yeah, most people like them. But dipping fries in Frosties—that's special."

"Jeez, I'm trying not to toss my crickets here."

"Come on. You don't like dipping fries in Frosties?"

"I'm afraid to say yes because then you'll want to marry me."

"I don't even want to marry Marley, and she likes *Friends* and baby goats too."

"No?"

"I mean, I'm not huge on the thought of marrying anyone ever at this point in my life."

"You seem like too much of a romantic to be so jaded."

"Surprise!"

"Now, see, *that* we have in common. Which is, ironically, a more important commonality than liking *Friends* or baby goats. Which, by the way, I do, because I'm not a monster."

"So now I ask you, Florence Bankhead: how *you* doin'?"

She looks at me.

"You know. From *Friends*."

"No, yeah, I know."

"But it was also kind of a serious question. How you doin'?"

"Who's asking? Joey Tribbiani or Jude Wheeler?"

"Jude Wheeler."

She smiles a little and sits up. "Better now."

"Better now as in *let's rally and make the most of the rest of this Sunrise Night*?"

"I guess that would depend on what we're talking about doing. Does it involve more"—she pulls out her phone and Googles something—"entomophagy?"

"Entomowhatthehell?"

"Entomophagy. Eating of insects."

"You could've just said *eating of insects*."

"When a word like *entomophagy* exists?"

"Fair point."

"So where we going?" Florence asks.

"Well, I was thinking of checking out this all-night diner that has really great cicada waffles. Oh wait, that's—"

"Yeah, that's almost exactly the thing I *don't* want to do."

"I was just softening you up to accept my offer of bowling. Because I'm sure you find it unbearably average, like loving baby goats," I say.

"Is there an all-night bowling alley?"

"Wait, you're entertaining this?"

"Again, I hope this doesn't lead you to propose."

"Only thing I'm proposing is whipping your ass at bowling."

Florence ponders for a while, looking at me, several different expressions passing over her face. Then she hops to her feet. "Lead on, Jiminy Cricket. You're about to learn the hard way that dance muscles and coordination have many uses."

FLORENCE
AT THE LAKER LANES BOWLING ALLEY THAT'S APPARENTLY GOING TO CLOSE IN THIRTY-FIVE MINUTES, 12:25 A.M.

"We'd like a lane, please."

"We close in thirty-five minutes," the girl says. "You still want a lane?"

"Oh. I thought you were an all-night alley?" Jude asks. "The sign outside says 'Welcome Hackers.' Which sort of seems like it could be a problem? Has anyone hacked into your bowling system?"

"Our . . . bowling system?" The girl looks unimpressed. "And do what? Change spares to strikes?"

"I didn't really think that joke through," Jude says.

Bowling alley girl doesn't look older than thirteen, but she's covered in tattoos. "We stay open late one day a year for . . . you guys. Then we close at one and when we close, everyone has to go. Doesn't matter if you aren't done. You hear those people bowling?"

We all go quiet, listening to the heavy thuds and muted cheers.

"They got here earlier," she says. "So bowl fast. You all need shoes?"

FLORENCE
BOWLING FAST, 12:30 A.M.

"Do you think her family owns this place?"

Jude is programming our names into the bowling system. "Probably," he says. "Or they're breaking like a million child labor laws."

"I wonder how much crap she takes from the patrons. She was all ready to take us on if she had to. Dukes out."

"Reminds me a little of you."

"Yeah?"

"Smart. Unimpressed. Prickly, kind of."

These are all things I like about myself. I'm pleased. I'm also uncomfortable. "Some people don't like prickly girls," I say.

"Boring people."

"Boring people," I agree, relieved.

"I like it that I know you're not just saying things you think I wanna hear," he says, fast. "I know when you like something, it's for real. You don't lie."

I think about my fake stomachache and try not to flinch. "What color ball you want?" I ask.

"Blue. Like yours."

"Blue balls all around. Eight pound?"

"Eight-pound blue balls."

"I think we've pretty much squeezed the blue balls joke dry."

"Squeezed. Dry."

"Yes, Jude, thank you. I see you have a pulse. Now, am I Thing One or Thing Two?" I ask, looking at the screen.

"Thing Two."

"Then roll that ball on down the hall. I'm getting us Slurpees."

FLORENCE
MAKING CRUCIAL SLURPEE DECISIONS, 12:34 A.M.

"You want blue raspberry or Coke?"

"I like both. You have a preference?"

I hate blue raspberry with a passion. But also he's so cute that I want to die. "Nope, no preference," I tell him.

"Cool," he says, and takes the Coke.

"Got fries too. Cheese fries."

"Okay, Stomach of Steel. Guess you're over that cricket donut."

"Nah, I'm just gonna coat my stomach in plastic cheese so I can't feel the crickets jumping around in there anymore. This is a medical decision."

"Cool."

"You bowl already?"

"I did."

"All the pins are still up."

"They replace them," he says, "after you knock them down."

"Oh."

I squint at the bowling system display.

"What does that slash mean?" I ask.

"Means I got a spare. Wait. Florence."

"What?"

"*Florence.*"

"Jude?"

"You have . . . bowled before, right?"

He has a lock of dark hair curling over his forehead. I am trying not to look at him. It's awkward not to look at him. I end up looking two inches to the left of his left ear.

"Yes," I say.

"*Liar.*"

"Oh my God it's not a big deal."

"It is so a big deal. You've never bowled before and I have twenty minutes to teach you how. Come on. Come to the end of the lane. I'll show you how to do it."

FLORENCE
GOOD STUDENT

In the TV show version, someone would put their arms
around someone else's body, show them how
to swing a baseball bat. *It's all in the extension,*

they'd say, too close, too low, head tucked
over the shoulder. Jude says, *I'll show you how*
and I go cold, go hot, hide my face in my Slurpee

and say, *yeah okay, okay* then stand stupidly.
You have to come to the end of the lane, he says,
what, you're gonna bowl from back there

and I shuffle up like maybe I'm about to get
pushed off a cliff in my clown shoes. Heft
the ball, scrunch up my face, swing back my arm—

is this where he steps in behind me? Do I even
want him to, boy-with-a-girlfriend, would I even
like him anymore?—and Jude takes a half-step forward

and stops, because I've achieved liftoff. The ball careens
down the lane, pins spinning wildly out, and I don't
even think about it, just pirouette twice like

the tool I am, drop into a curtsy for Jude. *Whoa,*

okay there, he says, *strikeland.*

      Dancer muscles, I tell him.

Looks like you don't need my help after all, he says, and we lock
eyes and from five feet away I can imagine his hot breath
in my ear, on my neck, his fingers tight in my hair, saying,

you've surprised me, saying, *this is what the beginning
of something feels like, Florence—*
and that's when I know

I need to end it.

JUDE
BAD BOYFRIEND

Did she really need my help
that badly? She's a natural.
She has great instincts
for bowling, and, like she said, *dancer muscles.*

Maybe I didn't need to draw close enough
to smell her hair (scented the way rain looks like
falling), and to run my hand down

her forearm, tasting the warm softness
of her skin with my fingertips as I showed her
how to position the (blue) ball for her best chance

of beating me, and to feel her nestle, if only briefly,
into the valley of my body, like she was trying
to map the contours of some new
country by taking an impression in clay.

And even all that left me greedy. I also wanted
the purr of her eyelashes
on my cheek; and to let my breath caress
the spot under her ear that becomes
the curve of her jaw.

She did just roll a strike, though.

So I'm not a bad teacher—
just a bad boyfriend. If only

that small mercy were enough to stop me
from descending the dark spiral staircase,

you know the one,
the one that only goes down.

JUDE
AT THE LAKER LANES BOWLING ALLEY THAT'S APPARENTLY GOING TO CLOSE IN FIVE MINUTES, AS ANNOUNCED CURTLY OVER THE FAILING LOUDSPEAKER, WHICH MAKES HUMAN SPEECH SOUND LIKE A PERCUSSIVE SERIES OF FARTS IN A SHEET-METAL AIR-CONDITIONING DUCT, 12:55 A.M.

"We were just getting warmed up," I say. "I guess we'll have to call this game a draw."

"Draw, my ass. With a dull pencil," Florence says. "We're finishing this."

"No time."

"Come on." She starts heading in the direction of the front desk and the surly employee working there.

"What are you doing?" I ask.

"Watch."

The employee glares at Florence. "Can I help you? We're closing in a couple minutes."

"What's your name?"

"Ravyn. With a 'y.' I'll know if you say it with an 'e.'"

"Ravyn. Hey. I'm Florence. So, my buddy Jude and I just got here and this is our last night together, and he's going blind, and we were hoping we could bowl for just a little longer."

"Sorry. That sucks, but I gotta close up. My boss. You know."

Florence nods. She rummages in a pocket and comes up with a crumpled twenty. She smooths it and snaps it a couple times, holding it from each end. Then she sets it on the glass counter and slides it toward Ravyn. "Listen. What if someone who outranked your boss told you we could stay for a couple hours longer. Someone like, say, former president Andrew Jackson."

"Andrew Jackson was an asshole like my boss." Ravyn furtively reaches out and slides the bill off the counter and pockets it. She motions with her head. "Go hide in the back there. Until I get everyone out. You got two hours."

"You sure it's cool?" Florence asks. "Your boss?"

"My boss and his minimum-wage-paying ass can blow me. I'll take a temporary pay raise to hang out and watch dance videos here instead of with my shitty roommates. Screw it. Hang on."

She leans over to a goose-neck microphone and depresses a button.

"ATTENTION PLEASE, BOWLERS. LAKER LANES WILL BE CLOSING IN THIRTY SECONDS. THAT MEANS EVERYONE NEEDS TO TURN IN THEIR SHOES IMMEDIATELY. Okay. Go hide."

JUDE
AT THE NOW-CLOSED LAKER LANES BOWLING ALLEY, WHICH WE NOW HAVE ALL TO OURSELVES FOR THE NEXT TWO HOURS LIKE A DELETED SCENE FROM *FERRIS BUELLER'S DAY OFF*, 1:07 A.M.

"Okay, everyone's gone," Ravyn calls back to us. "Go nuts." As we pass her, she says, "I assume the stuff about going blind is BS."

Florence smiles a little. "Sorta but sorta not."

"I don't care," Ravyn says, and pulls out a vape pen covered in silver skulls. She extends it to us. We politely decline and reassume our lane.

"Whose turn?" Florence asks.

"Yours."

"You guys want refills on your slushies, just come grab them," Ravyn calls over. She sounds in considerably higher spirits.

"You won't get in trouble?" I ask.

"Does this place look like the kind that keeps close track of anything?"

"Closing time," Florence responds.

Ravyn erupts into peals of laughter. "Yeah, closing time. But not, like, ounces of slushie mix."

"We may take you up on that," I call back. "Speaking of keeping track of things, we gotta make sure we don't blow check-in time."

"I'm keeping track."

I roll. Two pins left standing. I turn to Florence. "I'm gonna need to hear your explanation for why you've never been bowling before."

Florence hefts her ball and positions her fingers in the holes. "What? I need to explain myself?"

"I mean, kinda. Who hasn't *ever* been bowling?"

"Lots of people haven't done lots of things. Ever been skydiving?"

"I would if there were two skydiving alleys within ten minutes of each other where I live."

"My family's just not a big bowling family, I guess." Florence rolls. Immediate gutter ball. She stomps. "*Shit.*"

"I knew that beginner's luck was going to run out," I say as I step up to roll. "So y'all aren't a big bowling family. What kind are you?"

"My dad's an oncology nurse at the university hospital in Madison and my mom's a sociology professor at UW."

"So you went to football games?"

"So we went to Shakespeare in the Park. It was boring when I was a kid and then I started to really like it. I take it you were a bowling family?"

"Yep. My mom's a receptionist for an eye doctor and my dad's an electrician. Total bowling family. I have fond memories of bowling."

"Like?"

"Hang on." I roll a spare. "Like this one time—I think I was eleven, I wanna say—we found out my grandma had cancer. I was super upset because my grandma and I were really close—"

"Were?"

"Are. She's still alive. She survived and she's doing okay now."

"Whew."

"Were you, like, interrupting my story to offer preemptive condolences?"

"You're not mad, are you?"

"Of course not. What a sweetie pie to interrupt for that reason."

Florence smiles and flips me the bird as she walks up to roll. "Here's your sweetie pie."

"Now *that's* the Florence I've come to know and love over the last few hours," I say.

I feel a twinge in my gut as I say *love* out loud. I've just told Florence I love her more times in the last few hours than I've told Marley during the same time period. I *know* it was a joke *love* but the fact I'm having enough fun for a joke *love* still makes me feel like an awful boyfriend. I resume spiraling in my head.

Florence releases her ball with a teeth-jarring thud. It slinks its way down the lane, arriving at the pins with enough momentum to bashfully tap one or two over.

"Definitely try not to, like, break the bowling alley, though," Ravyn calls to us, tinny dance music issuing from the speakers of her phone. "I hate this job but there aren't millions available in this town."

"Sorry," Florence replies to Ravyn. "And sorry to you," she says to me. "Your story about your dad taking you bowling?"

"Oh. Yeah. My grandma got cancer and my dad took me bowling and let me win and it made me feel better. And then my grandma lived and still sends me a twenty-dollar bill in a birthday card every year. The end. It's not a great story."

"Well, your grandma lived. So that's good. And I suspect there aren't many great bowling stories out there. I don't think it's you, it's just that . . . I don't think bowling, as a sport, inherently lends itself to compelling stories."

"Once my friends and I went bowling and we gave each other

names like *Pooplord* and *Diarrhea Dan* on the scoreboard."

"Did you get kicked out?"

"Well, no."

"Did anything happen because of it?"

"Because of *Pooplord* and *Diarrhea Dan?*"

"Yeah."

"No, nothing happened."

"Okay so that story actually—"

"No, yeah, it also kinda proves your point," I say. "I wasn't trying to say it was great. But I do legit think bowling at 1:15 a.m. with someone you just met after you've paid off the bowling alley employee to let you stay past closing is about as good of a story as it gets."

Florence smiles a little. "I might give you that one." She sets herself up for her turn.

I return her smile. "Oh, you might give me that one, huh? Aren't you generous. Hang on. I can tell from the way you're holding the ball that you're about to do a whack roll." I get up and go to her. I position myself behind her, a lock of her hair tickling my nose. I put my hand on her wrist, almost on top of her ball hand. "So when you hold it like this, it's gonna spin off into the gutter. You gotta hold it like this." I position her hand.

She seems to welcome the touch. She makes a reasonably solid roll, knocking over about half the pins. She pumps her fist. "Boom!"

"Look at you go."

"Let's get celebratory slushie refills."

Ravyn doesn't even look up from her phone and waves us past to the slushie machine.

"I'm mixing Coke and blue raspberry this time," I say.

"Don't cause an explosion there, Oppenheimer."

"An explosion would probably be healthier than a second slushie."

"You guys want some of the leftover hot dogs?" Ravyn asks. "I'm pretty sure they're fresh from this morning." She makes air quotes around *fresh*.

"That's gonna be a pass from me, but thanks," Florence says.

"You sure? I think bacteria pretty much avoid these hot dogs. I know I've never caught ants eating one."

"Yeah, I think I'm team bacteria and ants on this one," Florence says.

Ravyn shrugs. "More for me and my roommates."

We get back to our lane and sit with our slushies.

"This would be such a bummer place to work," Florence says.

"I guess if you don't have many choices, better than starving," I say.

"Could you ever live in a place like this?"

"The bowling alley?"

"Why on *earth* would I be asking you if you wanted to live in a bowling alley?"

"I don't know! You said a place like this. We're in a place."

"I meant this town, you absolute goof."

I start giggling.

"Did you sneak a quick snort off of whatever Ravyn's vaping when I wasn't looking?" Florence asks.

My giggling intensifies. "No, it's late and I'm getting dumb and loopy."

"What does Marley say when you get like this?"

"You're obsessed with Marley."

"Am not. Just curious."

"Wouldn't know. Never been out this late with Marley."

"Seriously?"

"Not that I can think of." This is not helping my spiraling thoughts. I consider texting Marley. That would probably look bad, me texting her this late (early?). I change the subject. I say to Florence, "I kinda already do live in a town like this. Dickson isn't that much bigger than Harbor City."

"Don't you want to get out?" Florence asks.

"I dunno," I respond. "I guess someday? Haven't thought about it that much. What about you?"

FLORENCE
AT LAKER LANES, IGNORING RAVYN HAVING A REALLY LOUD PHONE CALL ABOUT HOCKEY WITH HER COUSIN BEHIND US, 1:30 A.M.

"I am, like, pathologically obsessed with getting out," I tell Jude.

He walks up to the line, does a waltz-step (*one two three*), knocks down all the pins but one.

"Yeah?" he asks.

"Yeah. For a long time it was the Bolshoi."

". . . Bolsheviks?"

"Bolshoi." I heft my ball, look at it instead of Jude. "Ballet company. In Russia."

"Are you even allowed to do that? Go to Russia?"

"I don't know if I'd want to, now."

"But your parents would let you if they did?"

I shrug. "They had me late," I say.

He pauses. "So they're . . . older? What does that have to do with anything?"

"No, I mean like it's something they tell me a lot. They had me late, so I was the plot twist in their lives. Air quotes. So sometimes I get . . . I get more leeway with stuff. Like if I moved to Moscow they'd be thrilled. If I moved to Moscow, Idaho, they'd be thrilled. It's almost like . . . like they don't have any vision of what my life is going to be like. I wasn't expected. They don't have expectations."

"Because they had you late."

"Because they had me late, and because when I was born there was a lot of shit wrong with my eyes, and now every day is a magical perfect present because I'm alive and I can see. For now. Or whatever."

It's my turn and I hit the gutter, hard. We listen as the ball-return machine chucks back up the ball. We keep looking at each other like we each expect the other to say something.

"I like you a lot," I tell him—I don't know why—like it's been punched out of me.

He blinks. Hard. Then he picks up the ball and takes it up to the lane and now I'm talking to his back.

"Not like that. I mean. I like you a lot. But I don't trust things not to go away. People. Things I love. Love *doing*, I mean. Not that I love you. Doing you. I mean. I like you."

Jude isn't bowling. He's listening while I ramble on like a fool.

"But you'll still be able to dance when your vision goes, right? You can still move your body?" He sounds genuinely confused. He still hasn't turned around. "I know it's different, but can you tell me how?"

I guess we're going to skate over the *I like you* thing, I think.

"Nystagmus means my eyes shake uncontrollably. But mine only do it when my eyes don't work together. So, like, if I shut one for more than a few seconds, the other shakes. Which wouldn't be a big deal, I have two eyes for a reason, except that one of my eyes is a—a lazy eye, I hate that term so much—my eye isn't sleeping in until noon or whatever—but it's a lazy eye, and when I'm stressed it drifts. It unfocuses. And then the other eye shakes. And it's like I'm in some bullshit carnival ride. I can't balance on two legs. Much less one. On pointe. I can't jump, I can't track my own movements. It's . . . I can't see anything and I just want to sleep."

"When you're stressed."

"Yeah. And if I'm not stressed there's no guarantee it won't happen—that my eye won't drift—but still for a long time my parents wanted me to, like, live in a padded room and do something with my brain, as if *that's* less stressful, and I had all this pent-up energy. That's what I remember from being a kid, and then thank God I got a doctor who told them that I need to get all the excitement out of my body. I was maybe five? My parents put me in a tap class. So then I took all the classes at the studio, every genre, they put me on pointe when I was ten. And I worked hard. I loved it. I was . . . good. And . . . I don't know, I had some real-talk conversations with my parents around when I was old enough to be a person, you know? I told them there are no guarantees. Said I wanted to dance competitively. No expectations, not from me, not from them. I just wanted to try it. So I had the surgery to fix my lazy eye and then I had it again after it wore off and now they can only do it one more time. They've, like, run out of muscle to work with. I didn't know that was a thing that could happen. I was thirteen the last time I had it done and now my eye's starting to drift again."

Jude has turned back to me now, holding the ball in his arms like it's a weight he's carrying.

"So the next time it happens that's it. I get one more shot. They told me three months ago, at my last ophthalmologist appointment. That's part of the reason my parents both work at UW, I get the really primo health insurance."

"That's good," he says, and I can tell he means it, even as he obviously doesn't know anything about what makes health insurance good or not.

I look at him. I try to put my whole self there, in that look. "And listen, like, kids used to call me Captain Jack Sparrow because I had to wear an eyepatch to try to make my lazy eye stronger."

"Captain Jack Sparrow? Who famously did *not* wear an eyepatch but instead had two prominent smoky eyes?"

"It's almost like it wasn't the smartest kids making fun of me. Anyway, all through middle school, every afternoon, I wore that goddamn eyepatch. In sixth grade I thought I had a lot of friends. In seventh grade I found out I was wrong. Now I have people who like me, but only from a safe distance, and I'm still kind of reeling from that . . . that ophthalmologist appointment. I keep waiting for them to call me again and tell me that they made a mistake. But my phone isn't ringing, and it won't ring, I know that, and now . . . I don't know. I guess what I'm trying to do is apologize. I haven't really talked to anyone about this yet and now there's you and . . . I'm sorry if I'm throwing too much your way. I'm here waiting for you to do the thing my brain keeps telling me you're gonna do."

"And what's that?"

"Leave. Bail. I don't know." I cough as cover and look away. "Is it still your turn?"

JUDE
AT LAKER LANES, BOWLING AND SPIRALING, 1:43 A.M.

The intimacy with which the word hits makes me feel funny. "Leave?" I say.

"Nothing. Never mind. Still your turn?"

"Hang on. What do you mean, leave?"

"I didn't mean anything."

I set my ball back on the rack. "That's just an odd word choice."

"Yeah, well, it's like two a.m."

I sit beside her. "Look—"

"Please don't make me regret opening up to you."

"It's just that *leave you* has romantic connotations."

"Well, any such connotations were extremely unintentional."

"You sure? I don't want us to have some misunderstanding."

Florence gives me a look. "Yes, Jude. I'm sure. You sure you're not engaging in some weird projection here?"

"What's projection?"

"When you've got something going on in your own brain that you think is coming from outside. From me."

"Never heard of that concept before."

"You know what they say: after you eat crickets for the first time, learning about projection isn't far behind."

"Do they say that?"

"Probably. So? Projecting?"

"I don't know. Maybe. My brain does funny things." *Maybe my brain is my version of your eyes*, I think, but don't say.

"Jude," Florence says quietly. "You've seemed off for the last little bit. Are you freaking out right now over something?"

I shift uncomfortably, moving my weight from one butt cheek to the other. My stomach roils.

"Kinda."

"You feel like telling me?"

I study my feet. "You think bowling shoes are intentionally ugly so people won't steal them?"

"They're not exactly the most functional shoes outside of the bowling alley context."

"Wouldn't want to run a marathon in them."

"Are you obsessing about Marley?"

I chew on the inside of my lip. "I'm feeling sorta guilty, I guess?"

"Why?"

"I feel like a bad boyfriend."

"You've been a perfect gentleman all night."

"I know, I just—"

"You just what?"

"I'm having more fun than I should be," I say.

Florence laughs. "My apologies?"

I laugh too. "You damn well better be sorry. How dare you."

"How about I start making gross mouth sounds for the rest of the night to dampen your fun." Florence starts smacking her lips and making sloppy chewing noises that sound like stirring mac and cheese.

I clamp my hands over my ears. "Stop. You're fine. I'm—wait for it—projecting. Did I do that right?"

"Perfectly. If you want, I can make a concerted effort to assure you that I'm not interested in you romantically. Would that help you feel better?"

Not remotely, I think. "No need," I say.

We sit there for a while without talking. It's quiet except for Ravyn snorting and guffawing over something she's watching on her phone.

"I shouldn't have reacted that way after you opened up to me," I say finally.

"It's okay," Florence murmurs.

"I really like you too."

FLORENCE
NEXT TIME

When we slide her our shoes, Ravyn gives us
a high-five each like we're in some eighties
sports flick. I slip her another twenty

when Jude isn't looking. I feel weird doing stuff like that,
feel weirder not doing it. Weeks into camp
and the only spending money I've spent

I spent tonight, so why shouldn't Ravyn
have it? She gave us this time, and I gave
Jude my heart, and—where the hell did *that*

come from? Am I channeling Emily Henry tonight
in northern Michigan? I need to stop. But still I'm
in some other story, because when Ravyn shuts off

the lights, the darkness crests toward us like
a horror film, *out* and *out* and *out*
until we're standing in the last patch

of light. Then we're outside, and Jude's not talking—
not like he's mad, but like he's on pause. Tapping together
his thumb and his middle finger in a quick pattern, *one*

two three, and I stop to tie up my hair. I'm thinking

about what isn't. Thinking *we didn't*
play chess, we didn't shoot any zombies, we

didn't kiss and we won't. The edge of it
in my throat. It's ten minutes
to final check-in, we'll make it if we run,

and before I tell Jude, the door behind us
opens. Ravyn says, locking up, *you know*
I meant to tell you, you two are really

cute together, and before I can sputter out
a word, before Jude can dig himself the hole
he clearly wants to die in, she's unlocking

her Hyundai Elantra that looks made of maroon lace.
Want a ride back to camp? I'm good to drive—Promise
I wasn't vaping the old wacky tobacky earlier, she says, and I get in
(zebra seat covers, "Tainted Love" on the stereo)

before Jude can say no. What on earth
would we have said to each other on our walk back?
He can't even look me in the eye.

JUDE
FINAL CHECK-IN

Name?

Jude Wheeler.

There you are, near the bottom.
Having fun tonight?

As a matter of fact, yes, more fun
than I've had with any other
human being for as long as I can
remember, which is a problem,
because good boyfriends don't
have more fun with girls who aren't
their girlfriend than with girls
who are.

And good guys don't become bad
boyfriends with some girl
they just met hours prior.

And they don't let themselves imagine
what it would be like to be with
that girl. It never crosses
their mind what it would feel like to hold

her hand, to brush her lips
with theirs. Because
they're better at relationships
than their parents (or at least more
determined to avoid the same
mistakes) and so they tend to
them with greater care
than their parents—who let their union

curdle and crumble for no apparent reason
or at least nothing they're willing to talk
about—even with the other people
invested in the success
of the relationship. Because they choose
carefully, otherwise both parties
to the relationship will be miserable
and good guys don't make

people miserable whenever they can
avoid doing so. Because being better
than what you came from is the best evidence
that your life belongs to you. When so little else does.

Don't forget, everyone's gathering at Lakeshore Park at six to
watch the sunrise. You don't want to miss it. It's a tradition.

JUDE
AT FINAL CHECK-IN, WAITING FOR FLORENCE, 3:03 A.M.

"Sorry, the lady couldn't find my name. She kept looking under 'F' for Florence instead of 'B' for Bankhead. I think it's past her bedtime."

"You know, I think it actually might be past mine too," I say.

"Jude."

"I just—I honestly don't think I have it in me to stay awake anymore." I yawn cartoonishly, one of those real yawns that's so energetic it comes off as fake. All I had to do was think about yawning and I did, like always.

"Jude. Unacceptable."

"It's three a.m. Like, going to sleep is possibly the *most* acceptable."

"Is it a lack of caffeine? Because we can get our hands on some. I know a guy."

"Don't say Dr Pepper."

"Oh this guy doesn't have his PhD. He went to the School of Hard Knocks. The School of the Streets."

"Don't say Mr. Pibb either. Do not."

"Oh this guy is actually an anthropomorphic mountain. Just a big ol' beefy rock boy. Big-ass ol' mountain. Mountain-lookin' ass."

I'm laughing now in spite of myself. Loopy Florence's shift appears to have started promptly at three a.m. And she's a lot of fun. Which isn't helping my resolve to duck out.

"Is it Mountain Dew?" I ask. "Is your big, caffeine-filled, ol' beefy rocky, mountain-lookin'-ass guy Mountain Dew?"

"It's Mountain Dew, bro. *Do the Dew*," she says in this awful, guttural bro voice. "*Do the Dew, Jude.* Ooo ooo ooo. Do the Dew, Jude. That's very alliterative. Is that what it's called when words all sound kinda similar?"

"I truly have no idea."

"Well Google *Jude, while you Do the Dew, Jude*." She cackles at her own joke and walks over to one of the coolers that's lying around, opens it, pulls out a dripping can of Mountain Dew, shakes off the droplets, and hands it to me. I hold it stupidly. I was prepared to say no to and walk away from tough, take-no-nonsense Florence. I'm wholly unprepared for goofy, sweet Florence.

"Did you get a contact high from touching Ravyn's seat cushions?" I ask.

Florence plucks another can of Mountain Dew from the cooler and holds it like a microphone. "*Noooooooo, it's just late as balls, bitches, and I wanna paaaaaaaaartaaaay*," she sings into the can-mic loudly. She has a surprisingly good voice, even clowning. She begins dancing wildly. She does a spin, jumps, and lands in the splits. We both dissolve into giggles.

"Okay," I say. "You are gonna get us busted for being drunk and neither of us have had a sip."

She topples sideways from her splits position and keeps giggling. "Come help me up, Jude Dew Doer."

I approach her and extend my hand. She grips it with her full weight and yanks. I tumble forward into the grass beside her and roll onto my back. We laugh for a long time, we're both so absurdly wired and slap-happy from our trash-food-and-drink bacchanalia.

Finally, we turn onto our sides to face each other. Florence puts her palms together and rests her cheek on the back of her hand like something out of a children's bedtime storybook. "Hey," she murmurs.

"Hey." I put my palms together and rest my face on the back of my hand, mirroring her.

She slowly extends her index finger and presses the tip of my nose and goes "*boop*."

"How did that become a thing?"

"What?"

"Associating noses with beeping."

"I distinctly just *boop*ed your nose."

"Yeah but you can beep noses too. Did old-timey car horns look like human noses?"

Florence absolutely loses her shit. She rolls onto her back, tears stream down her cheeks. "You're driving your old-timey Chitty-Chitty-Bang-Bang-ass car and there's this, like, disembodied hyper-realistic human nose in the middle of the steering wheel."

"Like it sneezes sometimes."

"Jude!"

We say nothing for a while as our latest spate of sleep-deprivation-induced giggles subsides.

Finally Florence asks quietly, "Were you really just too tired to want to hang out with me any more tonight? Was that the truth?"

"Yes," I lie.

"Promise?"

"Promise," I lie.

"It does feel damn good to be lying down."

"I know, right?"

"What if we took a little nap."

"Here?"

"Mmm-hmmm. Like an hour. We could set an alarm on our phones."

"Then what?"

"Then we hang out some more until sunrise. Deal?"

I let a long time pass before answering. Hopefully she'll chalk it up to diminished wee-hour brain function. I'm spiraling. Now I'm also racked with remorse for lying to her. I really can't win here.

Florence doesn't wait for me. "Snooze," she murmurs. "Snooze time."

I yawn and pull out my phone. "I'm setting my alarm for one hour."

"Perfect." She nestles into the ground, rolling onto her side and hugging her knees to her chest. Then she closes her eyes.

JUDE
FLORENCE SLEEPING

I lie awake for a few minutes
after she drifts off, listening
to the nocturne of crickets, watching

the rise and fall of her
slowing breath, soft like benediction,
her hair splayed in the summer

grass like handfuls
of windfall silk.

Let sleep end
this poem.

Let sleep end this.

Let sleep end.

Let sleep.

Let.

FLORENCE
THE DREAM WHERE

every few minutes you wake up
and you check
        that he's still there,
two feet away. Grass under my nose
like a feather, crickets rubbing
their legs together
        to sing. Dream
where my grandma, dead four years
now, gives me her favorite hat.
Went missing after
        the hospital.
She told me, *Florence, be brave,*
put a finger to the tip of my nose
and said *Beep.*
        Did she? That hat
was velvet, had a bow, I could go
to dance halls in that hat. I could
teach Jude how
        to Charleston. Dream
where we walk all night, we're in
some European city and there's only
hours until sunrise,
        other cities, other people
we're gonna be, and in the dream I think maybe
I'm teenage Julie Delpy, which would be

(honestly) an upgrade.

              Dream where I speak French
to a turtle. Dream where a truck is backing up
so slow, its high-pitched whine like
now, now, now,
               and it's my alarm, and eyes open
Jude is smiling at me.

FLORENCE
LAKESHORE, 4:28 A.M.

Only stragglers here to see the sunrise,
zombies on Rockstar energy drinks
and the few wonderful weirdos who went

to bed at nine p.m. and woke up
just for the rosy-fingered dawn. Jude and I are
the in-between, and he waited for me

outside my dorm while I grabbed the quilt
it's been too hot for until now. We'll spread it out
on the grass. Early morning has a fragility

to it, like the world is made of eggshell,
and I feel that sense of newness in me too—
like I've been carrying around this bag

of weapons for my own protection,
and I've just been told it's safe
to put it all down. I tell Jude

it's my grandma's quilt, made in some cold
Wisconsin winter half a century ago, that
she dropped in on a dream I had tonight

to say hello. *Hello*, Jude says. I'm a little afraid
to look him in the eyes, like I might
crack open. Like it might feel good.

JUDE
UNEXPECTED OCEANS

I wasn't ready for what I saw
the first time I saw it, a few days prior.
An expanse of water too vast to see
its end.

An ocean in Michigan.

An ocean of sweet water with actual waves
crashing on an actual sandy beach.

There's wonder to realizing that
there are oceans without
midnight-colored whales fighting
wound-colored squid in the nightmare abyss.

Oceans that don't taste like tears.
Oceans that can quench your thirst.
Oceans in Michigan.
Unexpected oceans.

If this is a world with gentle oceans
where you'd never imagine, then who knows
what other wonders
it holds, where you least expect
to find them.

There is so much possibility
in this world. There is nothing
but.

FLORENCE
WAITING FOR THE SUN AT LAKESHORE, 5:04 A.M.

"It's another hour away," I tell him, looking at my weather app.

"Sunrise?"

"Yup."

"Didn't realize you can check that there."

"Sunset too, down to the minute."

"What's the first thing you're gonna do when you get home?"

"Maybe go check in at the studio," I say. "They keep asking if I can teach one of the ballet classes for the little ones, the Sunday morning class, and I was worried about it being too much for this summer, what with HAC and all, but if they still need someone when I get back . . . I don't know. It might be fun."

"How little?"

"Little little."

"Fun-sized little?"

"Even littler."

"Can you put newborns on pointe?"

I laugh. "No. We're talking three-year-olds."

"I cannot imagine you teaching ballet to toddlers."

"It would be anarchy, I admit. But I like them. They're little hellions. You should see them cruising around the studio, they're like heat-seeking missiles. But the teaching's not hard. Mostly you just get them to bounce up and down. Parents like it when they come home tired."

"Kinda like puppies."

"Yup, exactly. Puppy ballet."

"I want a full report, like, every Sunday."

I dodge that one and ask, "What's the first thing you're gonna do when *you* get home?"

"Sleep for like a million years. And then I don't know. Depends if I'm at my mom's or my dad's. They're still figuring that stuff out, who gets me when. Kind of like I'm a suitcase or something."

"What's the difference between them? Your mom's and your dad's?"

"So far? Dad thinks we're, like, buddies in a buddy comedy. He wakes me up early to go fishing. He told me he had a surprise right before camp, and he drove me to this . . . axe-throwing place? An hour away? Everyone else was, like, thirty, and loud and drunk. And throwing axes."

"Oh my God," I say.

"Yes, exactly. It was exactly oh my God."

"Did you die?"

"Florence, I am literally sitting here telling you this story."

"Yes, but did you *almost* die?"

"I had a close shave."

"That's not even an axe joke. That's a razor joke. I don't know what to do with that."

"It was fine," he says. "It's just like the divorce has made him forget how to be my dad, and he's . . . staying up late writing some Judd Apatow script in his head for how we should talk to each other. Like at the axe place, he was like, *how are things with Marley?* With a big wink. And before the divorce he pretended like he couldn't remember her name."

"Really? That sucks."

"Yeah," Jude says. "It was his way of telling me he doesn't like her. And now he's acting like he does *and* he's possibly down to hear if, like, she and I are hooking up?"

"Nooooooo."

"I know. And obviously that's not what he means. I mean, at least, I hope to God it isn't. Anyway, my mom's house is better. She's the same, she's just . . . sadder. But also she's doing stuff I haven't seen her do for a while. And I guess that's kind of nice."

"Like what?"

"When I was a kid, we had a dog. Like a little curly white dog. And in our house we always had a family discussion before we made a big change, and my dad made it clear that he really didn't want her to get that dog, and they fought about it for weeks. And Muffin, the dog—"

"MUFFIN. MUFFIN the DOG."

"Yes, I clearly did not name the dog."

"I love it. I love it so much."

"Muffin only lived a few years. It was really sad, she had bone cancer."

"Oh man, I'm so sorry."

"Yeah. Me too. And when she died, my dad didn't even pretend that he wasn't relieved. It was really shitty. And so now, a few weeks ago my mom, like, went out and put a deposit on a new dog, and we're going to pick her up when I get back."

"A deposit? Can't she get one from a shelter? Adopt, don't shop?"

Jude shrugs. "Sometimes people need to be able to make a decision for themselves without the world coming down so hard on them about it."

"That's deep," I say, teasing. "But also I agree. Tell her not to put it on the internet. They'll tar and feather her."

"She wouldn't, she's not trying to make a statement or anything. Anyway, we have a cat, so we need a puppy that can be trained to not eat the cat. That's the reason."

"What are you going to name her? The dog?"

"My mom asked me if I wanted to name her," he says. "But I'm gonna let her do it. She's been auditioning names. The dog has red fur, so right now she's thinking Maple. Like a maple leaf."

"MAPLE. MAPLE the DOG."

"You like it?"

"I love it so much. I want to hug Maple the dog."

"We can make that happen."

JUDE
LAKESHORE, THE FIRST RAYS OF SUNRISE
PEEKING OUT OVER THE HORIZON, 5:49 A.M.

"Hey, come with me," I say to Florence. "Over here."

"Why?" She gets up.

"Because the light is awesome right now and I want to make your picture."

"*Make your picture?*"

I laugh. "I must be really tired to let that slip. That's Southern for *take your picture*," I explain. "Southerners don't get their pictures taken. They get their *pictures made.*"

"You know what?" Florence says. "I actually prefer that. Isn't art about making things rather than taking things?"

"Ideally. Although the mamaws and papaws who taught us all that expression probably didn't think of that."

"Can I start saying it?"

"What?"

"Get your picture made."

"I mean, sure. I don't think that, like, the Southern Language Police will come for you or anything. We've been generous with the *y'all* license."

"If I ever come visit you, I'll fit right in."

"No one will ever guess the truth. Wait, stand there."

"Here?"

"Little to the right."

"Here?"

"Little more."

"Good?"

"Perfect. Okay . . . now do something dancer-y."

"Dancer-y?" Florence cocks an eyebrow.

"I was kinda hoping you'd know what that meant."

"Uh . . . how about—" Florence balances on her left leg, lifts her right leg, and then raises it skyward along her body, holding the bottom of her high-top white Chuck Taylor.

"Holy whoa. You are *flexible*."

"I literally did the splits in front of you like an hour ago."

"I know but this feels even more next-level."

"By all means, let's keep discussing while I stand here on one leg."

"Sorry." I point my camera and start photographing her. She's a dark silhouette against the rose-purple dawn sky and new sun. She looks like a sculpture. No, better. Like a tree. I approach her, starting to look through the photos as I walk, and show them to her. I expect her to crack some joke about how they should say *Just Breathe* or *You Are Beautiful* in some script-style font on them. Honestly, she'd be well within her rights—no ground broken in these photos' composition.

But she doesn't. Instead, as she looks, she smiles faintly—maybe a little sadly—and murmurs, "These are really good, Jude. Will you send these to me?"

"Sure," I say.

FLORENCE
LAKESHORE, 6:18 A.M.

"Listen," I tell him.

Jude turns to face me. "What?"

"Nothing," I say, chickening out. But he's looking at me now. So, I say, "I've been thinking."

It's immediately clear from his expression that someone has said some version of that phrase to him recently, and that things didn't go well from there.

"Have you seen that movie *Before Sunrise*?" I ask.

"No," he says cautiously.

"It's great. It has Ethan Hawke and Julie Delpy. They're really young, it's an old movie. They're both exploring Europe, they meet on a train coming from like . . . Budapest."

"Buda-pesht?"

"That's how you say Budapest."

"How do you know?"

"Because I saw this movie."

"Oh. Do you also like to eat pesh-to on your pash-ta?"

"Jude."

"Sorry."

"Listen. In the movie, they're coming from Budapest and they're going to Vienna and they meet, for the first time, on the train. They have all night before Ethan Hawke's character goes back to America and Julie Delpy goes back to France, where she's from. And they don't have any money because they're college students, and so instead of, like, going to find a hostel, they decide to stay awake, and they walk around Vienna all night talking. And that's the whole movie."

The sun is beginning to rise. Jude's face is all lit up. "I love that," he says.

"Remind you of something?"

"A little, maybe," he says, laughing. "So what happens?"

"What do you mean?"

"Do they end up together?"

"Well, they're clearly in love. But the film ends with them saying that they're not going to stay in touch."

"What? Not at all?"

"No calls, no letters. I guess they didn't have text or email back then. But—they agree to meet back in Vienna in six months. If they both still feel the same way."

Jude just looks at me.

"Don't you love that?" I ask him.

"I don't know if I love that. Do they meet up, six months later?"

"You don't find out."

"Seriously?"

"There's a sequel. You find out then."

"Will you tell me?"

"You should watch them! I've already said too much. Listen, what if . . ."

Jude is so beautiful—cheekbones, dark eyes and smudges underneath them—and he belongs to somebody else. I don't want to say it, but I have to: "What if we do the same thing they did?"

JUDE
LAKESHORE, STARTING TO SPIRAL, 6:23 A.M.

"What, meet in Vienna in six months? And then make a movie about it?"

"No, what if we don't stay in touch and meet up next year and spend Sunrise Night together again?"

"Like at all? No texting, no talking, no anything?"

"Exactly."

"Total silence for a year."

"Precisely."

I want to tell Florence that this idea is breaking my heart for reasons I probably couldn't articulate even if I'd had more than about forty-three minutes of sleep but instead all I offer is a feeble "why would we do that?"

FLORENCE
WHY WE WOULD DO THAT

Every year on Christmas Eve the guy
my mom dated in college calls her up
and she takes the phone to our sunroom

and shuts the French doors. And they talk
for a little bit and it's not a secret—I can see her
twirling the fringe of the throw blanket

through the doors, a little pink in the face. And
that's it. My dad makes a cocktail and we play
Scrabble and when she comes out

we open one present before bed like
the British royal family, and I don't know
if my parents talk about it after they go to bed.

I don't know if the other guy is married. I don't even
know his name. If it should bother me. But the situation,
whatever it is, has a clear beginning and end. Somewhere

in Tennessee, Marley is probably sleeping under her own
quilt, made by another grandma's loving hands, and I
can't pull the ripcord on dancing, not yet, not when

I can wring the last shining moments out of this

sunset. Be right there, on the edge of it. I know
there's a chance I won't be dancing next summer

at HAC, or at all, and so I might not have to make good
on this promise. Meet up again with someone
who could become my favorite person, knowing

I can't be his. Call it self-preservation. Call it
pride. Call me a control freak, but at least
I can get out while the getting's good, and if I'm back

next summer we can have another night like this.
Something bounded by space and time. Instead of an impossible
year of wanting, impossible waiting, knowing all the while

that soon loss will creep into my house with its knives
and cut every last thing away from me
that I so stupidly pretended was mine to keep.

JUDE
AND IT MADE SENSE SOMEHOW

Call it sleep deprivation but it made sense
the way she explained it. *It's a chance to move*
through the world in a different way. Isn't that what we do
as artists? Seek unconventional modes of living? Explore
new experiences? So where any two
normal people who just walked around
and talked all night would obviously stay
in touch over the next year, we just don't. We choose
to live differently.

And that was well and good and sure,
yeah, we're artists, but it got me thinking too
that I don't have to feel
guilty when Marley looks me in the eyes
tonight and asks, *so, did you meet anyone cool at camp?*
Because I can casually respond, *sure but no one*
I'm gonna be writing letters to and I'll be telling
the whole truth.

But here's the other thing:
My parents did everything
the way you were supposed to
and look how it turned out
for them. Maybe a forced commitment
to doing things the way you weren't supposed to
would be some sort of blessing.

JUDE
FAREWELL

Okay, so I guess I won't put my number
in your phone and *no cyberstalking,*
that'll ruin it and then hugging,
hugging, hugging, breaking the hug to walk
away, but finding an excuse to hug again; sleeping

on the flight home, waking
in a start, checking my phone to see
if she texted somehow to say
I was just joking, Jude. Of course we're going
to stay in touch. I can't believe you bought
all that—you must have been really tired even though
she didn't have my number
and my phone was in airplane
mode anyway.

Watching her walk away, searching
myself for the single grand gesture
that would undo our newly solemnized
wedding to a year of silence and coming
up empty.

Taking a picture of the back of her
head. My photography teacher said
once, *Sometimes the most compelling thing*

is what a photo doesn't show.
Absence has power.

THE DESERT

JUDE
AN ACCOUNTING OF THE TIMES I ALMOST BROKE

I thought of her
not just on the nights that the blanket
was too thin to cover me and left me shivering,
the days that felt like chewing
tinfoil and kneeling on Legos, the hours
my mind clicked in circles
of dread like trying to start
a car with a dead battery—

but also on the warm and yellow days, the bright
and silver nights, the hours
that moved around me
like cool satin. I wanted nothing more

on this earth than to hear the voice of the girl I've known
for twelve hours; I wanted to hear her voice
on the dull afternoons in my dad's sad
new two-bedroom bachelor's apartment in a place
called Coventry Green, everything the color of lack—
cream-colored carpet, eggshell walls, ivory ceiling,
cheap off-white plastic blinds,
a community pool stinking of so much chlorine that it's obvious
someone made the calculation *if it singes nose hairs, it'll kill
algae*; fallen pine needles and drowned wasps floating

in it like an armada for an empire
of depression.

I wanted to hear her voice the nights
my mom and I sat on our couch, the house still feeling
newly absent of my dad, eating a bucket of KFC
and watching *Gilmore Girls*, our forced laughter
a hollow echo in the emptiness.

I wanted most of all to hear her voice
after Marley told me about Peyton's ultimate Christian social
    experiment—
he didn't film it for YouTube—which was to plant in her the seed

of a brand-new little Christian life (on the exact night, give
or take a week or two, that I was torturing myself
for having too much fun bowling with another
girl) just to see what Marley would do, to see if she would accept
the strange blessing she had been given,
and all I could say, dumbly, through my shock
was, *I knew it* and *Well I hope they fire his ass as youth pastor.*

And then the frost came and I didn't really
sleep for three days (my own Christian social experiment?),
and in the predawn hours I would spiral out, thinking
of how the common denominator in the collapse
of my parents' union and of Marley's
and mine is me, and the only thing

that would snap me out of it was thinking
about how the girl I couldn't talk to
for a year slept in the grass that summer night, curled up
like a comma in a story that would continue, or maybe
an apostrophe denoting something I could have had.

And then there were all the other
unimportant times I wanted to hear
her voice, if only in the form of a text, like
standing at the movie theater
concession, filling a cup with Mountain Dew
as I'm about to go see the kind of movie with my dad
that my mom always hated, and I'd take a picture
and text it to her and say something like,
Just checking in with our big ol' beefy rock boyfriend
or I could send her a photo I took that I'm particularly proud of
for no particular reason, maybe of a sunrise
for old times' sake. Maybe of her

in front of the sunrise, the one I never ended up
sending her because I had no place to send it, a picture
I looked at often, along with the one of her
in front of the fire and the one of her
walking away for the year.

My resolve slipped and I found her social media
profiles but she had them all prudently set
to private, which somehow only made me

like her more at the same time it sent me spinning out,
wondering if she had anticipated my weakness
of will, and I knew I couldn't be
the one to break, to capitulate and send
her a message; to request access
to her life; to renege on our vow of silence.

All I had to do was nothing
to stay as perfect as I could ever be to her.

FLORENCE
PLANS

For years I kept a journal and I cataloged
all of it, brain-dump, expressed my third-grade agonies
in words. I HATE NICKY I HATE HER SHE KEPT

TAGGING ME "IT" AT RECESS, pen
stabbing through the page. My mom used to call me
Big Feelings, like *slow your roll there, Big Feelings*

when I'd be slamming around the kitchen in my eyepatch
after a day getting teased at school. She thought it would
help to express them on paper, keep me calmer

in the long run. I mean, she also taught me how to throw
a punch after the first time I got catcalled by a dude—
pickup truck, Culver's parking lot—so, balance

in all things.® Ignore them, though, and they leave you.
I don't think I've had feelings maybe for months now. Just stood
outside of myself numbly, like I wasn't sure I was

at the right house.
             I thought I wouldn't be here again.
             I thought I had banished it

after those first few weeks in my bed, three a.m. like some

Taylor Swift song, un-asleep, picturing Jude with his hands
on that other girl's face—I couldn't even say her name

in my head, I was that taken apart. His hands that I knew so well
   after
just one night, tanned and sure and my God, I kept
imagining them around my waist, tight in my hair, if I'd pushed it

just a little, if I'd been a worse person and said, *please, Jude,*
please—and he'd hate me now for it but not more than I hated
myself. That fever, like a weakness, like a wildfire, I didn't have
   words

for it, I texted all my friends from camp asking for his number,
saying I'd lost my phone when they couldn't believe
I didn't have it already.

              No one did. I made an empty contact
with his name. I wrote

a hundred messages to him that were really to no one. *He has*
a girlfriend, I thought, *and you were the one to make this call, you*
   can't
break it. He didn't have social media, he was way too interesting

for that. Not like I spent hours looking for it. On Google Images
if you typed in "Jude Wheeler Tennessee" you got one grainy
   photo

of his school photography club, him in the back row. You could

see a few of his curls and not a lot else. I spent a long time looking
at those curls. There were four of them. Five? It's hard
to count curls. My mom walked in while I was doing it and

I stuffed my phone under the couch cushions and told myself,
enough. It was August. I went straight into my junior year and
found myself
a boyfriend. Rafe wasn't on exchange, his family had moved

from Scotland a few months back so his mom could teach
at UW, but he still had the accent and he was built
like a quarterback, blond hair, brown lace-up boots

and he painted his nails and played mandolin and everyone
wanted him and I told myself I wanted him too. Kind,
funny, sort of, but in a childish way, kept taking my hands

off the buttons of his shirt in the back of his father's Range Rover
while he said, *slowly, slowly, there isn't a rush, I want this but—*
and I pulled back and I shut my eyes and I thought about Jude

and then I forced myself to erase the thought of him
all the way down. Straightened my sweater. Told Rafe, *I'm sorry,
we'll take it slow*, and smiled. *Big Feelings*, I said.

That next week my eye started shaking again.

NIGHT
TWO

JUDE
DEFECTIVE SUN

I'm standing alone in front
of the Bonfire after looking for her
all week at camp in vain
and I'm waiting
for her to arrive but she's not
coming and what sort of sun am I

who can't keep anyone
in my orbit, even when I haven't
had an opportunity to screw things up
because I haven't spoken with them (her)
once in any form for almost precisely 365 days,
give or take thirty minutes.

And speaking of suns,
the fire is searing my face hot and tight like
I've spent too much time
in the sun and wind and I'm ready
to leave in defeat, to walk back
to my dorm to try to sleep, if
my whirlpooling thoughts will allow
it (they won't, it'll be my own private
Sunrise Night no matter what) and then

I hear her voice.

FLORENCE
MORE

I didn't get the lead in the Satie piece because
I didn't go out for it. They couldn't say no
because I didn't let them. Even tonight

flinging myself through the barrel turns
that I choreographed myself—that's what
I told Dr. Rojas, I didn't want to be *distracted*

by a *lead* from my *love for choreo*, which was a
big old lie—I can feel my feet landing badly, all
the weight on the inside, ankles rolling

in a way I'll pay for tomorrow, but at least
if I fall it'll be in the back somewhere,
they can just drag me out by my legs

and play that vaudeville hee-haw sound. At least
this far back they can't see my bad eye
well enough to get how it's probably

tilting off its axis; this is my consolation, while
I'm in the back landing badly and five-alarm-
fire freaking out because I know that Rafe

is watching me dance on the livestream. When

it's finally over, I skip the bow. Walk straight
through the wings to the stage door and outside

and no one's there yet, thank God, no one's there
to see me cry. Not even
Jude. I've managed it

this long. Mealtimes have been the hardest
to miss him—but we rehearse late, and so we eat
late, and when I see his head in the buffet line

I run. Have some granola in my room. To-go lunches,
no trips to town, no trivia night, just me in my cabin
sweating it out so I don't see his face, so he doesn't

see me like this. So weak. Rafe doesn't mind. I think
he kind of likes me this way, the new B student me,
me defanged, and it's a foggier way of being, sure,

Marvel matinees every Sunday instead of the gym,
no protein in my diet because who the hell cares.
We eat Rolos on my basement sofa and make out

to Phoebe Bridgers and he tells me about growing up
in Inverness. He likes me in soft sweaters and
sometimes I braid my hair all fancy in the mirror

and wear perfume to smell like the cupcake

I'm becoming. On FaceTime last night we were talking
about our days and then out of nowhere Rafe told me he loved me

no matter what, that I don't have to be special or perfect,
and I smiled and I also maybe sort of thought, *screw
you, I am special and perfect* but if I could have two good eyes

my God I'd be happy to be ordinary forever. Maybe then
my stomach wouldn't crawl up my spine every time
I see that boy in dark jeans with a camera strap around his neck,

maybe I wouldn't flee like a coward. Maybe I would
be spending this Sunrise Night in my cabin like I told Rafe
I would (does he know about Jude? No, he doesn't, he doesn't

need to, what's to know?) instead of warily walking
the path to Bonfire still in my stage makeup and my stupid
dance skirt and leggings and it's bigger than I remember, the fire,

it does something hard and hot to me, and flushed
from the realization I don't see Jude until I'm standing right
behind him. Him, like the shadow of something burning.

JUDE
BONFIRE, 9:03 P.M.

"Hey, Jude," Florence says. "Sorry, I know you hate that but I can't forgo one of the most common greetings just because of your name."

I turn and there she is. She looks different. I can't quite identify what it is. Softer somehow. "I'm too happy to see you to care," I tell her, knowing, if anything, I'm understating things. We hug for a long time.

"You came," Florence says into my chest.

"*You* came. I almost gave up on you," I say into the top of her head. She smells like sugar cookies.

"Jude. Why?"

"What do you mean, why? Look how late you are."

"We didn't say an exact time, did we?"

"I don't know."

"It's been a year and a lot's happened since then."

"It seemed like it was earlier last year when we met up."

"I was already here when we met, huh?"

"Turning a marshmallow into charcoal."

Florence looks at me again like she's seeing me for the first time. "Jude! You came!"

"Did you really think I wouldn't?"

"I don't know what I thought."

We look at each other shyly in the firelight. We both start to speak simultaneously.

"Go ahead," Florence says.

"No you."

"I didn't—"Florence shakes her head.

We both laugh.

"This is so weird," I say. "We weren't this awkward last year, when we'd barely even met."

"We were doing something right. It must have been marshmallows."

"Do we need an icebreaker marshmallow or three?"

"Maybe just to take the edge off."

We go over to one of the long tables they have set up with bags of store-brand marshmallows, graham crackers, Hershey bars, and wood-handled metal marshmallow roasting sticks. We each grab a stick and load it up with three marshmallows. We return to the fire and sit.

"Remember," I say. "Close to the fire but not too close. As soon as you see it smoking a little bit, pull out." *That's good advice for lots of things a guy and girl do together, right, Marley?* I think.

"I'm gonna get it right this time. Perfect golden marshmallow." Florence has a determined cast to her gaze.

"I can't believe this is exactly what we were doing exactly one year ago tonight."

"Isn't it so weird?"

"One year."

"One year since we've seen each other. Did you cheat?"

The question paralyzes me. Do I tell her about Marley? I really don't want to. It's humiliating.

"Did you cheat?" Florence asks again. "Did you look up social media?"

"Oh."

"What did you think I was referring to?"

"Um. Poker?"

"You sure froze up when I asked. Have you been cheating at Texas Hold 'Em? Around the campfire with all the other cow-pokes?"

"I missed you," I say, smiling.

"Enough to cheat?"

"Nope. Didn't slip," I lie, knowing it probably won't be the last of the night. "You?"

"Nope. Tempted?"

"Were you?"

"I asked first."

"You need to turn that marshmallow."

"I know what I'm doing. So. Tempted?"

I look at the fire and then at Florence. "Sure. Yeah. Your turn."

Florence lifts her lightly smoking marshmallow from the fire and gives it an appraising spin. "I mean of course."

"I told you I missed you. Did you miss me?"

FLORENCE
BONFIRE, 9:10 P.M.

"Duh, of course, I missed you," I tell him, and stick the marshmallow back into the fire. I don't want to look him in the eyes, so I force myself to do an exaggerated up-and-down take. "Are you taller? Is it weird for me to ask if you're taller?"

"I'm taller. Six one."

"What were you before?"

"Five ten."

"Did you spend this year, like, eating dozens of eggs like Gaston? Every morning a gigantic glass of milk? Big old milk mustache?"

"Yes, Florence, I was a commercial for the Dairy Farmers of America."

"Okay, but that would be amazing. I would buy cows from you."

"Cows?"

He's laughing. I reach out to touch his arm.

"You're definitely taller," I say, but it comes out quiet and weird.

"You look different too."

"I do? I mean yeah. My eye is worse, I guess."

"Not that. I didn't notice it."

"It's okay to notice it."

"I know," he says. "But I didn't. I mean—your hair?"

It's half-up with pins from the performance. I pull them out. My hair falls around my shoulders and Jude lifts up a hand and then puts it back down.

"I got curtain bangs," I tell him.

"Curtain bangs."

"Yeah. Like Stevie Nicks, I guess. I guess I'm leaning into the seventies thing. Plus it—it helps to hide my bad eye." This is something I've never said out loud.

"And it's longer too. Was it curly last year?"

"Yeah," I say. "It was."

"I remembered your hair in a different way. When I thought about you."

"You thought about me."

"Yeah, Florence," he says. "I thought about you all the time."

Why do I want to cry? I think.

JUDE
BONFIRE, 9:12 P.M.

"How about you?" I ask. "Did you think about me?"

"I said I missed you."

"That doesn't mean you ever thought about me."

"How would that work?"

"I've missed people who I didn't think about."

"Don't you have to think about them to miss them?"

"Not necessarily."

"Not sure I buy that."

"Well." I shrug.

"Okay, well, when you're done trying to argue your way out of the answer I know you want, I'll be right here."

"What do you think is the answer I want?"

"I didn't say *think*. I said *know*." Florence stares intently into the fire. Shadows dance across her face.

"Which is?"

"That I thought about you all the time too." Florence looks at me, sizing up my expression to see if I betray myself. I do.

"Yeah. Okay. Busted."

Florence looks back into the fire with an unreadable smile. "Yeah, Jude. I thought about you all the time. Happy now?"

JUDE
ALL THE TIME

If you're anything like me,
all the time never means all
the time. It means once

you saw a sunrise and you wished
I was there to take (make) a photo
of it for you, the way I did
that once, with your sole raised
heavenward like you were testing
the temperature of the sky.

It means once you walked down
a leaf-strewn hill in late October,
unsteady like you were
on a ship's heaving deck and you wished
you could borrow my arm because it came free
of obligation or explanation.

It means once over a donut you remembered
eating one crusted with crickets
and you wondered what I was doing
at that exact moment and if I ever thought
of that night. If you're anything

like me, it means once you awoke in the stillness

of three a.m. and the sound of the wind
against your window reminded you
of me, for some reason
or no reason.

JUDE
BONFIRE, 9:22 P.M.

"Yeah, I'm happy now," I say. Florence has a thin string of marshmallow on her chin. I reach out and wipe it away. Touching her face sends a charge through me.

"Mmm, thank you," she says around a mouthful of marshmallow.

"Didn't want you looking like you hooked up with Duke of Duke's Mayonnaise fame."

"Didn't we have almost this exact conversation last year, but not involving a famous mayonnaise duke? Also: there's a famous mayonnaise duke?"

"Do you not have Duke's in Wisconsin? Everyone loves it where I'm from."

"Why are you suddenly this huge mayonnaise guy?"

"A *huge mayonnaise guy*?"

"You've just basically revealed yourself to be part of the Duke's Mayonnaise fandom."

"By acknowledging the existence of Duke's Mayonnaise?"

"You clearly love it too."

"My grandma used to use it in deviled eggs and tomato sandwiches."

"Was this your grandma who had cancer and survived?"

"Good memory! Yep. She treated all other brands like they were radioactive waste."

"I can respect a woman who has fervent opinions on mayo."

"Now look who's a huge mayonnaise gal."

"I respect people with fervent opinions on a wide variety of topics. I think if an opinion's worth having at all, it's worth having fervently," Florence says.

"I know that about you," I say.

"I've never told you that about me."

"No, but I still know it somehow. Doesn't it feel like we've known each other for way longer than we have? We haven't even known each other for a full twenty-four hours."

"However many hours plus a year."

"Well, the year doesn't count, does it?"

"Yeah, guess not. So, Jude, what are we going to do with our one wild and precious Sunrise Night?"

"Did you just make that up?"

"It's from a poem. Mary Oliver."

"She wrote about Sunrise Night? Did she go to HAC?"

"You think you're funny, don't you."

"Honestly yes. Yes I do."

"For real, though. What should our first stop be?"

FLORENCE
STRATEGY

All week I've haunted the dance building morning
to night. Choreo, yes, modern class, yes, but also I sort of
started making the director and the pianist coffee

in the staff room. I stayed to mark the floor, to check
the light cues, to insist on taking another load of dirty towels
in the washer-dryer in the basement. Anything

to keep me there longer. Later. No chance to see Jude,
no time to call Rafe. Too late to play capture the flag
or sign up for a little walking trip through town, too late

for the hot line at the cafeteria. Just a salad in a to-go box
before it's me and Makayla back in the girls' dorm and she's
    looking
at me like I'm a human hazard sign. Maybe I am. But

he has to still be with Marley. I knew it in my stomach. Like
can you imagine Jude breaking up with someone? Can you
imagine *anyone* breaking up with Jude? How do you have

a casual conversation with someone who, after one night,
could draw you a map of your brain? No, it had to wait.
I already felt like a loser. I wasn't going to bail on this game

I insisted we play and prove it to him for sure.

FLORENCE
BONFIRE, 9:28 P.M.

"Pac-Man," he says confidently.

"Pac-Man?"

"Yup."

"Is this something you think that I wanna do or is it something you wanna do that you're attempting to, like, incept into my head?"

". . . Ms. Pac-Man?"

"Jude."

"I feel like we could go and eat a lot of ghosts."

"Haven't you ever thought about how weird it is that it's Ms. Pac-Man when it's her on the title of the machine and not Mr. Pac-Man when it's his? Like, is she just that much fancier than him?"

"No," he says. "I always just kinda figured it was the patriarchy."

I love him. No. I don't. Marley, he has Marley. And more importantly (duh) I have Rafe. I should call Rafe. Right now. I should call him right now.

"Basically," I tell him, "you're saying we should go eat ghosts in the name of the patriarchy?"

"And also I hear that the arcade has milkshakes on Sunrise Night. We should go, though, it's already nine thirty. We're like the last ones here."

"Cool, let's go." I say it breezily. "Is it okay though if I call my boyfriend first?"

JUDE
THE ONE THING THAT DIDN'T OCCUR TO ME

I had no designs
for tonight (I didn't),
only the hope that she would
show up at all. I knew

that from there I'd have to see
if we still were what we left
ourselves, whatever that was.

The one thing that didn't occur to me
is that Florence would show up
with a boyfriend.

And now I don't know
what this means, whether
we are what we left ourselves
or something less, whether

this dance
starts over completely.

JUDE
HEADING SLOWLY AWAY FROM THE BONFIRE IN THE APPROXIMATE DIRECTION OF THE ARCADE, 9:31 P.M.

I decide to go big and broad to hide my surprise (and its companion feelings that I'm having much more difficulty putting a name to). "*Boyfriend? Florence? You have a boyfriend? Ooooooh.*"

Florence rolls her eyes. "Go ahead. Tease me. I deserve it, I'm sure."

I don't really have anything else other than to keep repeating some variation of *ooooooh* along with *you have a boyfriend* like we're in fourth grade. I feel like that might get old quickly for both of us.

"So what's his name?" I ask, knowing I'll hate it, even (and especially) if it's "Jude."

"Rafe."

"Ray?"

"*Rafe.* With an 'f.' *Ray-fuh.*"

"Can I call him Ray?"

"Why would you want to call him Ray? Rafe is already one syllable. You're not saving any time by denying him his 'f.'"

"I refuse to make a joke about denying him his 'f' because I'm mature and above such youthful shenanigans," I say.

Florence scoffs.

"So his name is spelled R-a-y-f?" I ask.

"R-a-f-e," Florence says.

"Okay, so I'd be denying him an 'f-e' by calling him Ray. And also giving him an undeserved 'y.'"

"You have to earn 'y'?"

"Sometimes."

"Sometimes?"

"You have to earn 'a-e-i-o-u' and *sometimes* 'y.'"

Florence laughs like she doesn't want to but can't help it. "I take back what I said about missing you."

"No takebacks," I say, feeling very proud of how I've been able to sweep my unknowable mix of feelings over Florence's having a boyfriend under a carpet of jokes.

"I think we need to revisit briefly why you were so into calling him Ray."

"It just sounds like the name of an old man wearing overalls, with a toothpick sticking out of his mouth. Goin' fishin'."

"*Jude*. How *dare* you put me in a relationship with an old man in overalls who likes fishin'. *Ew*."

"How's that revisiting working out for you?"

"Badly," Florence says. "It's working out badly and I'm very sorry I asked to revisit. Hey, real quick—" She moves to my other side.

I look at her. "What was—"

"I need you on the side of my good eye. If you're on the side of my bad eye, I'll keep turning, trying to see you, and then I'll start veering off in that direction, and I'll run you right off the sidewalk."

"Probably to my death."

"Probably to your death, in a cataclysmic explosion."

"I'll stay on your good side. Hey, do you think that's where that phrase came from?"

"My condition seems very specific to have resulted in a phrase like that. It probably came from, like, when old-timey people would slaughter a goose and you had to stay on the good side of the goose when slaughtering it."

"The good side of the goose?"

"Am I gonna have to Google this for you? Also, this is officially the second time we've ended up discussing geese."

"That's sweet that you'd want to see me so badly you'd run me off the sidewalk trying."

"Well, don't flatter yourself *too* much. It happens with literally everyone. But I am happy to see you, and I want to literally see you. How's Marley, by the way?"

JUDE
LYING IS WRONG

But I need to lie.

JUDE
STILL HEADING FOR THE ARCADE, ERECTING A RICKETY SCAFFOLD OF FALSEHOOD ON WHICH TO STAND, 9:34 P.M.

"Marley's good. Yeah, we're good."

FLORENCE
WE'RE GOOD

Good like: they went apple picking maybe in the fall and Jude
made her picture under the trees.

Good like: Jude had Thanksgiving with his mom first and then
saw his dad for dessert and Marley rode along and held his
hand when it was hard. Then they had a slice of pie together in
the park.

Good like: they accidentally got each other the same thing for
Christmas, the same perfect thing, like a vintage Pepsi T-shirt
because they had Pepsis on their first date.

Good like: Jude's dad warmed up to Marley so much that he
makes her favorite dinner on Sundays, and he never cooks,
ever, except for when Jude and Marley come over.

(Her favorite dinner is mac and cheese casserole. I'm sorry, I can't
help it. She has to be kind of basic in my imagination or I'm
going to cry.)

Good like: Jude thought about me all the time, like he said, and
when he did, he thought how he likes Marley so much more
than he likes me.

FLORENCE
ABOUT FIVE FEET FARTHER DOWN THE SIDEWALK, 9:34 P.M.

"I can join the club now," I tell Jude.

"The club?"

"The old married folks club. You guys have been together for what, like, a year and a half now? Two years?"

"Yeah. That sounds right."

"Basically you're high school married. Is she one of those girls who wants to get hitched right out of high school?"

"That's kind of mean."

". . . I didn't mean it to be mean? Some girls are romantics."

"Well, some guys are romantics."

"Do *you* want to get hitched right out of high school? You could like . . . I don't know. You could have a square dance? With a caller and everything."

"Florence, you need to tell me exactly what you think courtship rituals are like in Tennessee. Should I, like, have to remove a piece of hay from my mouth when I kiss her? Should I be presenting her with a freshly caught bass before each date?"

"No, I don't mean it like that! Like, some of my family is from Scotland, my grandparents came over here on my dad's side. My boyfriend is from Scotland. At weddings and stuff we have ceilidhs. Someone calls the dances, which means they tell you the steps. And there's a band and it's loud and sweaty and really fun. The guys wear kilts."

Jude's eyes are a little glazed over. "Your boyfriend is from Scotland?"

"Yeah."

"Rafe. He's from Scotland?"

"From Inverness."

"Is that how you say it? INN-ver-nuss."

"I could do it with the accent but then I would sound like an asshole. Americans putting on accents always sound like assholes. It's like a law."

"Is he an exchange student?"

"No."

Jude seems weirdly relieved. "Oh so like he was born there and moved here when he was little or something."

"Actually he just came over last year. His mom got recruited by UW–Madison to do some kind of biomedical research. And the head of her department knew my dad was Scottish and so we had them over for dinner and then last fall we started hook—dating."

"So he has the accent."

"Yeah."

"That's how you learned how to say Inverness."

"Jude, I've always known how to say Inverness. Does Marley have an accent?"

"Marley doesn't have a Scottish accent. Marley has the kind of accent where she sounds like she's swallowed her tongue." He says it with an acidity that surprises me.

"Is it . . . cute?" I ask him.

"Yes. It's adorable."

JUDE
CONTINUING DOWN THE SIDEWALK ON FLORENCE'S GOOD SIDE, 9:39 P.M.

"What's something she says?" Florence asks.

I think for a few seconds. "Mmm. Uh. Sometimes she'll be like, *hey, come on over here.*"

"Hey, come on over here?"

"Yeah. Or like, *hey, get on out of here.*"

"Okay, so the first one sounds like a fairly normal and non-regionally-specific phrase. And the second one . . . is she always telling you to get on out of places?"

"Rarely."

"But it does occasionally happen where she'll say, *Jude, get on out of here?*"

"Occasionally."

"What's a place she'll tell you to get on out of?"

"Maybe if we're riding in a pickup truck down some gravel road."

"She'll tell you to get on out of a *moving pickup truck?*"

"On our way to go mudding."

"She won't let you get to the mudding before you have to get on out of the truck?"

"She's a very private mudder."

"A private mudder."

"Mudding is her thinking time. Like when people meditate."

"It seems like maybe she simply wouldn't invite you along in the first place as opposed to telling you to get on out of the truck."

"But she's also an impulse mudder."

I look at Florence. Her face is equally divided between credulity and outrageous incredulity. At this point Marley is whatever ridiculous person I want her to be. I don't feel any obligation to truth or reality. The real Marley can live her happy life with her new baby Jaxton or Chaxton or Kayleeee or NeighLee or Kayxton or Neighxton or whatever they'll be named.

"So what do you and Rafe do? Mostly kilt-friendly activities?"

FLORENCE
AFTER CHECKING MY PHONE MAP TO MAKE SURE WE ARE STILL HEADED TOWARD THE ARCADE AND NOT OFF INTO THE WILDERNESS TO BE MURDERED, 9:42 P.M.

"Kilt-friendly activities."

"Yeah," Jude says. "Like don't they say something about kilts?"

"That . . . you're not supposed to wear anything beneath your kilt? Are you about to ask me if Rafe wears underwear beneath his kilt?"

"No. No I'm not."

"Are you okay?"

Jude looks kind of ill. "No I am not going to ask you if you know whether Rafe wears underwear beneath his kilt."

"He does."

"Oh good. That's good to know."

"For the record, I have never seen Rafe in a kilt. But, like, what we actually do . . . Rafe likes to play, like, weird little instruments. He plays the mandolin, and the Fisher-Price accordion, and the harmonica."

"Harmonicas aren't weird."

"He plays the banjo with that little harmonica attachment."

"Are you sure he isn't from Tennessee?"

"No," I say, laughing. "He moves a lot, and he says that it's easier to bring small instruments along. He had to stop playing the piano because they lived a bunch of places where he couldn't have one."

"And you play music with him?"

"No. I mean, I sing sometimes. I'm not good or anything. But I'm thinking about taking lessons."

"Really? That's cool."

"Yeah."

"You sound kind of bummed about it."

"I mean I'm sort of just looking for other stuff I'm good at. I like to sing. I joined the choir. I go see a lot of movies."

"Movies."

"Yeah, like Marvel movies."

"You sound kind of bummed about Marvel movies."

"Am I supposed to sound a certain kind of way about Marvel movies?"

"I'm not like an evangelist or anything for Marvel movies. I actually sort of don't care about Marvel movies. I mean I'll go see them. That's pretty much the movies there are to go see."

"Which is how I also feel about Marvel movies. So I guess I'm kind of not sure why it's not okay to feel vaguely bummed about that?" I don't ask it meanly. I really want to know.

"You just . . . you just seemed kind of sad right there, and I was trying to figure out why, or if you wanted to talk about it," Jude says.

"That's funny."

"What?"

"Nothing."

"What?"

"Nothing. It's just that . . . sometimes I kind of think that Rafe likes that I'm sad. Like it's the way I *should* feel or something? Or he tells me to cheer up and, like, gets me ice cream."

"Oh."

"But he doesn't really want to know why I'm sad. Sometimes I think he's afraid to know why."

"Some people are wusses."

"But not you."

"No," Jude says.

"What does Marley do when you're sad?"

He looks like he's about to say something, and then shakes his head. "She says we should go to youth group," he tells me. "She says that'll cheer me right up." He says it with an ironic laugh.

JUDE
CHEER ME RIGHT UP

I never accepted Marley's kind offer
to cheer me up
through youth group attendance,

which of course proved a severe miscalculation
for many reasons, not the least of which being
that I had dramatically underestimated the amount
and sort of fun that could be had at youth group

or perhaps, more precisely, *after* youth group in the back
of a Ram diesel pickup with a "Rollin' Coal" bumper sticker,
although I strongly suspect this isn't the kind of fun
Marley was talking about.

She always said it like I've never been
to youth group, like I haven't
lived my whole life in Dickson, Tennessee, where
you just sort of end up at youth group a *lot*.

I went with my buddy Aiden once
and the youth pastor talked with us
casually, while bowling, about how
short we fall of perfection, which is why
we need Jesus's salvation,

and I thought, *okay I get why I need Jesus*
but why do I need youth group
when I have a little youth pastor in my head
all the time to remind me of how short
I fall of perfection?

and then as if on cue,
I rolled a gutter ball.

FLORENCE
AT THE ARCADE, WHICH IS ABSOLUTELY WALL-TO-WALL BURSTING WITH YELLING, OBNOXIOUS HACKERS, 9:50 P.M.

"Whoa," Jude says, peering through the door. "Maybe we should come back later."

"They close at eleven thirty. If we're gonna Pac-Man I think now is our time."

"Do you want to divide and conquer? You can go get us tokens and I can wait in the line for milkshakes?"

"I kind of feel like if we separate I'll never see you again."

"That's legit. Okay. Let me go first. I can, like, keep my elbows up, push people out of the way."

"My knight in shining armor."

Jude snorts. "If you really want to be the one to fight through this crowd I'll let you."

Last year I would have said yes, but I'm not in the mood to fight anymore. We muscle through to the line for the token machine. "People are watching us," I tell Jude.

"We must be the hot camp gossip."

"Are we?"

"I don't know. We didn't hang out all session." He doesn't say it like it's a criticism, more like a fact.

"And now we're hanging out? That's the gossip?"

"I guess."

"Makayla's over there with her girlfriend."

Both of us put up a hand to wave hi. Makayla immediately takes out her phone and rapid-fire texts someone. I pull out my phone. It's not me.

"Yikes," Jude says.

"I kind of feel like we're in a fishbowl. Like we're betta fish."

"Don't they die after like a day?"

"I think they fight. I don't know. I hate fish. Do you know if the machine only takes cash?"

Jude cranes his neck. "I can't see it yet."

One of the employees hurries by holding a giant stuffed bear. "Excuse me," I ask her, putting my hand out. "Do you know if this machine only—"

"I need you to move," the employee barks.

I step back and take a deep breath.

"Yikes," Jude says.

"Yikes," I say.

"It'll be fine. How much cash do you have?"

"I have two twenties," I tell him.

"I only have a five and my debit card."

"How about I get our tokens and then later you can pick up something else?"

"Twenty dollars' worth of tokens?"

"There are zombies to kill," I remind him. "We need to go do the Lord's work."

Jude laughs in a kind of dark way that I haven't heard before. "The Lord wants us to kill zombies?"

"It's something Rafe says. The Lord's work. Sorry. Is it offensive?"

"No," he says. "The Lord definitely wants us to kill zombies."

JUDE
WHAT YOU HOPE LOVE IS

For the first few minutes we played
The House of the Dead 2, she sparkled—

she was chatty, full of life. She blew away
zombie after zombie like it was what
she was born to do. One of us would die

while the other would frantically jam
more tokens in the machine to resurrect
ourselves. It made me want to go
with her to a house filled with monsters in real life

and show her how
I would fight
for her and see how
she would fight for me.

After a while, though, she grew
quiet and subdued. She began
to miss more and more. It was okay,

I wasn't thinking
about the game anymore.

I was thinking that this is what you hope

love is: you enter a house
full of monsters with someone
and then you fight for each other
until you can't fight anymore.

JUDE
AT THE ARCADE, WHICH IS ABSOLUTELY BURSTING WITH YELLING, OBNOXIOUS HACKERS, 10:24 P.M.

"Hey, how you doing?" I ask. On the screen I'm dead. Florence is still fighting.

"Is that your Joey Tribbiani again? Because it's still terrible," Florence says, squinting as she takes aim. "God, the graphics on this are worse than I remember."

"My Joey Trib—"

"Remember? Last year?"

"Ah, right! No. I was genuinely asking. You got quiet."

A zombie jumps from the shadows and slashes Florence to death with a sword. She sighs and puts her gun in the rack. "I'm having a hard time playing," she says finally. "I can't focus."

"Too loud?"

"No, I mean like—aim right. Because of my eye. Bright screen, dark room. It's hard."

"Oh."

"I'm a bad teammate."

"You're the best teammate. I never would have gotten that far without you. Wanna play something different?"

"Let's give Pac-Man a go. I think my eyes can handle that one."

We wait a few minutes for the Pac-Man machine to clear and then we step up. Florence starts having fun again—at least, it looks like she is. I start to ask her something but Miles walks by with Nolan and Henry; they're all from my dorm floor.

"Big upgrade from Marley, bro," Miles says loudly to me as he passes.

I freeze. They know the truth about Marley. Florence, however, shoots me a look.

"We're just friends, dude," I tell Miles. What I don't say (because they know the truth and will bust me): *We're just friends, dude. And besides, Marley and I are good.*

"Your friends are rude about Marley," Florence says after they've left earshot.

"Yeah, well."

"You not gonna stick up for your girl's honor with them?"

"What, I'm gonna fistfight them at the arcade? Pick them up by the seat of the pants and toss them out?"

"Not throw down, just—I don't know. Say *something.*"

"It's fine. Does Rafe kickbox everyone who's rude to you or about you?"

FLORENCE
SLAYING PAC-MAN LIKE IT'S MY JOB, 10:29 P.M.

"It doesn't have to be a fistfight," I say, and even I know I sound annoyingly prim. "You could have done *something*. You could have flipped them the bird and said, 'Marley's hot.'"

He laughs. "Because flipping someone off is the appropriate social response?"

"I mean yeah, sometimes."

"We were raised differently, I guess. That's just not my automatic response."

"If someone was being a jackass to me and I didn't flip them off, my dad would feel sad for me."

"That's kind of awesome," Jude says. He gets tagged by a ghost and dies. Again.

I stuff another handful of tokens into the machine. "My dad is pretty awesome. My mom is too."

"Do they like Rafe?"

"All these questions about Rafe."

"You said you were gonna call him and then you didn't."

Shit, I think.

"Got distracted. It's not a big deal if I don't call," I say. "He won't like freak out or anything. And yeah, my parents like him. At least I think so. They haven't really said anything one way or the other, they try to stay out of my personal life."

"Your personal life? Do they call it that?"

"They do, actually."

"That's cool. I think if I asked my mom to stay out of my personal life she'd take my bedroom door off its hinges."

I laugh at the image. "That's hardcore. Is she that afraid you're gonna get someone pregnant?" That familiar *wah-wah-wah* sound from the machine. Jude has been eaten by another ghost. This time he feeds the game tokens.

"Pregnant?" he asks.

"I mean. Yeah? Or like, she just doesn't want you hooking up with anyone or—"

Jude isn't talking. He jams his joystick left and right. The machine is beeping like a carnival ride.

"Your parents aren't like that?" he finally asks.

"Pack of condoms in my bathroom. Lots of talks about consent. Sex-positive gynecologist. I'm supposed to tell my mom when I finally do it, if I want, and we can go out for a sundae."

"A sundae."

"Yeah."

"Like a reward?"

"No, I mean—when my mom wants to have a serious talk with me, we go to the Frosty Treat and eat hot fudge sundaes in the car."

"Oh. That makes more sense than, like, having a parade to celebrate that you had sex."

"I don't know. I think having a big-ass parade sounds kinda nice. You should feel that good about sex when you decide to do it."

"But you haven't yet."

"Led a parade?" I say, misunderstanding on purpose. "You've never seen me twirl a baton. I'd be *amazing*."

Jude sees the dodge for what it is, and smiles.

And I appreciate him not pressing the issue, so I tell him the truth. "No, I haven't had sex."

"Me neither."

"Not with Marley? Really? After two years?"

"Oh, Marley's had—uh. No. Not after two years."

"Marley's had sex?"

He's kind of sweating a little. He really doesn't seem to want to talk about this stuff. I'm surprised he hasn't died again.

"Marley's more religious than me," he says. "And I don't know if I want to."

"At all?"

"With her."

JUDE
LYING IS WRONG REDUX

I heard a story once
about a girl who faked a British accent
on the first day of school
as a gag and got so much positive attention
she just kept up the charade

and for an entire school year had to speak
in a fake accent because committing to the lie
for as long as it took was less humiliating
than admitting the truth.

FLORENCE
THE NULL POINT

There's a place I can go to just by
turning my head. Far left, chin down, let
my right eye sit at its edge. The shaking

stops. All this wind-up-toy tension you didn't
know you were feeling, it vanishes. The null point.
It's how I spot when I pirouette, how I keep

my temper in check, how I imagine grace maybe feels
if you're seeking grace. Like finding your echo
in another person, except you've found it

in yourself. But I don't go there anymore. They train it
out of you. The eye doctors, specialists, the physical
therapists, they tell your parents to correct you

when you tilt your head. My mother tapping my shoulder
almost apologetically, every time she'd find me
like that—like a little Joan of Arc

listening to God, like a composer teasing out
a counterpoint to his melody, I'd stand there
far away in the ocean of it. Waves of quick release

and then a calming. The only way I could see

the way the rest of the world saw. I think love is
like that. I think sex might be like that, with the right

person. The still point in the shivering world. When I tilt
my head now, it feels wrong because I've been told
it's wrong. I want to know its rightness again.

JUDE

BEING SLAIN BY PAC-MAN, 10:34 P.M.

"Don't you think Marley's hot?" Florence says.

"Sure." *I hate this.*

"So aren't you tempted?"

"Yeah, but." *I really hate this.*

I die, finally, and step back from the console. "You want another turn?" I ask Florence.

"Know what I just realized?"

"What did you just realize?"

"I've never seen a picture of Marley."

"What? No. I showed you one."

"Didn't."

"Are you *sure?*" I study Florence's face for some indication that she's messing with me, the way she's been poking at me all night.

"I'm *positive.* I wanna see a picture of her."

"Now? You're finally interested enough to ask *now?*" *Sure would have been nice if you'd been this interested in seeing a photo of Marley last year, when I still had one and hadn't deleted every single last one of them off my phone and then blocked her on every social media platform.*

"Yes, now." Florence looks determined.

"I—not now."

"Why?"

"Because it's not . . . convenient."

"What? You need to hitch up a team of horses to pull one off your phone or something? You have to go to the bank to open a safety deposit box with her picture in it? You have to have someone turn a key simultaneously with you like launching a missile from a submarine?"

"How do you know how to launch a missile from a submarine?"

"Movies. Isn't Marley your lock screen?"

"No, just—"

"Hey, if you two aren't gonna play, you need to step away from the machine. Can't just stand there and chitchat," an arcade employee says, entirely too officiously. "Besides, we're closing in twenty minutes."

I see an opportunity for a diversion. "So y'all are closing in twenty minutes, but it's so important that someone else gets a chance to play Pac-Man that you have to crawl up our butts?" I ask.

"You wanna be a smart-ass, you can leave now," the employee says.

"I'm just asking a question," I say.

"I don't have time for questions from HAC brats," he says.

"If you hate dealing with camp brats," Florence says, "maybe don't work at an arcade in a campin' town. It's, like, a free country."

He comes around from the counter and jabs toward the door with his thumb. "Okay, out. Both of you. Bye-bye. Have a nice Sunrise Night. Have a nice life. But do it somewhere else."

"You're fun," Florence says.

"Out," he says, herding us toward the door.

"Hang on, I gotta pee," Florence says. "Can I pee so I don't piss myself?"

The employee rolls his eyes and waves her toward the restroom. "Then go. And after that, leave."

"I'll meet you out front," Florence tells me. "Hey, give me that five you mentioned earlier."

She says it with such purpose that I don't ask any questions and hand over my five-dollar bill. When she meets me outside, she's grinning.

"What?" I ask, realizing I blew my chance to try to find a picture of Marley.

"Right before I left I jammed the five in the jukebox and cued up 'My Humps' by the Black Eyed Peas."

"*Florence.* You didn't."

"I did."

"Five dollars? What else did you play?"

"'My Humps.' Five dollars' worth of 'My Humps.'"

"Florence."

"Yeah?"

"That's *twenty* times."

"So now they have their music to close by. Let's go."

We cackle while we speed walk away.

FLORENCE
WALKING NOWHERE, 10:52 P.M.

We're on the corner of Lake and Main and Jude looks like he's going to keel over. He props himself up against a lamppost, laughing.

I ask him, "Can you think of one single less sexually appealing song? Also she delivers it like she's an old-timey phone operator. Like, 'connecting please! Now dialing up . . . all that ass inside those jeans!' Zero conviction. If you're going to refer to your boobs as lady lumps, you better sell that shit. Kelis totally convinced me that her boobs could be milkshakes."

"Florence, you need to stop or I am going to die and at sunrise they're going to have to do, like, a Viking burial for me on the lake."

"Yes, because so many Vikings died for the sake of Fergie."

"I'm all about historical accuracy," Jude says. "It's sad. You know they can just unplug the jukebox."

"They have to move it first," I say confidently. "The plug's behind it, and that thing had to be five hundred pounds, easy."

"You checked."

"I did."

"You realize that that arcade was full of HACkers who hate us now."

"If they do, they have no taste."

"No taste?"

"Well. Maybe good taste. Anyway, your roommate was really rude about your girlfriend."

"Yeah," he says. He takes his phone out to check the time. "Do you wanna get some food? The diner should still be open."

"Is that your lock screen?"

He looks up at me fast.

I put my hands up. "I don't have to see if it's private."

"No, it's just—" Jude hands me his phone.

I touch the screen. It's a picture of a windowpane, lights behind it. Police lights? It's beautiful at first, like a Christmas tree, and then it's unsettling. "That's amazing. Did you take that?"

"Yeah," he says.

"I love it."

We look at each other.

"I don't have any pictures of Marley on my phone," he says, quietly, "because we broke up the minute I got home last summer."

"Jude."

"She'd been boning her youth pastor."

"Jude."

"And now she's pregnant. Or maybe she had the baby. I don't know."

"Jude."

He smiles wanly. "Is this a big enough deal for us to go get a sundae and have a serious talk about it?"

"Dear Lord, yes. I think that's the only thing we *can* do."

JUDE
THE GREAT DEFEAT

Now I get to go rummaging
in my pockets, to offer up
my lint-covered defeat for Florence
to examine with her magnifying glass.

Now I get to explain to Florence that I lied
to her about Marley and Me (the blockbuster
sad humiliation, not the blockbuster sad film
of the same name) because I wanted
so desperately not to seem
like something easy to cast aside
and abandon.

All I wanted was to look like someone
worth keeping. That's not so much
to ask. That's worth lying
to protect.

FLORENCE
REASONS

Sometimes I feel like I can't read people
at all. (It's a good opening for a depth-perception joke—
that girl can't see anyone clearly!—that's funny

only if I tell it, and then it's funny out of pity.)
All night I've been thinking that something's off.
That I'm trying to explain who I am too much,

that I'm talking about Rafe too much, that I'm
too much, period. It's not a new feeling, but tonight
I had it pinned on Jude. Like he snapped shut

right after I mentioned my boyfriend, like he went
kind of dark. Like he was a favorite book that I went
to reread and then suddenly it was in pig Latin

and did I like it? *Yes, Florence, you kind of liked it*—
after last year feeling like a fool, feeling like you'd made it
all up, just you pining, all July and August opening up

that blank text to him and wanting, wanting,
wanting—tonight I was a little high off the petty win of it,
the thought that he wanted now what he couldn't have.

That he was comparing me to Marley. That I was maybe

winning. And now I feel like such a loser, because
the boy I love—no, *a* boy I love, *Jesus, Florence*—was bleeding

in front of me and I was too up my own ass to see it.

JUDE
AT STAVROS' DINER, STUDYING LAMINATED MENUS, 11:05 P.M.

"So, Florence, in case you've forgotten what a chicken tender looks like, it appears that we have helpful photos of each menu item," I say.

"Honestly, that *is* helpful. So many times I order chicken tenders and they come out and I'm like, what *are* these things lying before me? Some sort of fuzzy brown paddles? Are these tiny beaver tails? Can I eat them?"

"I'm in a pancakes mood."

"Yeah?"

"Pancakes are maybe my favorite food," I say.

"Come on."

"What?"

"Pancakes aren't a favorite food."

"They can be."

Florence rolls her eyes. "No. But not only will I allow it tonight, I think I'll join you in a stack of cakes."

"I need a sundae too," I say.

"Then I shall join you in a sundae."

The waitress, who could somehow be anywhere in age from twenty-five to fifty-five, comes and takes our order. We both order the tall stack of pancakes with coffee and a hot fudge sundae. For a few moments we both look at each other like we expect the other to speak but neither of us does.

"So," Florence says.

"So," I say.

She toys with a spoon, turning it over in her fingers. "Would you . . . like to talk about Marley?"

"Not especially."

"Okay, but it feels like you need to." Florence sounds both like she really wants to hear about Marley and doesn't.

I pick up a plastic saltshaker. "Have you ever done that thing where you spin a quarter and then jam a saltshaker down on top of it so it breaks the bottom and when they go to pick up the salt-shaker, boom, salt everywhere."

"Why would I or anyone else do something like that?"

"Why would anyone put twenty plays of 'My Humps' on a juke-box? To be a force of chaotic evil in the world."

"Touché." Florence lets a beat pass and then says, "Nice try changing the subject. Thus only confirming that you need to open up about Marley."

"You're always jabbing at me about Marley. It feels like this is just you wanting the hot goss or something."

Florence smiles a little. "Yeah, well, I'm not averse to getting the odd bit of hot goss every now and again, but believe it or not, I do actually care about you and it feels like you're hurting still."

"Oh yeah?"

"Jude, I've known you for many hours longer than I would need to in order to see that you're hurting. Which is about zero hours and maybe five minutes. Like, I suspected something was up from the beginning."

My face grows hot and red and I look away.

"I really don't care that you lied about her, by the way," Florence says.

"Really?"

She looks me dead in the eyes. "Meditative mudding?"

"Meditative— Oh man, I forgot I said that."

"Marley! Mudditating!"

"Marley the mudditator!"

We laugh until we're both crying, but for me it turns into real crying. I hope Florence can't tell the difference.

The waitress arrives with our pancakes and coffee and sundaes. She leans in as though confiding some great secret: "You know you can dip bites of pancake in the sundae and that's really good."

Florence looks at her. "That's honestly a *great* idea and the sort of thing you don't think of to do unless someone tells you."

"You'd be surprised how many people order this exact order," she says, and leaves.

I wipe my eyes and sigh.

"Have you talked about this with anyone?" Florence asks.

I shake my head.

"Not your parents?"

I laugh. "They are both, like, so in their own shit and cynical about love, they'd be useless."

"What about friends?"

"Well. Here's the funny thing. I don't"—I make air quotes— "have many friends. The further along we get in high school the more I sorta grow apart from the ones I do have." *And then I was so into Marley that I let my friendships fizzle,* I almost say out loud but don't.

Florence dips a bite of pancake in melted ice cream and hot fudge and eats it. "Mmmmm, Jude, you gotta try this. The pancake is an ice cream and fudge sponge. This is my new favorite food."

"*Pancakes aren't a favorite food*, is what you said."

"Pancakes and ice cream and fudge are, though. So, you haven't talked about this with anyone?"

"No."

"It'll feel better to talk about it. Come on. Unload."

I slump in my chair. I stare at the wall behind Florence. There's a signed photo of an extremely hirsute man in a white apron with some tall, tan dude. It looks like it's from the eighties. Some celeb I don't recognize.

"It was extremely embarrassing. Like, here Marley is telling me she's saving herself for marriage, and it turns out she's very much not, just with me. And I wasn't, like, trying to sleep with her, but still."

"That sucks," Florence says quietly.

"But even more than that, it makes me think that I'm exactly like my parents, where I don't get to have relationships that last. And maybe I'm being told that now so I never get married and then put a kid through what my parents are putting me through."

"I bet you're not like your parents. At all. In fact, no, I *guarantee* you're not like your parents."

"How can you say that? You don't know them. You barely know me."

"I know you enough."

I look at the other wall. There's a clock in the mitten shape of Michigan. I take a sip of my liberally sugared coffee and let the bittersweetness dissolve on my tongue. Then I chase it with a gob of ice cream. Florence waits for me.

"Then here's—" I stop because this part is hard to say out loud, but Florence's eyes are soft toward me and look like an easy place to land. "Then here's the other thing. I wonder what's wrong with me. That you could say you love me and then do something like that to me. Like why am I so broken. Why do I deserve that."

"You don't," Florence says. "You don't at all. You're not broken."

FLORENCE
AFTER ORDERING A SECOND ROUND OF PANCAKES BECAUSE WE'RE IN IT FOR THE LONG HAUL, 11:18 P.M.

"That's why I lied about it," he says. "I couldn't have you looking at me too like I'm broken."

"Hey, you're talking about my friend Jude there. Go easy." I worry about threading the needle on the thing I'm about to say. That it might sound like I feel sorry for Marley. And maybe I do just a tiny bit, and maybe I don't at all. "The thing is . . ." I pause. "The thing is, Marley had to be coming into that relationship with you with just like a catastrophic amount of damage to behave the way she did."

"I hate that," Jude says hard and fast. "I hate when people use trauma as an excuse for bad behavior. It might be a reason, but it's not an excuse. It's not a get-out-of-jail-free card."

"I'm not excusing her."

"Okay," he says doubtfully.

"That's not what I'm saying. What I'm saying is that *you're* not the broken one. She's the one who grew up probably with everyone in her church and her family telling her that her only real worth was, like, her 'purity.' And then you're her boyfriend, and she can't have you looking at her like she's 'dirty' or anything; that would break her. So she pretends that she doesn't want sex. But she's, like, sixteen. She definitely wants to go to bone town like the rest of us—"

Jude clenches his teeth a little.

"Okay, bad choice of words. She, like, wants . . . physical stuff like anyone else, and so she does it with someone who she doesn't need respect from."

"Huh."

"I don't know. That doesn't excuse it. But from where I'm sitting it looks like, as messed up as this is, Marley's cheating has a lot to do with her and not a lot to do with you."

He's playing with the pancake on his plate. "Yeah," he says after a minute. "Yeah."

"And when I say that you deserve better, that's what I mean. You deserve someone who will think about you, and care about you, and do what they can to make your life better. Instead of just using you as some weird little crutch."

"Florence."

"What?"

"You kind of sound like a therapist."

"Well, I've been in therapy."

"Oh. Wait, really?"

"I'm a seventeen-year-old who's going kind of blind in a weird unpredictable way and my mom is a college professor in Madison, Wisconsin. Of course I've been to therapy."

"When you put it like that."

"Yeah."

"Does it help?"

Suddenly I feel exposed in that particular way that I hate. But I also feel like Jude maybe needs to hear this. "Yeah. It helps. It helps a lot, actually. I went for a while last year, in the fall. After my eye started shaking again. Me looking for other stuff I'm good at . . . it's my therapist's suggestion. And it's sort of like a cage I'm thrashing against, I feel like . . . violently resentful every time I think like *ha ha yeah of course I'll just mosey on over to the band room and become a first chair* tuba *player, thank you, Dr. Love—*"

"Is that your therapist? His name is Dr. Love?" Jude looks incredulous.

"Her name."

"Dr. Love. I love it."

"Me too. And some of my frustration with it probably speaks to this need I have to, like, smoke everyone. Leave everyone in the dust. That's on me. I can, like, find satisfaction in playing the tuba without being amazing at it. I can sing just because it feels good. I don't have to be, like, Adele—"

"And dance?"

I pause. "Dance?"

"Yeah. Is the goal to, like, be able to dance just because you love it, and not because you're good at it?"

I go hot, cold. I muscle down the urge to punch something. I do the thing I've learned to do instead: I smile as nice as I can and then hide my mouth. Sip my water. "I think that's the goal," I say, when I can talk again.

"Because you can just make art because it feeds your soul."

"I know."

"You don't need to be the best at it—"

"*I was the best at it.*" The words come out like projectiles. "I was. The best at it. I was going to be the *best*. And I can't go from that to going to some, like, scarf-waving bullshit in bare feet dancing to new age music for the old ladies in the nursing home. I can't do it! I can't. I would rather never do anything *at all*."

Jude reaches out and touches my shoulder, and I am not going to cry.

"So what you're saying is that your therapy's working really well," he says.

I snort. "It's a work in progress. But last year I couldn't even get this far with it. Have you—have you ever thought about it? Therapy?"

JUDE
PREPARING TO DIG INTO A SECOND ROUND OF PANCAKES, WHICH IS ALMOST IMMEDIATELY STARTING TO LOOK LIKE A GRAVE ERROR IN JUDGMENT, 11:26 P.M.

"*Therapy?*" I say, like the word is slimy on my tongue. "Because my high school girlfriend diddled around and got knocked up?"

"Does that not seem like enough?"

"I don't know."

"What about your thoughts, then."

"What about them?"

"Did you not tell me last year that you have these spiraling thought patterns you get stuck in?"

"Did I say that?"

"Why, is it not true?"

"Yeah, it is, but I don't remember telling you that."

"I wouldn't invent this."

"You're a good listener," I say, in awe of her memory.

"So therapists can help with that kinda thing. They can prescribe medication."

I take a bite of pancake and pull my hand away but accidentally leave my fork sticking out of my mouth.

Florence sees and giggles. "You skip fork day in school?"

I pull the fork out of my mouth. "You just witnessed a Classic Jude. I'm always putting my fork in my mouth and taking my hand away to go for another bite, but I accidentally leave the fork in my mouth."

"My thing is I'm always literally missing my mouth with my fork because of my jacked-up depth perception."

We laugh even though that's a bummer.

"So yeah, medication," I say. "I guess they probably do have medication for my deal."

"For sure they do," Florence says.

"I don't know if it's my thing."

"Why not?" Florence carefully nibbles a bite of pancake off her fork.

Now I notice how tentatively she eats. I don't think she ate this way last year.

I shrug. "I just worry. I don't know."

"About what?"

"Like . . . isn't the whole job of medication to make you different?" I ask.

"No. It's to make you who you are. It's your brain fritzing out that makes you different."

"I'm scared of it, like, changing who I am. What if I can't take good photos anymore?"

"Jude. Do you honestly believe that it's the parts of your mind that make you unhappy that are responsible for your art?" Florence sets down her fork and her eyes bore into mine. One of her pupils is larger than the other.

"What if it is?"

"No chance. Sorry. I don't buy that at *all*."

"You don't think if I started taking medication for my thoughts that it would affect my photography?"

"I so completely do not. Or if it does, it'll make you even better.

You'll see the world more clearly. Can't you see how not having spiraling thoughts would free you up to put energy other places?"

"Do you take medication for anything?" I ask.

"Not for mental health, but I take Advil when I get cramps. It's really no different."

"My brain is PMS-ing?"

"In its own beautiful way," Florence says.

"I'll think about it. And think about it. And think about it. And think about it. And think about it. And—"

"Good one, Jude."

"I do try."

JUDE
QUIET

Now I'm wondering if there could be
a place for me away
from the bedlam of my own thinking,

where I don't have to squint to see
over the whirlwind of my own thoughts.

I read somewhere once that there's more
of us that is not us than *is*
us, by which I mean that we contain
more bacteria than we contain
ourselves. How much
are my thoughts some self-
replicating bacteria? Is my brain more
not me than me?

What if I could take some
mental antibiotic and become
more myself? What would I find there?
What would be left? If there is only the murmur

of snowdrift; wind moving through grass;
the sound of nightfall;
of an hour turning into two.

What if my mind learned a new language
of stillness and was, just for a while, quiet?

I put down my debit card, pay,
and we leave under the moon, glowing
silent as a temple in its cradle of sky.

FLORENCE
MAP

The thing I'm learning about Harbor City, way up here
like a crown on Michigan's head, is that it can transform itself
into the place people need it to be. All summer long

it's a beach town for families on vacation, and so it's all fudge
    shops
and sunhat shops and places selling jam—and then in the winter
there's the liberal arts college, the reason for the dive bars and the
    little

indie bookstore (that sadly doesn't stay open for Sunrise Night)
and the coffee shop with the chess tables and the punk music
    playing
too loud on the speakers. Places from the shadow Harbor City

that you can only see traces of in the summer. And on Sunrise
    Night,
the last Sunday of every June, the two Harbor Cities both stay
    open
for us, like a gift. And yeah we're just teenagers with money to
    burn

after a week grinding away over at HAC, making art, wishing
we could just sneak out some night for an ice cream, and yeah
    we're probably

annoying on Sunrise Night because of it, the employees probably
  hate staying up

until two so we can drink coffee and feel cool about ourselves,
and yeah I overtip everyone because I feel guilty. Yeah it's kind of
  like
a cleaned-up curated Disneyland of a town, everything laid out

across four pristine blocks, all its city edges sanded off. But mostly
it's magic. I want to be done thinking about the ways that my life
could be better. After we check in at HAC and Jude offers me

his arm to walk back down the hill, I hold it all the way to the
  coffee shop,
my hand tucked in his elbow, and he keeps looking at me. Looking
at me like I'm the map to a place he can't quite believe he's found.

FLORENCE
AT THE ANARCHIST COFFEE SHOP THAT I'M SORT OF AFRAID TO GO INTO, 12:14 A.M.

"I can hear the music all the way out here," I say.

We're peering through the window. The sign says "Open," but the coffee shop is too dark to see anything inside.

"How do people talk in there?" Jude asks.

"I don't know," I say. "Isn't this the place people go to play chess?"

"To a soundtrack of Metallica. Bizarre."

"I don't know if it's Metallica. It sounds like Anti-Flag or something. It's like music that wants to eat you and then floss with your bones."

"Florence."

"What?"

"Are you scared of punk music?"

"I am not scared of punk music. I wouldn't know about Anti-Flag if I were."

"You kind of sound like you are."

"I just wanted to play chess with you," I tell him. "And I don't think I can play chess while the music is trying to overthrow the government."

"Come on," he says, "I'll buy you a coffee," and when he opens the door the song pretty much punches us in the face.

"No one's here," I tell him. I have to say it kind of loud to be heard. It's just like a floor that's never been mopped and a bunch of gross tables with chessboards painted on them that look like they're gonna tip over and all your chess pieces are going to fall off and this MUSIC.

"What?" Jude leans in.

"This music!"

"What?"

"This MUSIC!"

"WHAT?"

There's no one at the counter. The menu is written in a font I can't really read. I turn my head a little, which relieves the pressure on my bad eye.

"Is that drink called The Bender Ender?" I ask Jude.

"Yeah. It's a tea drink, looks like raspberry iced tea."

"Raspberry iced tea is a bender ender?"

"The decaf is called Kill Your Enthusiasm."

"Cool. This is a cool place," I say.

"Are you being sarcastic?"

"Honestly," I say, "I'm not sure. Do they have food?"

"How are you still hungry?"

"I'm not. I just want to know what they name their food."

Jude looks around. "Soup of the day!" he says. "Oh."

"What?"

"The soup of the day is Eff You."

"They didn't write out the word? This place seems too self-satisfied to not write out the word."

"No, they wrote out the word."

"Oh."

"I didn't want to give them the satisfaction of saying it," Jude says. "I hate this place."

"This place hates us."

"Eff this place!"

"Eff it! Eff it right to heck!"

There's a bell on the counter. I ring it hard but you can't hear it over the music. *Die die die die die!* the singer is chanting.

"HEY," I yell.

Jude looks momentarily horrified and then he looks delighted. "HEY," he yells.

"HEY!"

"HEY!"

"HEY. HEY HEY HEY," we both yell. "HEY. HELP US! HEY, SOMEBODY HELP US!"

JUDE
HELP ARRIVES, 12:15 A.M.

An employee comes out of the back.

"What the *hell*?" I say.

"Her! It's her!" Florence says.

"We know you!" I snap a couple times, jogging my memory. "From the bowling alley, right? Last year?"

"Ravyn!" Florence says. "I remember now. Your name rules. With a 'y.' Not an 'e.' You'll know if we say it with an 'e.'"

Recognition passes over the girl's face. She looks fairly stoned and as though memory may not be her strong suit. "Oh yeah," she says slowly. "I kept the alley open late for you guys."

"Yes! You gave us free access to the slushie machines!" I say.

"Hell yeah, dudes." Ravyn laughs a profoundly baked laugh. She is visibly happier than the last time we saw her.

"You digging the new job?" Florence asks.

"I make more now with tips. I don't have to disinfect stanky-ass bowling shoes. I'm the manager here."

"Sounds like karma's rewarded you with a better job after showing such kindness to us," I say.

"For sure, for sure," she says, laughing again. "We're open all night so you don't even have to pay me to stay open later. What can I get you?"

"Do you have to have been on a bender to order a Bender Ender?" Florence asks.

"We don't card," Ravyn says.

"A Bender Ender for me," Florence says.

"Make it two," I say.

"Two Bender Enders," Rayvn says. She prepares them.

Florence tries to hand her a ten. Ravyn waves her off. "Maybe with a little more good karma I can get an even better job," Ravyn says.

"Here's hoping," Florence says, and stuffs the ten in the tip jar.

"I'm gonna turn the music down a little so you guys can talk," Ravyn says with a puckish glint.

I then remember how convinced Ravyn was that Florence and I were a couple. We sit with our drinks at a table with a chessboard painted on it.

"You having fun?" I ask Florence.

"Yeah. You?"

"Yeah. I like this place now."

"Me too, especially now that we can hear ourselves think," she says. "Wanna play chess?"

"I suck."

"Good, because same." She gets a box of chess pieces off a nearby shelf and starts arranging them on the board.

"Hang on, the horsey guy—"

"Knight?"

"Yes."

"Okay, either you're hustling me or you were underselling how much you're not a chess player."

"How hard could it be?"

"Jude. Have you never played chess before?"

"What does 'played chess' even mean. Could we not just as easily say that chess plays us?"

"We could not and will not."

"Hey, you'd never been bowling."

"No, and you were an excellent instructor, and I'm now going to teach you how to play chess."

FLORENCE
THE QUEEN'S GAMBIT, 12:24 A.M.

"Okay. Pawns go two spaces the first time, one after that. They capture diagonally." I move my pieces around to illustrate. "Knights go in kind of an 'L' motion. Bishops zigzag. Rooks—that's those castle things—they go straight in any direction. Kings are like pawns, but if you capture the king you win the game. And queens can do anything they want."

"Anything?"

"Except hopscotch another piece. Queens rule. Queens are the murder hornets of chess."

"I'm not going to remember any of this, you know. I wouldn't even if it weren't after midnight."

"That's cool. I don't mind beating you."

Jude laughs. "This Bender Ender is not going to keep me awake. We're gonna need espresso next."

"Blech."

"You don't feel really sophisticated drinking it?"

"Not really. I don't know how people drink stuff that tastes like gasoline."

"I put a lot of cream in mine," he says. "A lot of sugar."

"How is that not just a latte?"

"It's cheaper," he says. "How does Rafe take his coffee?"

For the first time since he told me he was lying about Marley, I realize—fully realize—that Jude isn't actually dating anyone anymore. "I don't know," I say. *I do know that I'm blushing right now.*

"He doesn't drink it?"

"He drinks a lot of tea. English breakfast. PG Tips, two sugars and a splash of milk."

Jude moves a pawn three spaces diagonally. I don't correct him. "What's he like?" Jude asks. "I guess that's what I'm trying to figure out."

"Through his tea order?"

"Come on. I'm being real here."

"Rafe is . . . I don't know. He's really nice. His mom and dad are great. His little brother is thirteen and has red hair and likes *Minecraft*. He has a cat—"

"I mean, what's *Rafe* like."

I think about it. We play chess. By that I mean Jude moves his pieces around while I send my queen out hunting. "Rafe wants to know if people are happy," I say finally. "And he wants people to do things right."

"Those are good qualities," Jude says. "To have both of those qualities at the same time, I mean."

"You think?" They aren't really things I like about Rafe.

"Yeah. Marley never wanted me to be happy, but she did want me to do things right. Or at least, what was right in her head. Like we'd be driving and some guy would cut me off and I'd curse without meaning to, and then Marley would just . . . sort of stay silent? But it was a different kind of silence. I could hear her disapproving."

I make a little noise of disgust.

Jude continues. "It was like the air got cracked. She wanted me to feel weird. And bad."

"I think Rafe . . . is kind of comfortable with the idea that I'm, like, not a happy person. As long as it's a slow burn."

"I don't think of you as an unhappy person."

"Yeah. I guess I don't know if I am. He doesn't want me to have *problems*, I know that. Like he's always checking in with me, like 'you all right?' But he doesn't really want to hear the answer if it's no. Suddenly it's a fight. Like I'm blowing up his day if I'm, like, feeling queasy after lunch, or if I have an AP Chem test that I'm stressed about. He starts listing things I could do. Like, I can make notecards to learn the periodic table! I can get a tutor! To him it needs an immediate solution, even though, for me, it's just normal stress. But he can't just look at me and say, *you'll do great on the test*. Or, *chemistry sucks*. And . . ."

Jude captures my rook with a pawn, correctly. I'm surprised. "And?" he asks.

"I don't know. It sounds bad."

"You can tell me."

"Sometimes I think he kind of likes the fact that I'm, like, sick. That my eye stuff is going on."

"He *likes* it?"

"Not that he likes it. But that it makes him feel more . . . secure. Like I'm worth less because of it. Or, no, that's mean. More like— like there's less of a chance that I'm going to dump him. Like he thinks that *I* think he's the best I can do, boyfriend-wise."

"Wow."

"I'm probably reading way too much into it," I say quickly. "I'm probably making it up."

"Does he go to see you dance?" Jude asks.

"Yeah."

"What does he think?"

"I don't know."

"He's not into it? Your dancing?"

"No, I mean . . . I don't know. I used to be at the studio, like, every day, either taking classes or teaching or cleaning up. And now I'm just taking the one modern class, and teaching the little kids on Sundays. And I know he's happier that I'm around more."

"Okay," Jude says cautiously. "That's maybe a little selfish, but it's not bad."

"Right."

"But does he know how *you* feel about not dancing as much?"

"How *I* feel?"

"Yeah."

"Oh," I say. "I don't know if I know how I feel about it. Or if I feel . . . anything about it at all."

Jude moves his queen like a heat-seeking missile. "Check."

"Check? You know to say check when you have my king in jeopardy? Oh my God, have you actually been sharking me this whole time?"

Then I look at the board.

"Jude. You're nowhere near my king."

"Oh."

"Why did you say check?"

"People say check!"

"They say check?"

"When they play chess, they say check! Like, hey check out what I just did. Check yourself before you wreck yourself."

I sigh and pick up my bishop and make the move I could have made five turns ago.

"Checkmate," I tell him.

"That means I won, right."

"Yes, Jude," I say. "Congratulations. You won."

"Let me go get us some coffee. Ravyn?" he asks, at the counter.

She looks up from her book. She's reading *Naked Lunch*. "Yeah?"

"Can we have two lattes? I'll pay this time."

"Do y'all want some weed gummies with those? They're good. Peach slices."

"Like the candy? Or made from slices of a peach?"

"Like the candy," she says.

"We're okay. Thanks though."

Jude waits for the coffee at the counter. I look at his shoulders through his T-shirt, the slope of his arms, the tilt of him while he's thinking.

"Thank you," I say, when he returns with them.

"Can I tell you something?" he says.

"Yeah, of course."

"I think you're the coolest person I know."

I flush again. "Where'd that come from?"

"Nowhere. The air."

"Thanks," I say. "I think you're the coolest person I know."

"I wasn't fishing for that," he says. "I really want you to know it. You're cool because you know who you are. Even when you don't. You're cool because you listen when people talk and you're really smart and you move like—like gravity doesn't have a hold on you. And—"

"What?" I can't breathe.

Jude has been looking me dead in the eyes, but now he swallows and looks at his hands. "And you're beautiful," he says. "And if Rafe thinks he's the best you can do, I think he's about to get a really nasty wake-up call."

FLORENCE
BEAUTIFUL

I don't know a lot of things for sure. I mean, I know my mom
won't eat any desserts that have those little flecks
of coconut on them, that she won't even pretend

to like it, that she'll wash her mouth out in the sink
if she spots a single white shaving on her cake. I know
that if my dad is talking to someone with an accent

he'll be talking with their accent within minutes. To that
person's face. And that he won't notice even while
everyone around him is dying inside. I know that

the Earth circles the sun, that takeout sushi
from that place on State Street takes forty-five minutes
minimum, and I know that Rafe won't ever dump me,

ever, that I'll have to be the one to do it when
the time comes. And I know the time is going to come,
that I'm not marrying Rafe, that I would never marry anyone

who thinks I'm such a sure thing. I know that Jude
has waited all night to tell me that he wants
me. I knew it from the moment I saw him lit up

like a candle at Bonfire, I knew it, and I know too

that I can't stand his timing. I can't stand
the pity in his voice, *poor Florence got herself*

in a bad situation, poor Florence with bad taste
in men—I get enough pity as it is. I know
that as much as I want to kiss Jude right now

I just as badly want to pop him in the kisser.

JUDE
WITH CHESS PIECES NO LONGER THE ONLY THING ON THE TABLE, 12:30 A.M.

"A nasty wake-up call?" Florence asks archly, setting up the pieces on the chessboard again.

I immediately feel stupid for my late-night bravado. "Yeah."

"What sort? Who's administering it?"

"I don't know."

"You?"

"Why are you saying it like that. *You.*"

"How am I saying it?"

"Like with this little laugh."

"Sorry, but it's funny."

"What is?"

"You being all like *Rafe is gonna get a huge wake-up call.*" Florence says it in a mock deep voice like she's imitating me.

"Why are you like this?" I mutter, and go to move my pawn.

"Like?"

"I was just trying to give you a compliment. Sue me. Jeez."

"I forgot boys expect you to be so grateful for throwing you a few scraps."

"Boys?"

"Sorry. *Men.* Manly men like you."

"I called you beautiful."

"*Beautiful.* Famously the finest praise a manly man can pay a woman."

"Know what? Forget it. I take it back."

Florence shrugs and moves her pawn and doesn't reply.

"No, but seriously, why are you this way?" I ask. "Like, I'm actually kinda glad we didn't talk for the whole year."

"You are?"

"Yeah, I am." I press my hands to the sides of my head. "*Grrrrrrr.* This sucks. I hate that the nicest thing will set you off."

It's my turn to move, but I don't care about the game anymore.

"Calling me beautiful and then insulting me and my boyfriend in the same breath isn't quite what I'd call the *nicest* thing. It's definitely *a* thing. Nicest? No. Your move." She nods at the chess pieces.

"Hold up. Whoa. How did I—"

"Well, kinda obvious how you insulted Rafe."

"You were the one who was complaining about him. Sorry for agreeing with you. It'll never happen again. Plus, you were always insulting Marley last year."

Florence shakes her head. "Nope. Never happened. I'd remember."

"You did it implicitly."

"Nope."

"It was obvious. You kept asking about her in a snide way, like she was beneath you."

"She didn't sound very cool. She sounds even less cool now," Florence says.

She's not wrong, I think. "So what grave offense did I visit upon you?" I ask.

"I don't need you to fix me by telling me how beautiful I am. Whatever issue I have with Rafe has nothing to do with me not feeling beautiful. I don't need your pity. I don't need you throwing me a bone."

"I wasn't trying to fix you. I wasn't pitying you. When I say 'beautiful,' I mean it different."

"How?"

JUDE
BEAUTIFUL

The problem with words
is how you reach
the end of their meaning

Alone
Joy
Storm
Sweet

and then you travel out
from that circle of light
into the darkness
and hope you stay
on the path.

Ocean
Time
Lose
Door

When I say beautiful
it means something different
to me than when most people
say it; it has more

weight. I know this
from the way other people say
it, toss it around like it's featherlight,
like it's easy to bear,
like it costs nothing.

The problem is though
that when I try to explain it
I reach the end of meaning.

Horses
Wind
Love
Die

I journey into the darkness.
Nothing has a shape anymore.
I can't see the way back.

Eclipse
Mother
Tide
Fall

No word means more
to me than *beautiful* and sometimes it feels
like I'll spend my whole life trying
to explain what I mean
when I say it.

Jubilation
Vision
Murmur
Dusk

FLORENCE
PLAYING FAVORITES, 12:35 A.M.

"All of you," he says. "That's what I meant by beautiful. What I mean is, even when you are pissing me off, you're still my favorite person in the world."

Jude is looking at his feet, which is good, because I'm pretty sure I'm about to cry.

"That can't be true," I tell him. "Come on."

"Well, okay, like my favorite non-grandma person."

"You're very confident I'm not a grandmother."

"I mean, you're not *my* grandma."

"*Favorite* person?"

"Now I'm gonna stand my ground."

"Leaning into it? We've known each other for like fifteen hours total."

"When I was with Marley, I kinda shed my other friends. Not by choice, but you know. Drifted apart."

"Oh, so I'm your favorite by process of elimination?"

Jude looks me dead in the eyes now. "No."

He says it with a quiet firmness that makes me have to look away because I feel like crying again.

Jude continues. "I didn't mean what I said earlier in, like, a toxically masculine way. I don't know if that's a phrase."

"About Rafe?"

"Yeah. I didn't mean that, like, me or some big-ass dude was going to come in and teach him a lesson."

"Oh no? You're not going to roll up with MMA fundamentals

and make Rafe rue his birth?"

"No, I'm sparing him an MMA-administered life lesson."

"About me. A life lesson about me. I'm some footnote in someone else's story of, like, self-actualization."

"I'm pretty sure you know you're not a footnote."

"God, I hope not."

"You're gonna be one of those people with biographies about them, plural."

"Now you're just kissing my ass," I tell him.

"I am not. I'm always on the lookout for good biography names."

"Such as?"

Jude grins, suddenly. "*Mudditating: The Marley Sievers Story.*"

I snort into my latte. "*Marley and Me: The Jude Wheeler Story.*"

"Oh hell no. I'll be damned if I'm, like, the subtitle of *that* girl's biography—"

"*I'll Be Damned: The Jude Wheeler Story.*"

"*I Hate You So Much, Florence Bankhead: A Novel.*"

"A very long novel."

"A saga. A trilogy!"

"I hate trilogies. The second book always sucks."

"Hey. I didn't mean you could do better than Rafe," Jude says.

"You did though."

"I did though," he says, quiet.

We play chess for a while longer, not talking much, but laughing when Jude intentionally makes bad moves as a joke: *I don't care, the Queen is boning the Bishop. It's a huge scandal in Chessland. She wants to be next to him, even if it means she gets captured. She's a sucker for doomed love.*

"Hey," I say. "What else are we gonna do tonight? I just had all this caffeine, I feel like we should . . . move."

"Move?"

"Let's go somewhere! Let's get out of here. They always say that in movies but no one says that in real life. Let's get out of here. Somewhere we can talk."

"There's nobody else here."

"Let's go back to HAC. We have final check-in at three anyway. We'll be right there."

"What's worth doing at HAC?"

"Have you heard the legend? The haunted elevator in the dance building? They put it in so that they could move the baby grand between floors, and—"

Jude is looking at me like I'm killing him a little bit.

"—and they say that the ghost of Michael Flatley is in there," I say, a little frantic.

"Who . . . is Michael Flatley?"

"Michael Flatley. The Lord of the Dance? Jude."

"*What?* I don't know the various lords and ladies of dance."

"Not various lords and ladies. *The Lord,* singular, of the Dance. He led an Irish dance troupe in the nineties called Riverdance. They were *massive.* Then he struck out on his own."

"People in the nineties were into such weird stuff. My mom said people were into Gregorian chanting for a hot minute. Anyway, now he's dead?"

"I guess?"

"And he didn't resurrect or anything?"

"No, he haunts this elevator. Ooooooh. Spooky."

"Florence—"

"Jude."

"Don't you still need to call your boyfriend?"

"Why?"

"*Call Your Boyfriend*," Jude says. "*A Novel*."

"I can do that later," I tell him fast. "Come on. Come on, let's get out of here—"

JUDE
WITH A CLEAR DESTINATION, 1:47 A.M.

"Cool seeing you two again," Ravyn says as we make our way to the door. "Gives me hope to see young love survive."

Florence laughs at this more loudly than I'd have liked. "*Us?* Oh no, this is literally the second time we've ever hung out."

"Dude, no way." Ravyn laughs her smoke-hoarse pothead laugh. "For real though?"

"For real," I say.

"You guys hang out once a year?" Ravyn asks.

"Yep," Florence says.

"Weird," Ravyn says, but not unadmiringly.

I nod at Florence. "She has a boyfriend."

"Who's not *you?*" Ravyn says, aghast. "I guess obviously, if you're only hanging out once a year."

Florence nods and starts to say something, but I interrupt. "He's *Scottish* and wears kilts and thick sweaters. He looks like a young Gerard Butler and talks like Shrek. He smuggles his own haggis on movie dates and mixes it into the popcorn. He—"

"*Jude.* You're somehow making me so angry and turning me on all at the same time," Florence says.

"I was only shooting for angry," I say, truthfully.

"You two obviously have mad chemistry, though," Ravyn says.

"Cool? But we're not—" Florence says.

"No, no yeah. I'm just saying. No offense. I have no filter," Ravyn says, unnecessarily.

"Oh, none taken. Anyway, though. I guess we'll see you next year, probably?"

Ravyn laughs. "Looks like it, huh?"

We make our farewells, leave outside, and start toward HAC.

"Ah, Ravyn," I say.

"That's so Ravyn," Florence says.

"Did we not make that joke even once last year?"

"We didn't know her well enough for it to make sense."

"Now we all know each other well enough for her to opine on our chemistry," I say.

"How awkward was that?" Florence looks at her feet when she says it but I figure she's concentrating on her balance.

"I was glad Rafe wasn't here to become absolutely, unintelligibly enraged."

Florence scoffs. "I don't think I've ever seen him enraged or even mildly perturbed about anything, unintelligibly or otherwise."

"That must be nice," I say.

"Is it?" Florence doesn't look happy.

"I don't know. You tell me. I'm glad I don't have to deal with an enraged Scotsman at least for giving the perception of chemistry to semi-strangers."

"It's fine."

I chortle. "*It's fine.* A *rave* review from our judges."

"No, it's fine. I don't know. Haven't thought about it."

I study Florence's face. "That feels untrue," I tell her.

"So I'm a liar now?"

"Not, like, generally a liar. Not a fundamentally dishonest person."

"*Not a fundamentally dishonest person.* Wow, a favorable ruling from Judge Judy. Hey! No, Judge *Jude*-y. Your name but with a 'y' on the end."

"I thought that's what you were saying the first time. But yeah, back to our subject, I think you might not be coming totally clean about this." I know I'm risking Florence's anger, but I press on; I don't know why.

Florence shrugs it off. "I don't know what to tell you."

"You *really* haven't thought about whether it's nice that Rafe never gets angry?"

"Should I have?"

"I would've."

JUDE
I'VE THOUGHT ABOUT IT A LOT

Every time my parents stained
the night red,

they didn't yell, they seethed.
They didn't strike, they turned
their backs and locked themselves in
separate rooms, but still

they broke each other
like water breaks stone—they lapped
at each other slowly until there was nothing
left but a wide and desolate valley.

FLORENCE
A MONSTER

I'm not messy about it. I like it to be clean,
a direct line, like a death ray. You messed up?
Consequences. You said a jackass thing to me

in the cafeteria, like *God why are you so needy,*
Florence, then smiled your varsity smile and said,
just kidding haha? Consequences. Swift and fast,

make them bleed. How it has to be. You hook up
with my friend in the studio bathroom
and then tell everyone she's a slut? Oh, consequences,

my dear little deluded friend. How else are you
going to learn? No you can't come with us to the movies.
No we won't text you when we go to Jamba. Yes

I will tell any girl who even glances at you
what a piece of shit you are, so go sit in the corner
and think about what you've done. If you let people

step all over you, they won't stop. They'll railroad you
into an empty classroom, smash your glasses, call you
a freak. Keep it up the whole year. All of middle school

they'll smell blood in the water. You have to make it stop yourself,

put them in their place, and then you think it's over—but
it keeps on for the rest of your goddamn life. Fine. You break

the social contract, sit next to me on the #7 bus with your old-man
     knees
pressing into my thighs, tell me I'd be prettier if there was a smile
beneath all that blond hair, while my beautiful useless

boyfriend stares down at his Bukowski? Yes I will
grind my boot into your instep, will yell *you're not*
my father! stranger danger!, will laugh in your face because

you think you have a chance with me? and when I drag Rafe
off at the next stop and he asks *what just happened? Was that*
really necessary?—yeah, that'll be the first time I really feel small.

FLORENCE
BACK AT HAC, CONSIDERING THE DARKENED DANCE BUILDING, 2:01 A.M.

"How do we get in?" Jude is asking. "I guess all of those windows look like they just slide up. Do you think maybe you can give me a boost or—"

"I have the code," I tell him. "No need for heroics."

"I didn't know students got the codes to the arts buildings."

I let us in.

"Well, I choreographed a bunch of pieces this summer, and Dr. Rojas let me come in late to block stuff out on the stage."

"Man, it's dark in here."

"The lights should come on automatically. You just have to wave your arms."

"I'm waving my arms. No lights."

"You are?" I ask him. "Be careful. The ghost of Michael Flatley is going to get you."

"I am genuinely sort of interested in what's going to happen when the ghost of Michael Flatley does get me. Do I have to join an Irish dance troupe?"

"I think, actually, he's supposed to challenge you to a tap competition."

"For real?"

"No, not for real, Jude, because the ghost of Michael Flatley is not in the Harbor Arts Camp dance building. Actually I don't even think he's dead, come to think of it."

"Well, you're a killjoy."

"I get that a lot," I tell him. I'm fumbling on the wall for the elevator controls. When I find the down button, the doors blink open immediately.

Jude looks at me in the sudden light. "Hi," he says.

"Hi," I say. My stomach twists.

"After you. Why are the walls padded? Like it's move-in day."

"They haul a lot of stuff in here. Props for the performances, the piano. Other stuff. Here, sit, it's not uncomfortable."

"Okay. What's upstairs?"

"Studios, offices. One good secret about the dance building is that there's a big washer and dryer in the basement, and they're free to use."

"Seriously?"

"Yeah. Dancers go through a lot of clothes. Wait, whoa—" The lights switch off inside the elevator. Only the buttons are illuminated.

"You're not angry at me anymore," he says.

I can only sort of see his face. "I wasn't ever angry at you," I say, since it's easier for me to say it in the dark.

"Ever?"

"Tonight," I tell him. "I wasn't angry at you tonight. About Rafe. Or anything. I just think it's good to be direct. I try to say what I mean."

"You're 'not here to make friends'?"

I laugh. "Yeah, I would probably be really successful on a reality show, unfortunately."

"I still don't buy that thing you said earlier, about not minding that Rafe doesn't get mad."

"You're pushing on that a little."

"You pushed a little about Marley. More than a little. This is push reciprocation."

"Okay. Yeah. I have thought about it. But I'm not sure my opinion on it makes sense."

"What do you mean?"

"I don't like angry people," I say. "But I also don't like that Rafe doesn't get angry."

"Yeah, my least favorite kind of guy is the guy who gets angry. Who slams around and talks over people and, like, can't contain himself."

"I hate that guy too."

"But you want Rafe to be that way?"

"No, I—I hate being the only one who's affected by something. Like, Rafe will get upset if something happens to him, he gets all moody and quiet. But if something shitty happens to me, then he takes a giant step back."

"You need, like, communal anger."

"I need to not always be the asshole," I tell him. "Sometimes I need my boyfriend to *also* be the asshole. Just for a minute. Behind a closed door or something. Like I wish I could say 'eff that guy!' and he would be like, 'yeah, eff that guy!' and then we can just move on, instead of him explaining to me that I should feel differently than the way I do."

"Well," Jude says. "Eff that guy."

"Eff that guy."

"I really don't like anger."

"Yeah?"

"Yeah. I feel like it's a kind of scorekeeping."

"What do you mean?"

"I watched my mom keep this record in her head of all the ways my dad messed up. Like, he left a mug on the counter? One point. He didn't fill up the truck when it was on empty? One point. He forgot about my dentist appointment or left me at school and some-body called her to ask where I was—that was the worst, when *she'd* get a call for something my dad did, that's when things usually got bad—five big fat points."

"You could usually tell? How many points something was worth?"

"Yeah, it's like survival stuff," Jude says. "You know? You keep track of it so you know when to hide in your room to avoid the fallout. Like, bad silence has a different quality than good silence. I don't know how else to explain it."

"And she'd yell at him?"

"No. She'd get quiet. Bad quiet. And it was like my dad didn't care. Or like he was expecting it, maybe, and so it didn't bother him? I've never said this out loud before, I guess. Sometimes I won-dered if he was determined to go ahead and do exactly what he wanted, and he was willing to pay the price, if the price was that my mom wouldn't talk to him sometimes."

"But it affected you."

"What did?"

"You. You were the one left at school. You didn't get your teeth cleaned. And then you were the one hiding under your bed when there was bad silence."

"I wasn't under my bed."

"It's a metaphor."

"I usually just hid in the closet."

"Jude—"

"I'm fine. It's not like I'm not fine."

"How long was it like that?"

"I don't know. A long time."

"And you and Marley never fought?"

"I mean, not like that. I'm never going to fight like that with anyone. I want . . ." He trails off. "I don't know what I want," he says finally.

"I think—I think I don't want someone who's angry," I say. "I think I want someone who knows how to defuse me."

"Yeah?"

"Maybe it's an unfair thing to wish for. I shouldn't put it on someone else."

JUDE
DEFUSE

I wonder if people who defuse
bombs ever wish instead

that they were indestructible
and could take the bomb
to some quiet place

with no one around
and let it explode
around them

so they could feel
its full heat and power.

JUDE
IN THE DARK OF THE DANCE BUILDING'S FREIGHT ELEVATOR, ILLUMINATED ONLY SLIGHTLY BY THE GHOSTLY GLOW OF THE BUTTON PANEL, 2:08 A.M.

"I like how it smells in here," I say.

"What, like a moldy basement?" Florence asks, wrinkling her nose theatrically.

"Exactly. It reminds me of the crawlspace where I hide the bodies."

"The bodies of your dead attempts to sell a joke?"

"Zing, Florence. Zing. No, but it reminds me of this old building in downtown Dickson where I had my first photography class. It smells like old building in here."

Florence sits cross-legged, her back against the padded wall. "I like how the cushioning dampens sound. It's cozy."

"What if this was your house. All my life I've been obsessed with tiny houses."

"What, like the ones on HGTV or whatever? That people buy to brag about how few shoes they own?"

"No, I mean like how you see a tiny shack beside railroad tracks and you wonder if, like, a railroad keeper lives in it."

"Oh, gotcha."

"It feels sort of like a confessional in here."

"Confess your sins, Jude. Be absolved."

"I . . . I'm too tired to think of anything funny."

"That didn't prevent your crawlspace joke a minute ago."

"Oooh, Florence. Zing redux."

"I used to go to confession."

"Really?"

"Sure. From your tone you'd think I just told you I used to make animal sacrifices."

"No, it's just I didn't think you were—"

"A lapsed Catholic."

"That makes you sound so world-weary."

"Even went to Catholic school for a few years."

"Wild! Did you wear the outfit?"

"The one perverts like? Yep. Are you a pervert? Is that why you asked?"

"I was more looking for something to zing you back about. I went to Christmas Eve midnight Mass once when I was a kid, with one of my friends."

"You realize like three-fourths of your stories involve going to church with a friend?"

I laugh. "Sorry, did I not mention I'm from a town of fifteen thousand in Tennessee? So: confession. Is it like on TV?"

"For the most part. Obviously I wasn't confessing as dramatic of stuff as on TV, but there's the screen thingy and that whole deal."

"Was it weird? Confessing your sins to someone?"

"I guess maybe if I were spilling more outrageous stuff."

"What kinda sins we talkin'?"

"What, I'm supposed to confess to you now, Father Jude?"

"If you already confessed it, it's not a live sin anymore. It's like a spent shotgun shell."

Florence laughs and thinks for a while, a little smile on her face.

"Oh. You know. Jealousy. Anger. Your light smattering of the Seven Deadly Sins. Cursing God for making me so imperfect. The usual. Okay. Now I've confessed. You confess something."

"Now I'll sound like a big copycat if I say I curse God for my imperfections."

"No way do you do that."

"So confident."

"I am."

"How do you know?"

She turns her head to me slowly. "Jude. I know."

"But how?"

She turns her head back, looking forward. "Because I don't think you believe in cursing imperfection. I think you're drawn to it. I think you love it."

"What makes you think that?"

"Am I wrong?"

"No."

"Okay, so I just confessed for you. You still owe me one. Here, how about this: do you think our experiment worked?" Florence sounds hesitant as she asks.

"What experiment?"

"The one where we taught rats to speak English. Jude. Come on. I know it's like two thirty a.m. but keep up here."

"What? I don't know."

"Where we didn't, you know, *speak* for an entire calendar year."

"Oh. What does 'worked' mean in this context?"

"Was it successful? Was it a good thing? Did it lessen the pain of existence? Did it make the world more beautiful?"

FLORENCE
TEASING OUT THE TRUTH IN THE DARK,
2:14 A.M.

"It's kind of funny that you're describing it that way," Jude says.

"Like what?"

"Like it was a bad idea. Which sort of makes it sound like you think it was my bad idea."

"So you think it was a bad idea."

"I got on the plane and the woman next to me was eating her bag of peanuts one peanut at a time. She'd like bite into it with her front teeth, like a squirrel, and then she'd hold it out and consider it like it was something she was considering displaying in the MOMA. And then she'd eat the rest. And I thought . . ." He trails off.

"What?"

"I thought, *oh my God I need to text Florence about Squirrel Woman*. And I couldn't. And then I had that feeling every ten minutes for the next year."

"Oh."

"So yeah, in short, I think it was a really bad idea. Why, did you enjoy it?"

When he gives me something like this, an opening, a confession, I want to give him something in return. I also want to snap up closed like a clam. I breathe through it. "Can I show you something?" I ask him.

"Yeah."

I pull out my phone.

Jude looks at the screen. "Why are you showing me your contacts list? Um, wait. How many contacts do you have? Who is Brendan Sunday?"

"A guy named Brendan who I met on a Sunday, probably. I don't know. I don't remember."

"But you put the 'Sunday' in there so you would remember?"

"Seems like it, doesn't it."

". . . Who is Evie Ice Cream? Harrison My Mom?"

"Evie works at the Frosty Treat. We keep meaning to hang out, she wants to show me this movie called *Barbarella*. Harrison My Mom . . . oh. That's one of my mom's TAs. I went to her office to help her move some bookcases and I met him. He wanted to take me out when I turn eighteen."

"Oh."

"Don't worry. He's like twenty-two and that's gross, and also he looks like he hasn't seen daylight in years."

"Why did you keep his number?"

"Probably so I remember not to answer his texts. I am not going out with anyone whose name comes up as Harrison My Mom."

"*When* he texts."

"They usually do."

"Florence."

"What?"

"Are you secretly a psycho?"

"I mean, is it a secret?"

"Wait. Hold on. Jude. *Jude Wheeler*."

"Yeah."

"My name is in your phone. Unless I'm your second Jude Wheeler."

"You're my first. My only Jude."

"But my number isn't there? It's just like an empty contact."

"I know."

"So . . . why?"

"I was like losing my mind wanting to talk to you, I wrote all these texts even though I couldn't send them."

"Florence."

"You think I'm pathetic."

"I could never think you're pathetic."

"These were pathetic texts that I wanted to send."

"Like what?"

My face is hot. At least he can't see it in the dark. "Like I missed you. I miss you. Three a.m. texts. That stuff. I don't know. Can we not talk about it?"

"I think we're talking about it. Why didn't you just get my number from someone?"

"I didn't want to bother you. And Marley."

"Clearly Marley was bothered in other ways. And you could never bother me."

"That's not true."

"I mean if you poke me in the side like a hundred times in a row I might be sort of bothered."

"Fair. But . . . I mean. Jude, you're a lot nicer than me."

"So?"

"Don't you think I would walk all over you? In, like, a monster way."

"I don't think I'm a doormat."

"You're not."

"Do you think I'm a doormat?"

"I don't. I totally don't. I just know that while things are getting weirder and worse with my eye that I like . . . I don't, sometimes I'm good and fine and I feel like myself and sometimes I'm just angry."

"Hence the therapy. Isn't that what therapy's for?"

"I mean, yeah, therapy's made me aware of it. Therapy's given me words for it, and I'm trying not to be that way. But I'm not, like, cured. I still get angry. I don't want to get angry with you."

"Is it getting worse?"

"What? The anger?"

"Your eye. What does it mean when your eye gets worse?"

"Like the sensation? What it feels like?"

"Yeah. Does the world dim, or—I mean you don't need to talk about it if you don't want to."

"No. It's okay. The world doesn't dim or anything like that. It gets kind of blurry. I lose . . . spatial awareness, that's the term. I clip myself on corners, I miss doorknobs. I miss, like, drinking glasses when I reach for them. I can't balance on one leg anymore. Stuff like that. And I get tired."

"Tired? Emotionally?"

"I mean, yeah, but also . . . I don't know if it's like this for anyone else. I've never met anyone else who deals with this. But like, my eyes get tired. My face gets tired. Walking around is hard. I just want to wear soft things and listen to audiobooks with my eyes closed and sleep."

"That makes sense."

"But it means that I'm disconnected from everything. From my life."

"Does Rafe help?"

"He doesn't hurt, I guess. We kind of disconnect together. He's a good person to fall asleep on the couch with. I've seen the first half of a lot of movies this year."

"I watched the *Sunrise* movies."

"You did?"

"All of them."

"What did you think?"

"I loved them. I want to go to Europe."

"You should go to Europe."

"We should go. Let's go to Vienna. Let's skip HAC next year and just do it. Backpack around."

"We're still in high school. My parents would never let me, Jude," I say, laughing.

"Mine wouldn't either. Let's do it."

"With what money?"

"My photo contest money. We'll get on a plane, we'll go. Let's do it—"

JUDE
CONTINUING TO CONFESS, 2:21 A.M.

"Hold on, hold on," Florence says. "Photo contest money?"

"I thought I told you," I say.

"And when would you have done that? Obviously we can rule out immediately after the contest winners were announced."

"In the hours leading up to this present moment."

"Dude, we both know you didn't mention it. So can we dispense with the evasion so I can congratulate you?"

"I won a thousand dollars in a photo contest."

"*A thousand dollars?!* Jude! I need details. Now."

I hope she can't see me blushing, but we've somehow inched so close together in the dark that she can probably feel it radiating from my cheeks. Maybe it's like the thing where if you walk on the wrong side of her, she keeps getting closer until she runs you off the sidewalk. I try to sound casual. "So Tennessee State Parks was running a photo contest where you could win stuff and the grand prize was a thousand dollars and I took a photo last fall at Montgomery Bell State Park, right near where I live."

"Can I see it?"

"Sure." I pull out my phone and scroll until I find it. "Here you go."

Florence leans over to look at it and I can feel the warmth of her skin. She holds my wrist to steady my hand and stares at the photo for a long time without saying anything.

"You trying to think of a joke or——" I ask.

"Not at all," she says quietly. "This is a really, really good picture."

"I couldn't believe I won."

"Was this a statewide contest?" Florence still holds my wrist—I'm not complaining.

"Yeah. A buncha people entered. Pros and stuff."

"I think you're a pro now, Jude."

"I'm honestly shocked I won. Whatever. Art is subjective, right?"

"I mean, sure, but this is objectively one of the most beautiful nature photos I've ever seen."

My face burns. "That means a lot to me."

"I'm not just saying that. I'm not blowing sunshine up your ass. This is your future. This is the beginning. You're going to make a living doing art and getting paid for it."

"You think?"

"I think."

It occurs to me how incredibly gracious she is, even as her ability to dance as she used to is ebbing. "Hey, let's get a picture of you," I say.

"Now?"

"The light is really cool. It'll be tricky but I think I can—here, move a little—" I stand and gently nudge Florence closer toward the light of the button panel. I crouch with my phone. "Okay. I'm gonna get one of you silhouetted against the panel. Good. Okay, now—" I shift positions. "I'm getting one of your face now." I take a few pictures and look at what we've gotten. "Oh yeah," I murmur. "Yeah. These are really good."

"Let me see," Florence says. She kneels beside me, our shoulders touching. She holds my wrist again while I show her the pictures. We're very close and she smells like the peppery vanilla of an old paperback book. She says something but I miss it because she's almost absentmindedly stroking my wristbone with the pad of her index finger and her scent and and and and it's making me dizzy.

JUDE
I CONFESS

Florence, like the city.

Florence, city of Renaissance painting.

Florence, looking like a Renaissance
painting herself in the gray solstice light
of the elevator button panel, illuminated
like an object of adoration.

And what surrounds worship
but confession? And so

I confess: in this delirium
of mid-night I have never seen
anyone so beautiful.

I confess: in this small and soft chamber,
made for the lifting of heavy things,
my heart is the lift of birds into sky.

I confess: in this second collection of hours of knowing
you, my skin craves exploring the country
of yours, my fingers mapping your boulevards and rivers.

I confess: in this closeness, my lips sing
for yours, blood beats close
to the surface. Hot and lush like August.

FLORENCE
THE NULL POINT, TWO

My head goes quiet in the dark.
The order of it is all wrong,
there isn't a screen between me

and this heat. No form to it,
just flame, his dark hair, rucked
curls I could twist my fingers into.

I am wrong. This is right. Right
here and if I tilt my head a little
to the left, chin down, my turning

heart will still. He is looking at
my mouth. Every edge I have
he knows now, finds the grace

in it anyway. In me, wild, wounded,
and with someone else, and when
I remember, I make myself pull back

and breathe. Face it. Again the world
shakes. Blindness isn't a metaphor for
blindness. I know, I've seen it all along.

JUDE
IN THE FALL

I make a quarter turn to face her, her hand still clutching
my wrist and the ghostly electric image of her.

And she turns too to hold my gaze.
Her lips part as though at the cusp
of speaking but she keeps silent.

I remember a time—I was young,
on a scout trip, canoeing a river.

We came to high bluffs where you could
plunge into the spring-clear water below.

I ascended with the others
and watched as they took their turns,
whooping until the river silenced them
and they bobbed back up, exhilarated cries
echoing from the rocks.

Finally it was my turn. I toed the edge.
Someone behind me said, *it's time
to jump. Sometimes you have to
just jump.*

I did; I jumped, and while I plummeted

through the bright empty between
sky and water, my mind was clean
like starlight, unstained by worry.

Sometimes you have to just leap
and find quiet in the fall.

I leap.

JUDE
LEAPING AND FALLING, 2:28 A.M.

She withdraws, releasing my wrist. "Jude," she says softly.

I yank myself back. "I'm sorry. I'm sorry. I'm—" I run my fingers through my hair.

"No, it's—"

"I wasn't—I mean I—" I press the heels of my hands to my temples. "Sorry. I'm sorry." I can feel my face absolutely throbbing with blood.

"No, Jude, it's—I need to do something. Can you—" She won't meet my eyes.

"Yeah."

"Can you hang on a little bit?"

"Sure. Listen, I don't know what I was—"

"No, no worries, just—hang on." Florence punches the button to open the doors. They open and the exit-sign-illuminated hallway feels bright compared to the elevator. "I'll just be a sec and then we can—"

"Yeah yeah, take whatever time. I'll just be—"

"Okay. One sec." Florence leaves the elevator. She doesn't look back as she pulls out her phone and starts typing furiously as she hurries up the corridor.

I watch her until the doors close and I'm in the dark again. My pulse thrums in my ears in the close silence. This space now feels like a mausoleum. Stifling. No air. Minutes drip past. Suddenly the elevator starts descending.

FLORENCE
CATASTROPHE

I'm going to try for casual. It's almost three a.m.
but I can still sound casual, right? I'm going to call
and get his voicemail, he has Do Not Disturb on

this late anyway, straight to voicemail! I'll just explain
that I've been doing a lot of thinking while I've been
here, that the dancing has been hard, knowing

I have to give it up, hard, the blind thing, hard (hard!),
that I need some space inside my own head. All of this is true.
None of this is lying. Is it?

It'll be fine, even if

he answers, even if he says he loves me—I really need him
to not say that he loves me. I don't want to end this
being the bad guy. But I *am* the bad guy, being with Rafe,

wanting Jude, wanting Jude so much that it burns and
we'll—God I don't know what we'll do when I hang up this
   phone.
We'll do something. God. Then I'll go home. Home,

where I'll be for the next ten months, even if I spend my senior
   year

doing long distance with Jude, nine hours away
in Dickson, Tennessee, and after fifteen hours together

we'll spend twice that time a week on FaceTime, but I guess
the math is fine. I guess it's drivable, though honestly it's moot
because I can't really drive. Jude drives. Jude can come

see me, stay in the guest room, we can sneak around Willy Street
one weekend a month and I won't do that thing I always do,
where I'm so determined that we're going to have a good time

that I talk things up too much, say, *this restaurant will change
your life*, like I'm some character from a Zach Braff movie
where I'm really just a letdown. No. I'll behave. I'll sparkle.

I know I won't screw it up. I mean
                    actually, no, I know I'm going
to screw it all up, and standing here in the stairwell, my field of
    vision

does that thing where it lurches hard to the right, that thing
that isn't anxiety and isn't nystagmus, is instead the sweet spot
between them both, and yes, I am catastrophizing—my therapist

calls this catastrophizing—and I know if I rip up the plan now
I'll careen into the sea. So I stay the course. Stay the course!
Steady on, Florence! I lean against the cinder-block wall

and I call him. Once, twice, it's going to go to voicemail—
see? Fine! It's all fine! And then, of course, he answers.

JUDE
DESCENDING, 2:30 A.M.

The doors open to another darkened corridor and standing there is a girl, dressed like a dancer, who looks slightly too old to be a HACker. She holds a laundry bag and is texting. She looks surprised but not shocked to see me when she looks up.

"Hi," I say awkwardly.

"Ghost of Michael Flatley?" she asks, getting on. She hits the first-floor button. The doors close and we start ascending again.

I could have used a minute or two without further humiliation, I think. "Yep," I reply. "I mean that's why I'm here. I'm not the ghost. Obviously."

"There's no mistaking the Lord of the Dance."

"I'd guess not."

"You know Michael Flatley's very much alive, right? As much so as the HAC legend."

"I didn't even know before tonight that he was the Lord of the Dance, much less alive or dead."

"Seems like someone could have Googled that before the legend got started."

The elevator stops.

"Anyway," the girl says. "Happy Sunrise Night." The doors open and she leaves.

I can hear Florence up the hallway over the girl's footfalls. She's talking with someone on the phone—it must be Rafe. I can hear her faintly but I can still make out what she's saying. The doors start to close but I hold them open so I can eavesdrop.

FLORENCE
CATASTROPHE, TWO

Hey it's me.

No I know it's late, I'm sorry. Were you—

No, I'm okay. Nothing happened. I mean something happened.
But not, like, *to* me.

More like I—I mean, I've been thinking. I feel like I . . . I don't
want us to be together anymore. I mean that I want to be
alone.
I'm lying. I don't want to be alone.

I've done a lot of thinking and now it's the night before camp
ends and I just—I don't think it's fair to you. Everything that's
happening to me. I need some space to deal with it.

Yeah. Yeah, I mean the eye stuff.

No, but you know what? That's not the only thing. I'm tired of
feeling like I'm too much for someone. I'm tired of feeling
like I need to be small. I have, like, big feelings, it's not like
something I can help—

No.
Well I didn't call you a bad person, did I?

Stop. No, stop. I don't *think* you're a bad person, either. I just don't know if we should be together right now.

Later? I mean I don't know about later.

Rafe, I'm not changing my mind about us.

JUDE
IN THE FALL, TWO

I'm not changing my mind about us.

As in: *I entered this elevator with Jude*
in love with you, and I'm still in love
with you and always will be.

My heart feels like it's just jammed
a fork handle in an electrical socket.
And I would know, because I did it
when I was four.

The elevator doors slide shut
like an overly on-the-nose
metaphor about the closing off
of possibility, silencing the sound
of Florence telling Rafe, *I'm not changing*
my mind about us.

I repeat it in my head so many times
the words start to dissolve, like dialogue
when you're watching TV half-asleep.

I begin to wonder if I actually heard it
or if my quick-to-punish brain conjured it
to hurt me. Wouldn't be the first time.

I'm going to wait. I won't rush
to judgment. No maddening
rom-com miscommunications here.

Or maybe I won't wait. There's only one way
to know for sure whether I heard
what I heard. I hit the button
to open the elevator doors—

FLORENCE
CATASTROPHE, THREE

I love you too.

Yes, asshole, I do mean it. You've been really good to me, in so
many ways. And I've thought about you a lot these last few
weeks.

I tried.

I really did.

> I'm telling the truth.

We can get into it more when I get back, okay?

Fine, then, you decide. Just let me know. If you want to take a
walk and talk about it more—

Yeah. Yeah, okay. Bye.

JUDE
FALLEN

I love you too.

I hit the button to close
the elevator doors like they'd just opened
onto a lobby packed with people and I
was standing on the elevator completely
naked, which is a great way to describe
how I feel at this moment.

I sit in the dark with my mortification; face burning—
now the elevator button panel mocks me
with the dimness of its light:

*You can almost see. You're so close. You can make
things out just well enough to know that you're alone
in this darkness and someone will always be better
than you. Peyton. Rafe. There will always be someone
they prefer to you.* And how much better

than Peyton am I anyway? Trying to kiss a girl
who has a boyfriend? How could I let this moment
overcome me like that? So much that I made Florence
feel compelled to reaffirm

her love for Rafe. *You've ruined everything,*

my spiraling thoughts chant. *At least with Marley,*
your hands were clean. There's no coming back from this.
My mind won't give me a moment's rest. The one grace here

is that she's someone I don't have to see anymore.
I don't have to wait for her to get back and tell me
what I already know, which is that I made a grave
misstep while intoxicated on pancakes and lack
of sleep and the heady exhilaration of being near her. We never
    have

to talk again, in fact. I can leave this elevator, return
to check-in, tell them I'm turning in for the night,
then, in the solitude (hopefully) of my dorm,
replay the events of the last few minutes
on a loop in my mind until I'm too exhausted
to stay awake and capitulate to sleep,

where the dream shift can take over
the endless cyclical ruminating, waking me
every hour until it's time to throw things in a
bag and get to the airport shuttle. I think
that's exactly what I'll do. It's all I can do.

(It would have been so easy
not to screw this up.)

(All I needed to do was not

try to kiss her, something I've
been doing successfully almost
my whole life.)

Look on the bright side:
maybe you're not as toxic
to love in your orbit
as you think. After all,
you seem to have driven Florence
right back into Rafe's arms.

Leaving without goodbye or explanation
is wrong, but I need to leave.

FLORENCE
I'M NOT CHANGING MY MIND ABOUT US

He's not there when I get back, but you knew that
already. It's the logical end to the story. The doors open,
they close. I sit on the floor and after a minute

it's dark again. Maybe he stepped out
for some air, went to the bathroom. I stick
my head in the men's down in the basement

but it's empty. Wave hi to Chloe the TA washing
her leotards in the laundry room, try not
to look like a fool. The heat of wanting, the heat

of shame. Probably I deserve this. I probably
did something wrong, like maybe it was building
in him all night, the acid in his belly, listening

to me being me, all prickly and sad and wrong
for him, and I'm pretty, so I get why he wanted me,
but I guess then he thought better. Take the haunted elevator

to the top floor to search the studios, like it's hide-
and-seek. Part of me wants to look under the grand piano
and so I do, like a child, and what did I do wrong? I did

something. No—what if he's hurt? What if he's spiraling,

lost in himself somewhere, feeling guilty maybe that I went
to end it with Rafe? That would be like Jude, flagellating

away for no good reason. What if he heard me dumping
Rafe and went off to feel all sinner-y about it? I feel awful.
I feel like I would have found him already. I could just

text him—but no, I can't. What if I've misread all
of this? Fantasy then, staring up into the strings and hammers
of this thing that makes music, thinking

Florence, don't be a fool. Don't believe them when they say
they like you for who you are.
          And then the mind-bending

rush of anger, the one where I'm time-traveling
without going anywhere, just flat in my dance skirt
in a place that doesn't want me anymore and then

I say no. *I'm not doing this. Get up.* Make myself
get up. There's a door to the roof, what if
he's waiting for me on the roof? What if he thinks

that's romantic? That would be like Jude, and I hate
that I'm hoping, now, at the end of the hall slamming
open the door to the stairwell, and I want to run

all the way up, but stairs are my enemy. Cool air,

five minutes to three, not much of a view and
of course no Jude. Why am I such a fool? Was this

some kind of power play, Jude wanting to see
how far I'd go for something he was never going
to give me? Dump the good-enough boyfriend

so that we're both lonely and alone. I should
call Rafe back. I should tell him I was drunk,
afraid. Maybe he'd even like that. What the hell

is wrong with me? I thought at least I was pretty.
I thought I was a good listener. Probably I'm pretty
like something that will eat you after. Probably

the reward isn't worth the risk, and now another
sure thing isn't. Sure like steady, sure like seeing
me as my best self, the girl that would've picked up

a sword for him, fought any battle. The girl
who wasn't worth it. The girl who never was,
and from my vantage point on the roof I watch
all the little idiot artists scurrying back to their idiot

check-in and I'm crying now, in this place I'll never
get back to, and when I take out my phone
to delete *Jude Wheeler* I tell myself I'll never be

this naive again, this broken, not ever.

THE DESERT

FLORENCE
LIKE DISASTER

It's hard to know what to do after the universe
tapes a "Kick Me" sign to your back. Usually
I wise up fast. I'm a fighter—have you noticed

that that's what they call you when you're a chronically
sick kid? *She's a fighter.* Like, buddy, I'm six,
I'm pretty sure I'm also an astronaut. Ophthalmologists

didn't make me a fighter, or three trips under
anesthesia before eighth grade. No, other kids made me
a fighter. Other people. The sheer unfairness

of other people, who say they like you and they love
you and then they leave you for dead on the side
of the road. Maybe I'm being dramatic

but honestly, last summer, that was the way it felt.
Last summer it was like the universe was giving me
this endless cosmic swirlie. When I got home

I couldn't dance. I couldn't eat. I couldn't do much
but walk up and down Atwood Avenue and think
about all the things this street used to be. The indie theater

used to show porn, I guess, before I was born.

Artists used to live out here. Some still do but mostly
now it's condos. People can't stop talking about the way

things were before, like it was better by default. Why am I
the only one who feels like I walk around with my mistakes
tied to my ankles, rattling away like tin cans? In August,

Rafe started dating my friend Ichika. I was dropped
by my friend group because it was awkward, them
and Alexis and Desiree and Mason all at homecoming

without me, and then one week later I dropped my pointe class
after I misjudged a jump and crashed into the standing barre,
and I did something, I think, to my back, but the doctors

couldn't see anything on the scans and told me to take
Tylenol for the pain. Sleeping was hard, there was no way
to get comfortable, and why would I want to sleep anyway

when it was straight teleportation into another school day
with nothing else to look forward to? My dad watched me
ghouling around the house and bought me *The Bell Jar*

to make me feel less alone, which I read in one glorious brain-on-
    fire
night, sleepless but electrified, and then I got Plath's book *Ariel*,
    and then
The Colossus, and I stood in the indie bookstore off State

staring at the biographies thinking, *oh my God, am I becoming
a Plath person?* and so I went to the poetry section instead.
Didn't know where to start, everything was about trees

and I like trees okay, but nature is hard for me. Hiking is hard
with my eyes. Mostly nature wants me to die. Instead I got
a book by Terrance Hayes and then one by Alison Stine and then

stacks of them from the library, stuff that made me want to *do*
   something
after I read it, pound out the rhythms on the wall. I needed
to take some kind of action, but I didn't know what. Sometimes

after I read a poem I loved I'd do push-ups on my bedroom floor.
Sometimes I'd write down my favorite lines and then some
of my own stuff below it, riffing, nothing real. Not like art.

Just—feelings. Big feelings. I dropped my other dance classes.
A handful, then the rest, the modern too, sat there kicking my
   feet
in the director's office while she fought back tears. I'd danced for
   her

since I was five, and then I just walked out, like it was simple,
like you could drive away from your past all at once. I wrote
about that too. About deferring the decision to get surgery

again, at least for now, since there was no ticking clock

on my dance career. I could be kind of blind forever. Blindness
isn't a metaphor, except when it is, and so that fall I was exactly
   that:

kind of blind. On a whim I signed up for a writing class
and then I dropped it like a bomb. Sharing my poetry felt like
I was stripping off my skin on stage. Spent that weekend reading

Elizabeth Bishop and crying because I'd also mastered the art
of losing and yes, it looked exactly like disaster, and that was when
   my mom
let herself into my room and said, *Florence. Stop.* She had

a sabbatical in the spring. She was going to San Francisco
for research, and she'd thought maybe she'd fly back weekends
but "seeing the way things were" with me—maybe I could go too,

do school out there. Would I want that? And I looked at myself
in the mirror, snotty and puffy and crying over poetry
in my bed, and thought, *what the hell do I have to lose?*

FLORENCE
ASIDE

Have you noticed I haven't mentioned Jude once?
Yeah. I'm proud of that.

JUDE
THE NEW YEAR

Without realizing it, I'd started measuring
each new year not from January to January
but from June to June. After all, I'd lately
lived each year for the promise of HAC,

that week out of fifty-two where I felt
like the fullest, best version
of myself. Where my mind was
quietest. And that was even before
I met Florence and certainly before I lost her.

So I ended my year watching the dawn break
through a mineral-spotted dorm window, feeling as broken
as I've ever felt, wondering if God made me
a photographer because the only beautiful things safe

from me are the ones I press onto pixels and film
like a dead violet pressed between the pages of a book.
Never had I felt less newness
and possibility at the rising of the day.

What's wrong? my mom asked
when she picked me up that night
at the Nashville airport. *I think I might be done
with HAC,* I said. *I don't want to go back
next year.* She was quiet

for a while and didn't ask
why, which I appreciated because I had neither
the energy to tell the story nor to invent
a lie. She just said, *a year is a long time. Maybe you'll change
your mind.* For a few weeks, I held

the wild and absurd hope
that at some moment, my phone would light
up like the fireflies that spotted the dusk
of that waning summer, glowing with a message
from Florence—*It's okay, Jude, there's a final
Sunrise Night for us.*
But nothing came.

I couldn't bear to look up
her social media. The only thing worse
than it still being a private cipher would be seeing her
with Rafe, his arm around her, hugging
their bodies together, while they both wore
easy, joyous smiles, knowing that she sacrificed her privacy
just to show me this.

In the fall, in October, my grandma died.
The survivor. The one I told Florence about
while we were bowling. She died. And so there was
one fewer person in the world I could love.

I grieved her. There was no rest

for my mind. Every rare occasion it went still
I would immediately remember something
like how she always kept out
a jar of those rectangular oatmeal cookies
with cream filling that they only sell
to grandmas and how there was never
any point in my life
when that didn't seem important.

Or how once when I was five
she read me the story of Cinderella
and changed every part mentioning
fancy gowns to fancy overalls
and I laughed until I got a case
of hiccups that lasted for fifteen minutes.

When someone you love is gone you realize
how you'd lived in only fleeting grace.

Then in the winter I got accepted
to a fancy art school—my first choice—
on a photography scholarship. A photo

of my grandma, the last time
I saw her alive—dying and afraid
in her hospital bed, wreathed
in tubes like a whale fighting

a squid—was part of my application.
So was the photo of Florence,
I guess also technically the last time
I saw her alive, her face in the chiaroscuro

of the elevator button panel
as though painted in some twenty-first-century
Caravaggio. I'd thought,
if I don't get in, it won't be because
I kept back what most wounded me—

I figured there might be
some fiendish magic in the record
of the costs I'd paid.

If all you have to offer is blood, offer blood.

Winter yielded to spring. I let my hair grow.

I finally went to see a therapist, like Florence
suggested. A guy on my mom's health plan
who wore rumpled khakis with blue
Chuck Taylors, in an obvious attempt
to appear nonthreatening. And you know

what? It worked. He diagnosed me
with OCD and anxiety and put me on
a medication that made my scalp tingle

and helped me feel less like a rubber band
about to be shot at the back of someone's neck.

I went to prom with a girl who loved
manga and K-pop. She had streaks in her hair
the color of bowling alley blue raspberry slushie
and a septum piercing. We dressed ourselves
from Goodwill; she painted my fingernails

the blue of her hair; and we ended up back
at her house with a group of friends, watching
Cats and yelling at the screen. It was fun
and meaningless. She still had a year

of high school left. We kissed
like we were expected to, but only the once,
and I spent the duration wondering
what Florence was doing

at that moment, like I'd done countless other times
that year. My OCD medication was good
for some things but it didn't make it impossible
to obsess over anything. I knew then

that my mom was right; that I wasn't quite done
with HAC. Sometimes
you have to take the photo from different angles
before your mind will finally let you

rest. Sometimes you have to turn
back for one more shot
before your light goes.

FLORENCE
SAN FRANCISCO

We had a one-bedroom in the Haight.

There was a place on the corner that sold sushi burritos.

I went to a high school that looked like a spaceship and they
offered Mandarin classes and yoga.

I definitely took the intro to Mandarin class. And the advanced
yoga.

Also a poetry class. No one knew me there. What did it matter?

My top-choice school deferred my early application and I didn't
apply anywhere else.

I thought I'd take a year away.

I thought I'd get a job somewhere. Maybe I could work on a farm
in Italy.

A boy named Carlos fell in the middle of warrior three in yoga
class and started snort-laughing and he immediately became
my new best friend.

I had trouble walking up and down the hills, placing my feet, but I
almost didn't care.

I loved it there that much.

Carlos let me hold on to his arm. We went to a gay bar in the
Castro and I had a sneaky beer.

I didn't like it. The beer. I loved watching Carlos dance.

I almost wanted to dance with him.

I wrote a poem about it.

We went to City Lights and I discovered I didn't really like the
Beats but I pretended I did because Carlos really loved Ginsberg.

From what I could tell, the Beats were mostly gross dudes. I
bought a Lyn Hejinian book instead.

At night my mom started brushing my hair again.

I wrote a poem about it.

She didn't ask about my college apps, and I didn't tell her.

Most Sundays Carlos and I ate sushi burritos outside the Palace
of Fine Arts.

Then in March he got a boyfriend and so we mostly just hung out
at lunch.

I had time to think again, and that turned out to be bad news
bears.

I wrote a poem about Jude. It was like looking under a bandage
and seeing that the wound had gone black at the edges.

I wrote another. Another. My teacher liked them. They made me
want to vomit.

I didn't know what I was feeling and so I shut the box inside my
heart marked Jude and hid it away.

In April I got an email from my top-choice college.

I'd gotten in, regular decision.

I cried. My mom let me have a glass of champagne. She thought it
was my first ever drink and I let her think that.

I wrote a poem about a farm in Italy.

I thought maybe I'd stay in San Francisco over the summer.

Then my poetry teacher grabbed me on the last day of class.

She said, do you know about this great arts camp?

It's up in Michigan.

Maybe you'd like it there.

NIGHT
THREE

JUDE
THE RULE OF THIRDS

One thing about Christianity
that I always liked
(SPOILER ALERT: it's not cool youth pastors):

the whole Trinity thing.

There was always something
about the symmetry of threes
that appealed to me, that felt powerful.

It only made sense when I learned
about the Rule of Thirds in photography—
mentally divide your photos
into a grid with three groups of three.
Place the important parts
of your photo at the meeting points
of the gridlines.

Two Sunrise Nights felt incomplete.
There was none of my kind of symmetry—
the kind I needed, that would let my mind stop
gnawing away at me. I had to position the last part
of the picture where the gridlines met.

I looked for her all week.
I didn't see her. But that was nothing

new—I've never seen her at HAC before
Sunrise Night. I knew that seeing her
once more, from afar,

might be all that I had courage for, so I went
to the dance showcase that happens just before
Bonfire. I sat in the audience and looked
for her on the stage. And if not there,
then in the audience.
She wasn't there, anywhere.

I bowed under her absence like I did
under the weight of all my new losses
and I wondered again what she was doing
at that moment, if she was seeking the same
sort of symmetry as I was.

Probably not, I thought. *Good old
bilateral symmetry for her. If it's good
enough for most
multicellular organisms, it's good
enough for Sunrise Nights.*

Perhaps it was for the best—
Seeing her dance as the last time
I saw her might have done me in.

I guess you don't always get
to follow the Rule of Thirds.

Maybe sometimes your lot is to live
with an ill-composed photo.
Lord knows I've learned
that much.

With a last look (or two) (or three)
(or, you know what, don't worry about it)
back over my shoulder, I leave
the dance showcase into
the long-shadowed gloaming and follow
the smell of woodsmoke to Bonfire,

where I'll have my paltry satisfaction
of the Rule of Thirds. Where I'll make
some eulogy for unfed hunger, where I'll lay
to rest what needs to be laid
to rest, to start a new year
and a new life, clean and free.
(Are you allowed to say LOL
in a poem? If so, LOL.)

I'm standing alone in front
of the fire, close enough
to be uncomfortable, watching the dance
of flames. I turn
from the sting of smoke in my eyes

and there she is.

JUDE
SHE'S REAL

We fall into a wordless hug.
The kind where
what you want most
is to make sure
someone is real.

JUDE
IN FRONT OF THE BONFIRE, IMPROBABLY, FOR A THIRD TIME, RECONNECTING FONDLY, 8:53 P.M.

"*Asshole*," Florence hisses, breaking our hug with enough force to push me back.

"I know. I'm sorry."

"You don't get to do that."

"What?"

"*What.*"

"I'm serious. Tell me what I don't get to do and I won't do it."

"This whole thing. *I'm sorry. I'm so full of regret. Please forgive me.*" Florence says the words like they're made of earwax.

"Do you not want me to be sorry?"

"No, I do, but I also don't want it cast back on me to where now the ball is in my court to forgive you or I'm the bitch."

"Okay."

"Okay then."

Silence pools around us. We each wait for the other to step out of it.

"I'm standing here quietly feeling sorry, expecting no absolution," I say tentatively.

"Good. How does it feel?"

"Bad. Very shitty."

"Good."

"Jeez."

"I mean it. Good."

"Kinda harsh."

"Do you really think you're in a position to be judging things to be harsh?"

"Probably not."

"Try again."

"Definitely not."

"Better. You know that I literally struggled with whether I was coming here to see you and hang out or chew your ass out and leave?"

"I guess I know now."

"And, like, even at this moment, I don't know why I'm here." Florence looks into the fire as she says this. She looks different. Her features are softer, rounder. Her hair is shorter. It's hard to tell in this light but she might have a nose stud.

"I don't really know how to respond to that," I say.

"Don't then. Maybe just listen."

"Okay. I'm listening."

Florence looks at the flames for a long time. "I'm still thinking," she says.

"I'll just be over here listening. We have until sunrise."

After a pause, she says, "It's that I am so, *so* sick of being abandoned. I hate it so much. And, like, last summer was *that*. You. My friends. Even dance, honestly."

"I didn't—"

"Weren't you just going to listen?"

"Yeah, but I feel like I need to—"

"Are you about to tell me that you didn't desert me last year?"

"Sorta, I—"

"Oh, so you didn't leave that elevator with zero notice?"

"No, I—"

"You didn't slink off into the night like some possum that got caught eating moldy cold cuts from a dumpster? And instead your flesh transformed and you became a being of pure incorporeal energy, able to exist outside of the strictures of time and space, seeing and knowing all things at once?"

"Not that," I say quietly.

"Because I was gonna say, you've really taken a demotion since then."

"Fair enough."

"So you did abandon me."

"I—yes." I manage to tamp down the urge to reflexively apologize.

"Remember last year when we were talking about whether our thing—where we don't communicate for a year—is a good idea?"

"Yes."

"You didn't think it was a good idea."

"I recall that."

"I never said what I thought," Florence says.

"I recall that too."

"I liked it. I thought it was a good idea. I mean, sure, there were lots of times I wished we could have talked, but ultimately, it was an opportunity to see if there was *anyone* in my life who would just *be there* without my constantly pulling them back, you know? Constantly making the case for myself with them. I wanted someone who would just *show up. Be present.*"

"And that was me."

"*Was.*"

"Can I say something?" I ask.

"I don't know." Florence folds her arms in front of her chest.

"How about I'll say it and then you can decide after if I was allowed to say it."

"Fine."

"I really missed you. That's all."

Florence is quiet while she considers what I've said, or maybe something else. "You ditched me," she says quietly. "Middle of the night."

"Okay, but, like, it wasn't for kicks. Notice me not apologizing again."

"I noticed. Why, then?"

"Well . . ." I let a long time pass while I figure out what to say. "I really should have rehearsed this."

"Well?"

"I was embarrassed."

"Because you tried to kiss me?"

"I mean, *obviously*, but then you and Rafe."

"Me and Rafe what?"

"You, like, reaffirming your love for him or whatever."

"What are you talking about?"

"I heard you."

"You—*what*? How did you hear a thing that didn't happen?"

"I heard you. While I was waiting for you some girl called the elevator to the basement and got on. When she got back off on the first floor, the doors opened and I could hear you up the hall and you were telling Rafe something about how you still felt the same about him. And how you still loved him."

Florence starts laughing. She goes to say something but laughs some more. She covers her face with one hand and shakes her head.

"Being laughed at was exactly the reaction I was hoping for," I say. "That definitely helps my retroactive humiliation."

Florence's laughter subsides into a sigh. "What I was saying to Rafe was that I still loved him in a way where I didn't want to be with him anymore and I wasn't changing my mind about him and me *breaking up*."

I'm not sure I heard her right (and almost hoping I didn't), so I ask, "Do what now?"

"Breaking up, Jude. Ending our relationship."

"That's what that phone call was?"

"I don't believe this."

"Florence?"

"Yes."

"Okay, *how* was I supposed to know that?"

Florence raises her arms like she's showing me how huge the fish she caught was. "Oh, gee, Jude, I don't know. Maybe if you *stuck around long enough for me to come back to the elevator and say, 'hey I just broke up with my boyfriend, now where were we?'*"

"Um. So, I don't really have a great answer for that, I guess."

We both start laughing and we do that together for a while. It feels good.

"Make you a marshmallow?" I ask.

"Make three," she says.

FLORENCE
OFF INTO THE NIGHT TO TRY TO OUTRUN OUR FEELINGS, 9:12 P.M.

"Where are you going?" Jude asks.

"I don't know. I feel like I need to be moving or I'm somehow going to slip back into last summer's temporal reality. I'm antsy."

"You're using lots of science metaphors tonight."

"I had a really good physics teacher in San Francisco."

"Whoa. What?"

"What?"

"San Francisco? Did you guys move?"

"My mom was on sabbatical, and I went with her."

"Wow. That's . . . not a small thing."

"Yeah, it wasn't really part of the plan."

"Why did you go?"

I take a deep breath and try very, very hard not to tear his head off. "I was having kind of a bad fall semester," I tell him.

"Sorry."

"Can you please not apologize? And anyway, I'm not giving you ownership over it. Last fall's . . . badness, I mean. Rafe has joint ownership, and my stupid friends, and my stupid eye, and the fact that it started blizzarding in Wisconsin in October—"

"Ouch."

"So yeah, I went to San Francisco. No snow there."

"Did you find a studio there? To dance with, I mean?"

"No. I was . . . I was writing poetry."

"You're laughing like it's funny."

"It's kind of funny. Me being sensitive enough to write poetry."

"I don't know, you're pretty sensitive."

"Hey, you're the one with the dreamy hair."

"You pierced your nose!"

"Dude, it's a stud so small that my mom didn't notice for *two weeks*. You listen to sad boy music."

"We have literally never talked about music."

"I distinctly recall discussing 'My Humps' by the Black Eyed Peas so don't say never."

We're laughing again.

"You listen to Dearly. Admit it," I say. "You're required by law as a Sad Southern Boy."

"Dearly is *amazing*."

"I didn't say Dearly wasn't amazing! Something can be amazing and, like, all-caps VERY SAD all at the same time. Some people love being sad."

"Like poets?"

"You're hilarious."

"Yep, I totally am."

"Listen, I'm not interested in being professionally sad," I tell him. "Or professionally angry. Or professionally anything. Wouldn't that be terrible, to have only one way of being? One way of seeing the world? Like oh, Jude Wheeler, they go to him when they need..."

"What?" He looks a little afraid. "What would they go to me when they need?"

"Joy," I say, finally. "They'd go to you when they need joy."

"You're sort of talking like you've forgiven me."

"I know. Weird, isn't it?" I tell him. We round a corner and—

"Why are we at a gas station?" Jude asks.

"Oh. Uh—"

"Florence."

"What?"

"You were walking like you had someplace really specific to be."

"I mean. Maybe I was walking like I really specifically needed us to get Slurpees."

"Downtown is literally in the other direction."

"Slurpees AND mini donuts? And I'm buying?"

"Wow," he says. "I love a gas station."

"Who knew. Oh my God, wait—is that a Plymouth Barracuda?"

"That cool old red car?"

"Yeah, I think it is! Candy-apple red."

"And you're just casually able to identify it?"

"Every girl is entitled to one implausible dream car—it's in the Constitution—and that one's mine."

JUDE
STAYING JUST FAR ENOUGH AHEAD OF OUR FEELINGS THAT WE MIGHT MANAGE TO DROWN THEM IN SLURPEES AND POWDERED MINI DONUTS, 9:19 P.M.

"So hang on," I say. "I wanna hear more about this poetry you're writing now."

"What do you want to know?"

"Is this, like, your new deal?"

"I mean, it's why I'm here, if that's what you mean," she says casually.

"You're not here for dance?"

"Nope."

"Like, at all?"

"Nope. Told you that a few minutes ago."

"You just said you didn't find a dance studio because you were writing poetry."

"Well, that's what I meant. I hope they have Coke Slurpees. You ever mixed Coke Slurpee with coconut Slurpee?"

"That explains that," I mutter out loud, without really meaning to.

"What explains what?"

"To answer your earlier question, of course I've mixed Coke Slurpee with coconut Slurpee. How incurious do you think I am?"

"Jude. What explains what?"

I hesitate to answer because I think it makes me seem pathetic. "That explains why you weren't at the dance showcase," I say.

"And you were?"

"Obviously."

"Jude!"

"Don't act like it was some cute rom-com gesture. I didn't know if I was ever going to see you again. It was going to be a silent good-bye."

"Can we start a band called A Silent Goodbye?"

"Get it all out of your system."

"Can I play tambourine? No! Triangle! No! Accordion! Banjo?"

"Go on. All out."

"Aw. Are you annoyed?"

"No."

"You sound annoyed," Florence says.

"I hate that we talk once a year and so I learn about your life in this weird feast-and-famine way." We walk into the mini-mart.

"Yeah but if we—" Florence starts to say, but a familiar-sounding voice cuts her short.

"*Dude. What?!* You guys!"

We look over to the snack aisle. Well, one of the snack aisles. "No way. Ravyn?" I say incredulously.

"What's up, dudes. Third Sunrise Night in a row," Ravyn says. "Hell yeah."

"You work here now?" Florence asks.

Ravyn laughs her stoner laugh. "Nah. Just dipping in for some Hot Cheetos to chase some edibles later."

"Thinking ahead," Florence says.

"Don't get Cheetos dust on the upholstery of your sweet ride out there," I say, nodding out the window at the Barracuda.

"All good. Got it restored with vinyl upholstery. You can wipe it off easy." Ravyn doesn't appear to be joking in the slightest.

"Wait, I was kidding. You for real? That's your Barracuda?" I ask.

"1970 Hemi Cuda, baby. It's stupid fast. You're all *vrooooom*."

"Hold up. Are you still working at the coffee shop?"

"Yeah, no. Like a month after you guys came in, one of my friends gave me a FartCoin for my birthday."

"A what?"

"FartCoin. Crypto. Anyway, I turned around and sold it at exactly the right time and made a buttload of cash, which I invested in a chain of dispensaries with a couple partners. Things took off. I mean capitalism still sucks but."

"But now you're making it work for you," Florence says.

"American dream, baby."

"It's official, Ravyn. I've now encountered you as many times as I've encountered Jude here."

"*Stop*," Ravyn says. "Hanging out once a year?! Still?? What's you two's deal?"

"Collectively or individually?" I ask.

"Either."

"How much time do you have?" Florence asks.

"For real though, I gotta run to Target and get a birthday present for my nephew before they close. You guys need a ride anywhere?"

Florence looks to me. "Jude? Remember the night we met? You said you loved Target because you weren't a monster?"

"I said that?"

"Is it not true?"

"It is. I am not a monster."

Florence turns to Ravyn. "Would you mind terribly if we accompanied you to Target? What Jude didn't tell you was that you own my dream car and I would very much like to ride in it."

"You can drive it."

"Riding shotgun is fine."

"Get in, losers, we're going shopping. *Mean Girls?*"

"Got the reference. Great movie," Florence says. "Can we grab Slurpees real quick?"

"For sure. By the way, little pro tip: they have Coke and piña colada back there. You mix them? Daaaamn."

FLORENCE
HAVING SUCCESSFULLY OUTRUN OUR FEELINGS ALL THE WAY TO TARGET IN MY DREAM CAR, 9:32 P.M.

"I'll just drop you two out front and go find parking," Ravyn says. "Wow. Isn't that a mom thing to say?"

"It totally is," Jude says. "But you don't have to drop us. We can walk."

"Nah dude," Ravyn says. "I park this thing in the ass-end of nowhere. Can't have anyone pull up next to me and scratch my baby. You go ahead. We can meet out front at ten thirty?"

"Sounds great," Florence says, and we hop out. Inside, we bask for a minute in the rush of air-conditioning.

"Target," Jude says.

"What's the first thing you do inside a Target?"

"I go look at the big pen aisle."

"I'm down," I tell him. "Do you ever buy any?"

"Pens?"

"Yeah."

"No. Because—well, does that thing ever happen to you? When you're in a store looking at, like, a big wall of sweaters, and they have every good color, and they're all lined up next to each other, folded really nicely, and you're like, I have to have one of those."

"I know exactly what you're talking about."

"Right? And then you pick one up, like a blue one, a nice color, a color you wear all the time, even, and you take it home and—"

"And you don't know why you bought it."

"Exactly. It's not as good. Because you didn't want the one sweater. You wanted the wall of sweaters."

"That's why you don't buy pens," I say.

"Yeah. I don't want the one package of pens. I want the big pen aisle. All of it. And you can't take it home with you."

We consider the highlighter section.

"It's really hard to resist buying myself a bunch of highlighters," I tell him.

"You'd have to buy them all," he says, "to scratch that itch you're feeling." Jude takes out his phone and leans back a little, aiming it upward.

"Wait."

"What?" he asks, still looking at his screen.

"Wait. Wait!"

"What?"

"Is this the feeling that makes you want to take a photograph? Like, is this where it starts for you?"

He looks thrilled and also a little embarrassed. "I mean—I mean yeah," he says. "I can take the whole wall with me."

"You can take the whole wall with you."

Jude snaps the picture. "Where does the poetry feeling come from?" he asks.

"I'm really not an authority on it."

"I mean, you're here for poetry. It's competitive to get in. You have *some* authority."

I want to squirm. "No, like. I knew what I was talking about with dance. I did it for thirteen years. You know? I knew all the terms, I could talk about it. I could *do* it. I knew when I landed wrong, I knew what a good extension felt like. With poetry I—I don't know. I don't know what I'm doing."

"That's so cool."

"What do you mean?"

"Haven't you ever wanted to experience an amazing thing for the first time again?"

"Like a movie?"

"Or a song. Your favorite song. Or like—like meeting someone who's going to change your life. Having that life-changing night all over again. For the first time." He's looking at me now, intently.

Heat flushes through me, and then an unexpected stab of anger. I'm thinking about how embarrassing it was to search the dance building for him, alone. "That was the whole point of the no-communication thing," I say as breezily as I can. "Wasn't it?"

Jude nods. "Yeah, I guess it was. But we were talking about the poem itch. What makes you wanna write a poem?"

"I mean. At first it was because I was, like . . . intensely feeling something. I would write it right there in the moment in one big rush. And that *felt* good, getting it out, but I didn't like the way the poem turned out."

"Yeah?"

"Yeah. And then as I kept going, I found new poets to read, and I'd pick up something that made me want to write. Like I had to put the book down and find a pen. So poems happened that way for a while."

"Did you like those?"

"I liked them better," I tell him. "But I was still starting from a feeling. And I'm figuring out that . . . at least for me, I can't start with a feeling. I need to see something, or experience something, that makes me feel something, but then I have to wait. I write it down somewhere and leave it. Let it grow, almost. I come back to it later and see if there's something there for a poem."

"If the idea has sticking power."

"Not ideas," I tell him. "Images. Images first."

"Did you hear that?"

"Hear what?"

"Confidence. That was confidence. That was authority."

"I'm just quoting my teacher!"

"Confidence."

"False confidence," I tell him. "Like, I am always the person in the parking garage who thinks the car is over there."

"And it's not over there."

"Never. But I charge off confidently in the wrong direction anyway."

We're walking again. Jude isn't quite looking at me. "I looked for you tonight," he says. "I looked for you on stage. And—"

I don't say anything. I don't breathe.

"And it sort of broke my heart," he says, "when I thought you didn't come."

JUDE
ON THE BINARY NATURE OF HEARTBREAK

But something I've learned:
hearts don't get sort of
broken. That's just something
you say to hide the extent
of your fragility.

(Speaking in second person
is also a great way
to hide fragility.)

It's like how
something can't be "very
unique." Something is either
unique or it isn't.
The switch is on
or off. The glass is shattered
or not.

Your heart is either broken
or it isn't. Sure, you can be sad.
There are infinite shades of sadness.
But the minute you say your heart
is broken, you're committed.

Especially if you're saying it
to the person who did
the breaking.

JUDE
WHEREIN OUR FEELINGS FOUND A GREAT PARKING SPACE RIGHT NEAR THE FRONT AND CAUGHT UP WITH US IN THE BIG PEN AISLE, 9:46 P.M.

"Jude," Florence murmurs.

"Hey look at the size of this pen! It's, like, comically huge," I say. "It'd be really funny to sign an important document with this while wearing a tiny cowboy hat."

"It kinda breaks my heart to think about you sitting there at the showcase, looking for me. Tell me you weren't alone at least. I can't think of a lonelier feeling on earth than looking for someone you really want to see and not finding them. Especially when you're alone."

"No, there were lots of other people there."

"You know what I meant."

"Because imagine if it were just me, sitting there all by myself in the middle of the auditorium."

"With some, like, wildly inappropriate and conspicuous snack."

"A huge dill pickle."

"*What?*"

"Yeah, this kid who moved to my school from Texas says people there get huge pickles to eat during movies."

"During *movies?*"

"That's what he said. He could have been joking."

"Honestly I don't hate it?" Florence catches my eye and there's weight in her gaze.

I look at her for a while, with what I hope is an expression of openness, to leave her space to say whatever she obviously wants to tell me.

"I looked for you too," she says quietly, looking away.

"At the dance showcase?"

She shakes her head. She looks like she wants to say something but also doesn't. She toys with a package of pens. "I looked for you a bunch of places. Dumb places where you couldn't have been. Looked there too."

"In a package of pens?"

She smiles a little and shakes her head.

"The elevator?"

She nods. We hold a few seconds of silence between us like it's fragile.

"Anyway," she says. She won't make eye contact.

"Hey." I touch her shoulder.

She finally looks at me and I can see the fierce hurt in her eyes.

"Hey," I say again. "Now can I tell you I'm sorry?"

She nods.

"I'm sorry." I hug her and we hug for a long time, swaying back and forth in the big pen aisle like we're slow dancing.

FLORENCE
ANTICIPATION

They say if you want to go on vacation,
you should plan it a year in advance. The longer

you wait, the better you feel when you get on that plane
to Paris, or whatever. I don't know if it's true,

because I was pretty sure I was never coming back
to Michigan again, curse the land and salt the earth, etc.,

after I dragged myself crying back to my dorm last June
at 3 a.m. to sleep straight through the sunrise. But here I am,

feeling better. I test the feeling out. I mean, coming back to HAC
was a gamble, and honestly my mom wanted it more than I did—

well, she wanted me to want *something*. Maybe it was out of
    respect
that she'd stopped talking to me about dancing altogether, but

it was like I'd buried the me-that-danced in the yard at blackest
midnight, never to be spoken of again, and I don't know why

I'm thinking about it now in the home decor section of the
    Harbor City
Target, holding out a rose candle under Jude's nose. I'd do

a pirouette for him, but I'm not sure I'd read him a poem.
I'd tell him how badly I was hurt, but I'm not sure I would let him

kiss me. But I want him to, I want him to—oh, at least I think
I want him to. Dancing used to be the thing I did for myself,
    damn

the world, and later it was a bomb I carried around—afraid it
    would
go off, afraid to put it down—and then when I left HAC last year

it was like I left my dancer self there, too. She's still standing
on the roof of the dance building, all alone. But I don't know

if I miss her. I think I'm something else now. Tonight,
in the candle aisle, holding out a candle to Jude like

it's a flower, I get the sense of how good it will feel
to one day write a poem about right now.

FLORENCE
CARRYING OUR FEELINGS AROUND IN A RED PLASTIC TARGET BASKET, 10:12 P.M.

"That candle reminds me of my grandma," Jude says.

"The rose one?"

"Yeah. Gimme that again." He inhales. "I think that's her perfume," he says. "Or was, I guess."

"Was?"

"She died last year." Jude says it in that casual way that people sometimes say things they're afraid will make them cry.

"Oh, Jude. She's the one you told me about?"

"Yeah. The cancer came back. It happened pretty fast. Though, I don't know."

"What?"

"It's funny, they didn't even put it in the obituary. How she died. I read the whole page of them in the paper, and I noticed that if people die after they turn eighty, it's like it almost doesn't matter what they die from."

"It should matter," I say.

"Maybe sometimes they don't know why they died. Maybe that's why." Jude takes one more whiff and puts the candle back on the shelf.

"She was the one who sent you a twenty-dollar bill on your birthday every year."

"Yeah," he says. "She had great stories. She told me when she had my mom, my uncle, who was seventeen at the time, drove her to the hospital in the back of his buddy's Mustang convertible, no time to put the top up, dropped her off, and then went on to school."

"Wow."

"First period waits for no man. Or baby."

"It's really hard to know how to feel about death."

"I mean, I think it's . . . a bad thing, Florence."

"Oh for sure. I don't mean that. I just mean like . . . it's so impossible to imagine what it's like to not be here anymore. Not be conscious, I mean. Who knows if there's a heaven or whatever."

"Well, I think there's a heaven."

"I *want* to think there's a heaven. And then this, like, jerk part of my brain wonders if we believe in heaven just because it's too scary not to believe in heaven."

"I just don't know if the 'real' answer always has to be the scary one. You know? I mean, it's not like I want to be treated like I'm a kid. I don't need to believe in Santa Claus. I like it when things are complicated. But I don't think—"

"That the universe trends toward chaos?"

"I mean, you're the one with the good physics teacher," Jude says. "You tell me."

"Well, entropy exists. Things do kind of . . . slide toward disorder. But also, we're here, somehow. The big bang happened and the planet started spinning and we stand on the ground and we breathe this air and we're here. That happened too."

"And they don't know why."

"They don't know why."

"I don't like being told how to feel. You know? People assume that I'm sad about my grandma. And I am, and I miss her, but there's more to it than that."

"What do you mean?"

"I don't—" He frowns, trying to sort it out. "She made amazing biscuits," he says, finally. "When I was seven, she made me a scarf in my favorite colors, blue and green. And she loved me. So I'm . . . okay. I'm okay about it too. But it was still a bad year."

Jude picks up a lavender candle and sniffs.

"Here," he says. "Smell this one."

JUDE
STIMULATING THE OLFACTORY CENTERS OF OUR BRAINS, FOR BETTER OR WORSE, 10:21 P.M.

Florence takes a whiff, squinches her nose, and waves me away. "Oh. Nuh-uh."

I sniff it again. "This smells amazing. How can you not love this. It's like so comforting."

"Not to me. Opposite, in fact."

"Seriously? Why?"

"Because."

"Now I'm really curious."

"Don't worry about it."

"What, is this what Rafe smelled like or—"

"No. Okay. Just to get you off my back? This is what the Epsom salts smelled like that I used to use for muscle aches after an especially gnarly dance session and that's why I really didn't want to talk about it, so I hope you're happy." Florence stares me down defiantly.

I cap the candle and put it back on the shelf. "I am happy, actually."

"Oh yeah?"

"Yeah, I am."

"Even though I clearly did not want to talk about it."

"I'm glad you opened up to me."

"Under duress."

"Okay." I face her. "Look, Florence? Normally this is where I'd apologize—"

"Okay."

"—And fold. But not this time. Wanna know why?"

"Why?"

"Because I *care* about you. Like *deeply* care and I know we've known each other for literally two days or less, blah blah blah. But that's not my choice, you know? If it were up to me, we'd be talking every day. Every hour. We wouldn't have to spend half of our one night a year together catching up and getting to know each other again. We'd tell each other everything. Because it feels good to tell you things. And I would hope that it feels good to tell *me* things because I care about you and your life. When you hurt, I want to help you carry that. I want to hurt with you and for you. I want to be that person in your life and I don't care how crazy that sounds after how long we've known each other. I don't know what to tell you—you've gotten to me. *Obviously.* I hope for nothing more than you feeling the same about me." I look at Florence, suddenly grateful that I spilled that in a largely deserted Target.

Florence stares at me for a long time. While still making unbroken eye contact she reaches over to the shelf, picks up a candle, and takes a long sniff. "This smells like a yoga studio in a truck stop," she murmurs.

"You're so—" I say, throwing my hands in the air. I turn.

Florence grabs my arm and turns me back around. "Jude. Just—"

"You don't take me seriously at all."

"I do." She pauses for what feels like a long time. "Listen, I—I have a hard time opening up."

"You've spilled to me before about things."

"Yeah, but this is different."

"How?"

"Because I'm still coming to terms with it. This is . . . a death of a piece of me. Like my whole identity up until this point. Here I felt like I was just getting to know myself, and then that's gone. Taken away. And not in any sort of dignified, glorious way. I just started falling too much to keep doing it. I couldn't keep my balance. My skin was just a sea of bruises. It hurt so much. I thought I broke my wrist for a few days there. And my eyes still aren't done crapping out, by the way. It's hard feeling like you're sliding down a hill and you can't stop and you don't know where the bottom is. It's—it's really scary, and I'm scared. Okay?"

"I'm so, so sorry about all that, Florence."

"Yeah," she whispers.

"There's nothing I want more than to throw myself down that hill with you and try to beat you to the bottom so I can cushion your fall. Like Westley from *Princess Bride*."

"It was Buttercup who threw herself down the hill."

"I would if I could. Do you believe me?"

Florence meets my eyes. "Yeah. I do. You're the first person I've ever said that all out loud to, you know."

"You don't like to feel vulnerable."

"And you do?"

"No, I'm just saying I know you especially don't like it. But I dunno. Sometimes you gotta make yourself vulnerable to heal, you know what I mean? Like getting emotional surgery. I would've killed to be able to talk to you after my grandma died. Even though I was one big raw wound. I felt like I was mourning alone."

Florence doesn't reply but gets the rose candle off the shelf. She hands it to me. She pulls out her phone and holds it to her ear.

"Okay," she says. "I'm here now."

"What, like—"

"Yeah. Go ahead."

I hesitate but she doesn't seem to be joking. I laugh a little anyway, in case she is, and open the rose candle. I hesitate and then raise it to my nose. My eyes start filling with tears almost spontaneously. I quickly wipe them away and cough. "This is what happens to me when I watch Mr. Rogers videos on YouTube."

Florence stands there looking at me, her phone to her ear.

"So—" I start to say.

"Sorry, I can't hear you. I'm two thousand miles away. Better use the phone."

"Right. Forgot." I pull out my phone and put it to my ear. *"Brrrring brrrring."*

"Hello?" Florence says.

"Hey, uh. Florence?"

"Is this a telemarketer?"

"Oh right, you don't have my number in your phone, huh? It's Jude."

"Who?"

"Come on."

"I'm kidding. Hey, Jude. It's good to hear from you even though you're breaking our rules."

"Yeah, I know but I wouldn't be calling if it weren't important."

"What's up?"

"So, ah." I start to choke up and I try to play it off with a laugh. "This is dumb, right?" I turn away from Florence toward the candle shelves. "My, um, grandma—" The lump rises again and I clear my throat.

"It's okay, Jude," Florence says gently. "Take all the time you need."

"My grandma. She, uh. She died. Yesterday. We kinda knew it was gonna happen but. At least it was quick, right? That's what everyone says."

"Jude. I'm so sorry. Are you okay?"

Now tears are fully streaming down my cheeks. I think, *This sucks but also it doesn't?* "Man, I'm glad there's no one looking for candles at almost midnight," I say.

"What do you mean? Are you at a Target sniffing candles?"

"Yeah, how did you know I was at a Target specifically?"

"Because I figured Dickson, Tennessee, doesn't have a Diptyque store that's open that late."

"Oh yeah, you're right about that. I don't know what 'Diptyque' is, but I know we don't have it."

"I wish I could be there with you. I love sniffing candles and hanging out with you. Are you okay?"

"Yeah. I mean no, but yeah."

"You wanna talk about it?"

"I just miss her. That's all. And I'm tired of things in my life falling apart and I really miss you also. I wish I could see you."

"I miss you too, Jude."

FLORENCE
IN THE SELF-CHECKOUT, 10:32 P.M.

"Ugh, come on, *scan*."

"Ravyn will understand if we're a few minutes late," Jude says. "She doesn't seem like someone who's ever in a rush."

"I know, it's just, like, pathological. I hate making people feel put out because of me."

Jude coughs a little. "I'm having some trouble getting how that squares with your, like, general ethos."

The receipt prints. I hand him the travel-sized rose candle and put the lavender one in my pocket. "I mean, she's doing us a favor. I don't want her to think I'm not grateful."

"Right. But, like, one thing I like about you is that you're so 'I'm going to do what I need to do, and damn the consequences,'" Jude says.

"I think about the consequences all the time."

"You do?"

The night air is cool and sweet. We wait by the big red balls at the entrance.

"Yeah. I'm not, like, the way I am on purpose," I say. "Some of it . . . I don't know, some of it is probably just impulse control. I think it and then I'm saying it. And then I have to deal with the aftermath."

"I think about everything I say forever before I say it. I, like, rehearse it to death." Jude fishes the rose candle out of the bag and sniffs it again.

"What's that like?"

He laughs. "Oh wait," he says. "You're serious."

"I am! I mean, I don't think you do that with me?"

"Not in the moment. But I definitely carved out some rehearsal time in the weeks before HAC. In case I was gonna see you again."

"You did?"

Jude's not looking at me. "Yeah. Like, there were scenarios. Different scenarios."

"Like what?"

He looks a little like he's desperate for a trapdoor out of this conversation. "I mean, there was a scenario where I'd just come find you on the first day back. Like, forget Sunrise Night. I'd go to your dorm room, and maybe you'd be rooming with Makayla again, but in my head I'd planned it for when I knew she'd have Shakespeare rehearsal. Like the hour before dinner. And you'd have that quilt on your bed, and a little ceramic lamp, from like—"

"Target?"

"Target, and so your overhead light would be off. And you'd have that shadow play on your face. You have the cheekbones for it. For good lighting. And yeah, I don't know, you'd be like stretching on a yoga mat or something because I imagine that's what dancers do after rehearsal, a cooldown or something, and I'd knock, and you'd look up at me, and—"

"And what?"

He's staring doggedly at his feet. "And I'd make some joke."

"What joke?"

"This is a really bad idea."

"What is? Is that that joke?"

"Florence." Jude looks up at me, then over my shoulder, and blanches.

"Jude. What's the joke?"

"The joke is," he says, "that I want to—"

I take a breath. I lean in.

"—Oh. It's Ravyn," Jude says.

On cue, she honks, then rolls down her window. "What's up," she says.

Jude and I are staring at each other.

"Did someone die?" she asks.

Jude mutters something that I can't quite make out. It sounds like *romance*.

"Ravyn," I say, not looking at her. "Listen. We're, like, starving—"

Jude raises his eyebrows.

"And there's a, um. There's an Olde Style Buffet in this mall parking lot and I love Olde Style Buffet," I continue.

Ravyn laughs. "Oh wait," she says, "you're serious."

"Yeah. They have the best—"

"Mac and cheese," Jude supplies.

"The best mac and cheese."

"Okay but like, Olde Style Buffet is the place that they bus entire nursing homes to after bingo night. You're fifty years too young to go to Olde Style Buffet," Ravyn says.

"Late-night restaurants are, like, the inner part of the Venn diagram of teenagers and the elderly," I say. "Think about Perkins. Think about *Denny's*, for crying out loud."

"Can't argue with that logic," Ravyn says. "Especially since you . . . seem like you care a lot about this."

"She has Big Feelings," Jude says.

"Sorry," I say, "I'm just, um—"

"Hangry," Jude supplies.

"I'm hangry. And you are so awesome for giving us a ride here. I really appreciate it. But we're gonna get some food and then we can, like, walk back downtown. It's only a few miles."

"Cool," Ravyn says. "I'll see you next Sunrise Night."

"This is our last one," Jude says.

"For real? Wow. I sort of got to the place where I looked forward to seeing you two every year. Sometimes it'd be, like, Christmas, and out of nowhere I'd wonder what you two were doing, Blondie and Diet Timothée Chalamet."

"*Right?* Oh my God," I say, in wonder. "Diet Chalamet."

Jude turns bright red. "I will kill you both. Especially if Chalamet ever turns out to be a creep."

"Let me give you my number just in case." Ravyn reaches out for my phone. "For real, though," she says as she's typing. "This is the last time I'm gonna see you. That's a bummer. You guys were always such good tippers."

"It's my finest quality," I say.

Ravyn hands it back. "Blondie," she says. "Diet Chalamet. It's been a pleasure."

I sort of want to cry. I look at my phone. "Wait, is this CashMo transfer from you?"

Ravyn makes a clicking noise and points a finger gun. "You kids have fun."

"Is this your real last name?"

Clicking and finger gun again.

"That is incredible. Bye, Ravyn," I say, as she drives off.

Jude is staring at my lock screen. "Ravyn just sent you a CashMo transfer?"

"Yes. And look at her last name."

"It's McHaven."

JUDE
THE JOKE IS

The joke is that I want
to kiss you right now
really, really badly.

The joke is that
would have been a terrible
idea, but I would have done
it anyway.

The joke is that I've come
to feel like I can't trust
the one thing everyone says
you should trust most,
which is my heart.

The joke is that I could
have sworn you leaned
toward me, as though you knew
what I was going to say
before I knew I was going to say it.

The joke is that I don't know
whether you were leaning in for a kiss
or losing your balance.

The joke is that I don't know
if there's a difference
between the two.

JUDE
GOING TO THE OLDE STYLE BUFFET, WHICH, AT ALMOST 11:00 P.M. IS APPEARING TO BE SOMEHOW EVEN MORE QUESTIONABLE A CHOICE THAN IT WOULD NORMALLY BE, 10:49 P.M.

We look at each other in wonder. *"Ravyn McHaven,"* we say simultaneously.

"Why is Ravyn McHaven CashMo-ing you money? Has it come through yet?" I ask.

"Still pending," she says.

"We gotta get us some Olde Style Buffet now," I say. "And see what Ravyn McHaven sent us."

"Oh good," Florence says as we enter. "I was worried after our candle-smelling session that an absolutely soul-scorching reek of battered codfish wouldn't be permeating every molecule of oxygen in here. Wouldn't want my nose to get spoiled and soft."

"There's really just no doubt that there's codfish served here, is there?" I say.

"Like if you had some sort of rare medical condition where you had to have a big steamy hunk of battered cod in your mouth at all times or you would die, you would be rejoicing in the knowledge that you had at least a few more hours to live."

"Please don't say 'big steamy hunk of battered cod.'"

The hostess regards us wearily. "Two?"

"Two," I say.

"Booth or table?"

"Booth please," Florence says.

"This way." She leads us back to a booth in the corner. We're too far from HAC for other HACkers to have landed here, but there are a few other raucous tables of teenagers.

The hostess nods in the direction of a few sneeze-guard-covered warming tables. "Buffet's that way. Plates're there. Get you a new one each trip."

"Thank you, ma'am," I say.

Florence waits until she leaves. "*Thank you, ma'am,*" she says. Her eyes gleam with delight.

"I'm Southern."

"It's adorable!"

We make our way over to the warming tables and take plates.

"I'm so hungry I could eat . . . well, at an Olde Style Buffet," Florence says.

"I thought you loved this place."

"I thought so too. I think maybe I loved the one specific Olde Style Buffet with which I'm familiar and which I haven't eaten at since I quit dancing."

"I feel like a buffet shouldn't lean too hard into the 'olde' business," I say.

"Why?" Florence slops a heaping, gloppy scoop of traffic-cone-colored mac and cheese onto her plate.

I peel a slice of graying ham from atop a ham pile. "Well, because it's like 'hey we do things the way they did before they discovered germs and handwashing.'"

"I mean, it's honest at least?"

We fill our plates and sit.

Florence bites into a fried shrimp. "So many times when I was dancing I would have eaten through a stack of angora sweaters to get to a plate of buffet fried shrimp."

I finish a bite of soupy lasagna. "Con: the death of a dream. Pro: get to indulge in Olde Style Buffet shrimp. Seems like a fair trade."

Florence laughs.

"Sorry if that's a terrible joke."

"Nah, I like it when you show your sharp edges," Florence says. "Makes me less afraid to show mine."

We eat for a while without saying anything. I take a bite of a rib that tastes like it was cooked by being sat on for a long time on a bus and say, "Here we are again. Third time."

"Third time."

"This has now been the highlight of my year for three years."

"Mine too."

"I'm gonna miss it a lot."

"Same. But you know what? I bet there are a lot of highlights waiting for both of us in the years to come."

I hesitate to bring it up because I've been scared to. But I do anyway: "We haven't talked about college."

"No we haven't."

"Should . . . we?"

Florence prods her mac and cheese with her fork like she's checking it for signs of life while thinking. "Not yet," she says finally. "Until we do, as far we know, we're going to the same college, where we'll hang out like this every night. I love living in that space of possibility. If only for a few hours."

"You mean that?"

"About possibility?"

"About us hanging out every night."

"Of course."

"Not of course. We could have been texting every night until now. But you didn't want to."

Florence smiles ruefully. "This might shock you, but texting every night with me is not the recipe for happiness you might think. Ask Rafe."

"That's a risk I'd be willing to take," I say. "I wouldn't even need to check in with Rafe."

"You say that now."

"I say it any time."

"Wanna have a contest?"

"I suck at contests," I say.

"Huh, that's funny because I feel like you told me how you won a four-figure sum in a contest once."

"Oh, are you proposing a photo contest?"

"No."

"Then I stand by what I said."

Florence holds out her hands like she's holding an unseen box. "Here are the rules: we see who can create the most objectively disgusting dish from the buffet options available."

"Okay. What do I win?"

"Oooh cocky now! I like it! The loser has to do one thing of the winner's choice. Anything they say. How you like them stakes?"

I start to say how I like them better than the chicken-fried steaks here.

Florence cuts me off before I manage a word. "Don't say you

like them better than the steaks here or some other dad-joke shit. I won't have you sullying the Olde Style Buffet in such a manner."

"I was going to ask who judges," I lie.

"We do. Honor system."

"You trust me?"

"Completely. You trust me?" Florence asks.

"Sure."

"Let's do this. Cover your plate with a napkin. Absolutely no peeking before the unveiling."

We go to the buffet. I fill a dish with vanilla-chocolate swirl soft serve. I top it with hardboiled egg yolk crumbles from the salad bar and drizzle it all with cocktail sauce. I ring it with fried shrimp. I'm practically dry-heaving in my mouth by the time I reach our table, thinking about what I'm going to make Florence do. I might make her text me every single night for a year. I smile smugly at Florence, who's beaten me back to our booth and sits with a serene expression.

"You first," Florence says.

I whip the napkin off my dish. "I present . . . the shrimp cocktail sundae."

"Ugh, Jude, are those hardboiled egg crumbles?"

"Indeed they are."

"Well done, Wheeler. Sweetness combined with insectile creature is almost a riff on the cricket donuts of night one."

"Didn't even think of that. Your turn. Hope you came ready to play. This will be hard to beat."

"Yes it will. However—" Florence whips the napkin off her plate. It's covered in sushi rolls. They don't seem to have been adulterated in any way.

I stare at Florence's entry. "Did you make those?!"

"Nope. Got them from over there." She points at a table some distance separate from the warming tables. "And by the way, I win."

"What?! Hang on."

"No, Jude, I absolutely win."

"Hang on though. No artistry went into this. No authorship."

"You're veering dangerously into 'my kid could paint that' territory. Sometimes the creativity comes in knowing when something is already perfect and doesn't need to be messed with."

"Is that *ham* on one of the rolls?"

"And mayo. And Jude, look." She points. A long, curly black hair sticks out from one of the rolls.

"Oh man. Oh." My stomach does a quarter turn. I cover my mouth.

"Imagine slathering that roll—which has been sitting out for hours—in some soy and wasabi and feeling that hair in the back of your throat, just beyond your reach. Tickle tickle."

"Oh, Florence. Dude. No."

"Or stuck between your back molars."

"You gotta stop. I'm gonna yak."

"Do you concede?"

"I concede. You win. Can you—"

"Sure." Florence sets the plate on a table behind her, out of my view. "You're the color of the key lime pie they have on the dessert table. Want a piece?"

"I'm gonna need a minute."

"Remember: slow, deep breaths. While you recover, I'm gonna cash in my demand."

"Okay."

"Thanks for not making this more difficult than it needed to be."

"Sure," I say queasily. "I am nothing if not a man of honor."

"*Man of honor.*" Florence's eyes bring mine into their gravity. She looks suddenly serious. "I want you to go talk to a therapist, at least once, about your obsessive thoughts," she says quietly.

I can't help it. I smile at her. "I did," I say.

"I know it's weird, but think about my eyes. It's the way I am. But I still see a doctor for them. And look—maybe you'll see a therapist and they'll say there's nothing clinical going on. But then you're still talking to someone a little—"

"Florence."

"What?"

"I did. I talked to someone."

"Oh."

"Oh," I say, fondly.

"Are you telling me I found and presented this pube sushi for nothing?"

"Not nothing. You did almost make me vomit. That's a thing."

"How was it—"

"Almost vomiting? Not great."

"You didn't let me finish. Going to therapy."

"I'm on this medication now. It helps—I mean, I'm still kind of an anxious person. I think I'll probably always be an anxious person. But it's almost like I can get up above it now. I'm getting better at interrupting myself. I'm trying not to take my thoughts too seriously."

"That must be hard."

"Yeah. I'm still working on it. Getting my head right. But I . . . I don't know."

"What?"

"I don't know if it'll be a place I—I arrive at. Does that make sense? I'm still having some trouble with that idea. That some days are just going to be harder than others. That there's not, like, a destination."

"It is kind of sad. But also there's something kind of beautiful about it."

"You think?"

"Yeah."

"It's too bad."

"What is?"

"Can you imagine? If I hadn't already seen a therapist? *Vhat brings you to my office, Mr. Vheeler?*" I say in a German accent. "*Well, it all started with a piece of sushi with a pube in it,*" I say in my normal voice.

"That hair was too long to be a pube," Florence says.

"We probably don't need to analyze it any further."

"Okay."

"Hey, not to move on prematurely from the delightful topics of my crappy mental health and possibly non-pubes in buffet sushi, but what did Ravyn McHaven send you?"

"Oh! I didn't even check! Got distracted." Florence pulls out her phone. Her eyes widen. She covers her mouth with a little gasp.

"Florence?"

"Jude." She holds the screen toward me.

"I gotta be reading that wrong."

"I thought that at first." A two followed by a comma and three zeros, then a dot and two more zeros. "That's two thousand dollars."

"Is it a joke?"

"The note with it says, 'Karma for always being good tippers. Go have another Sunrise Night somewhere on me.'"

FLORENCE
HITCHING A RIDE, 11:20 P.M.

"Two thousand dollars."

"Two thousand dollars," Jude echoes. "I wonder how many Fart-Coins that is."

"A thousand bucks each."

We pay our bill at the register and drift outside.

"I sort of feel like I should put it toward college," Jude says. "But . . . I got a pretty big scholarship. If I have a job in the summers I can pay for the rest, easy."

"Yeah. My parents have a college fund for me. Which is a privilege, I know, and I feel weird about it—"

"Don't apologize for something nice your parents did for you."

"Okay. I won't."

"If we needed it, I'd say we should use it for school. But we don't, and—well, Ravyn said to go have another Sunrise Night."

He flops down on the warped bench by the entrance, and I sit down next to him.

"So this time next year?" I say.

"Where? We'll be too old for HAC," Jude says.

"Right, and anyway, I want us to be done with 'next year.' I want next week." I laugh a little. "I can't go on like an epic adventure to Six Flags or to the moon or whatever! I have to work."

"Work where? And wait—I don't even know where you're living right now. Like, do you realize how messed up that is? It's so messed up! Like, are you going back to San Francisco or Madison?"

"Madison. My mom's sabbatical is over, she moved back while

I was here. I was gonna see if the dance studio could let me teach the toddlers again, but—honestly I think it would bum me out. So I don't know. Maybe I'll scoop ice cream or something. Are you working?"

Jude's face shifts a little. "Yeah," he says.

"Wait. What's your job?"

"I've told you about my job."

"You haven't told me about your job."

"I take pictures," he says.

I raise my eyebrows. "Yes I do in fact know that. Who is paying you to take these pictures?"

"People."

"You do realize that not telling me is worse than telling me. Because honestly right now I am imagining you taking pictures of people's guinea pigs in, like, tiny tuxedos, against one of those mall photography laser light backgrounds—"

"Idomotherandbabyshoots." He says it really fast, like he's flinging it away from him.

"Oh my God." I can't mask my delight.

"Okay, I knew you were going to react like—"

"Oh my God, you photograph BABIES and you have never told me this before? Wait! How does this work? Do they wear little shoes?! Do you put the babies in like those pea pod outfits with little green mittens on and—JUDE."

He's laughing. "No it's a lot of young moms in white dresses in fields, holding like a little snoozing baby in a knit cap."

"Dads too?"

"Dads too, sometimes. Mostly moms."

"Do you have a go-to field? Like a field that you go to?"

"That's the same question twice."

"Jude, I need details. I am dying."

"I have my camera, and a little light bounce, if I need it. And a tripod. I advertise on Facebook. Are you happy?"

"I am so happy."

"Why do you love this so much?"

"You're my favorite person," I say. "I guess that's why." The air between us changes. "Okay I can still smell the fish from the buffet," I tell him, because all of a sudden I'm feeling shy. "Let's just hitchhike back to campus? Check-in's soon enough."

"Wait, what? Hitchhike?"

"Yeah. It's not a big deal, we're both old enough now."

"And we weren't last year? To hitchhike?"

"Well, you have to be eighteen."

"What? Is this actually happening?"

I pull out my phone. "I'll just put in for a ride. How have you never hitchhiked before?"

"Um. No? I have no desire to hitchhike. I don't wanna be axe murdered. I don't wanna be the subject of some weird grisly podcast that millennials listen to on their sad commutes."

"That was weirdly specific."

"I live my life by that motto. Don't do things that'll make you the subject of a podcast. Hitchhiking is one of them."

"Literally no one has ever died hitchhiking. There was a news article about it. It's the safest rideshare app out there."

"Wait, hold up. An app?" Jude looks at me quizzically.

I turn my phone to show him. "See? Even in Harbor City. Our

Hitchhike is—look, two minutes out."

"The name of that app," Jude says, "is cruel and misleading. App names should be an abstraction."

I grin at him. "I know. I kind of love it."

"Of course you do."

"How are we gonna spend this money, Jude?"

"We have the next four and a half hours to decide."

"I'm going to buy us both ponies."

We sit for a long minute.

"Is that it?" he asks. "The Ford SUV pulling up?"

"That's it."

The car has the little HITCHHIKE light in the window. Jude opens the back door for me.

"Sunrise Night?" the driver asks.

"Yup," Jude says. "Headed back to HAC."

"I saw, that's why I asked," he says, and he punches a button. The SUV is filled with pulsating disco lights. Donna Summer is blasting from—everywhere.

"WELCOME TO THE SECRET DISCO HITCHHIKE," the driver yells.

"Oh my God," I say.

"CONGRATULATIONS!" the driver yells. He's into yelling.

"I am so sorry."

"WHAT?" Jude says.

"I can't say it louder. I don't wanna offend—"

"WHAT? WHAT ARE YOU SAYING?"

"I THINK THIS IS THE BAD KIND OF HITCHHIK-ING," I shout back at him, as we tear out of the parking lot at high velocity.

JUDE
ODE TO SITTING TOO CLOSE IN A CAR

I want to sit too close
to you in this car,

our thighs rubbing
electric against each other,
separated only by thin
denim, our ravenous skin aching
to chew through and meet.

You smell like hot oil
and vanilla perfume
and a late summer night
humid with reckless decisions;
your body hums
against mine.

Who's kidding who.
I know you as hunger.

I want to devour you.

FLORENCE
THE QUIET GAME

There is no talking in the Disco Hitchhike. We learn this
quickly. In the backseat Jude holds up his phone and gestures
with his thumbs. *Text?* he mouths. When I put my number

into his contacts, I write FLORENCE 🗡
and I kind of feel like I'm taking off my clothes. I hit save,
pass it back. My screen lights up immediately. *This is weird,*

it reads. Then three dots. I watch his hands while he types.
Every five seconds his face is strobed pink, white, blue, green
and I think the driver is maybe trying to talk to us

but it's hard to tell over the Bee Gees. *Not weird,* I write.
It's just me. He smiles, head tipped down. *That's why. All the nights
I wanted to do this and I couldn't. I could text any other girl*

in the world. Just not you. The lights go white, white, white.
The driver is saying something about Lake Michigan in winter,
how rarely it freezes. The Bee Gees are telling us to dance

and when I write, *I like that you use punctuation,* Jude writes back,
Of course I do. Who do you think I am? I breathe, steady myself.
You're someone who wants to tell me secrets in the backseat of a taxi,

I tell him. *You're someone I might never see again after tonight.*

The music swells up high and loud, a giddy disco orchestra,
and Jude is reaching out his hand for mine. I fumble for his
    fingers,

intertwine. We don't let go. He's holding his screen at an angle,
    texting
with his left thumb, and my phone lights up. Says, *there are trains
    and buses*
and planes, Florence, says, *we're adults now and we get to make*

the call, says, *WE do, the two of us,* says, *I want to go back
to the dance building* and the taxi's pulled up in front of HAC
and the driver flicks off the music right when I turn and say out
    loud,

"why the dance building?" And Jude is hoarse when he says,
"because I think I need a do-over."

JUDE
DO-OVER

Name a sweeter grace
than the chance
to write a new and joyous
history into the leatherbound
volume of memory—I'll wait.

How often do you get to vanish
the red scar, un-dry the black ink,
stand at the tomb's mouth,
and call Lazarus to come hang.

I'm not taking inventory now
about all the ways I've been
unlucky in my life.

Right now I'm only thinking
of how I'm the luckiest
guy on earth.

It's midnight and I'm standing
in the blazing sun.

JUDE
WALKING TOWARD THE DANCE BUILDING, AND
MORE SPECIFICALLY ITS ELEVATORS, READY
FOR SECOND CHANCES, GHOST OF MICHAEL
FLATLEY BE DAMNED, EVEN THOUGH HE IS AS
ALIVE AS EVER, 12:06 A.M.

"That was our last first check-in," I say.

"Hey, that's true," Florence says.

"Makes me kinda sad."

"Aw."

"I know. I get sentimental about dumb stuff. Like you do not want to see how it destroys me to see an abandoned shoe by the roadside."

"On the contrary, there's maybe nothing I'd rather see?"

"Hey!"

"Jude! Hey!"

"Wanna hear something cool?"

"I always appreciate when I'm given the opportunity to avoid hearing something cool nonconsensually."

"And?"

"Tell me something cool."

"Let me see if I remember this right. Okay: light from Earth from forty-five hundred years ago has only traveled 4.5 percent of the way across our galaxy, so if you could teleport to a spot 4.5 percent of the way across our galaxy, you could see the pyramids being built."

"Wait." Florence shakes her head. "So—is it like the reverse of the light-from-dead-stars thing that every romantic person loves?"

"Exactly!"

"That *is* pretty cool."

"I memorized that fact specifically because I thought you'd like it."

"You're like one of those crows who befriends a human and then brings them gifts like cool rocks and little pieces of metal."

"Crows do that?!"

"I may have memorized *that* fact specifically because I thought *you'd* like it. I even knew you wouldn't mind being compared to a gift-giving crow."

"You were right."

FLORENCE
WHAT'S LYING AHEAD, 12:15 A.M.

At the dance building, I punch in the code to unlock the door.

"They're too lazy to change it. First time in the dance building in a year."

"You feel okay?"

"Yeah. I don't know. Maybe. This might be the last time I walk through here."

"You think?"

"When will I ever be here again?"

"You never know. You could come back and be a TA. Or straight-up teach here."

"Not dance."

"I don't think it's against the law for poets to be in the dance building."

"It feels illegal. God, it still smells the same in here. Whatever they use to clean the floors. That waxy smell. Kind of bleachy. Wow, I . . ."

"What?"

"Do you wanna go sit by the lake instead? Or—I bet the coffee shop is empty. The one that hates us. We could have a chess rematch."

"Florence."

"I'll let you win. You can checkmate me all you want."

We're standing at the elevator doors. Jude says, "You really don't want to be here, do you."

"I want to be here."

"That doesn't feel really true, though—"

"I want to be here with you. I don't want to be, like, seeing my own ghost."

"Teaming up with Michael Flatley's ghost?"

"Oh God, that would probably happen, huh?"

"I gotta think so. You two teaming up like Sherlock Holmes and Dr. Watson. Solving ghost mysteries. Anyway sorry. You were saying."

"I don't know. It's like, there I am, right around the corner, in a bun and a unitard. Ghost or real? Two years ago everyone in the dance program hated me. Did I ever tell you that? That's why I was sitting by myself at that first Sunrise Night, it wasn't because I, like, made that decision all on my own. Like I was too cool for everyone else. It was because they hated me, Jude. And I liked it. How messed up is that? They hated me because I was *good* and I knew it and I didn't, like, feed them some bullshit about how I was just lucky and that they'd get the lead next year. That's their problem. It's not my job to make someone else feel better about their own bullshit."

"I—"

"No one ever held my hand through it."

Jude reaches out and takes mine. I blink back the wet in my eyes.

"Sometimes I think dance made me a bad person," I tell him. "Or maybe I was one all along."

"Don't give me that."

"But—"

"I think you're competitive. That's all. You've always played to win. And now, instead of holding off the whole world with your big-ass sword, you've realized you're just playing against yourself."

"I don't know how to win that game."

"Me neither. I think you just say 'check' and hope for the best."

I laugh. "That seems like your solution to a lot of problems."

"Just keep lining 'em up, I'll keep knocking 'em down. I'm here all night."

"Just tonight?" I mean for the question to come out lightly, but it doesn't.

"I don't know."

We stare at the elevator panel, glowing in the dark.

"Up or down?" I ask, but he doesn't respond.

JUDE
GUARDRAILS

Ah, there you are, Intrusive Thought, Thief
of Joy, showing up
at just the right time like you
always used to. How I'd missed you
after mostly medicating you
into tranquility; after learning all manner
of wonderful coping mechanisms to wrestle
you into meek submission.

How nice to see you again, old friend,
Oh Intrusive Thought that this might be
the best things ever get. This moment;
this immaculate, snow-covered field of potential
without track or spot;

when I exist to Florence as someone
for whom she saves up factoids
about crows, like a crow gathering
shiny pieces of metal and buttons to offer
as gifts.

I don't get better than this.

Night one, we had Marley
as a guardrail. Night two,

it was Rafe. Now we're driving
ninety on a mountain road that falls
off into chasms on either side.

If my parents had walked away
from each other in this moment
they could have been unstained;
spared all of us the pain of watching
something beautiful go to rot like
the green-fuzzed clementine always lurking
at the bottom of the net bag.

If I had turned from Marley
at this point, there would have been
no bruise of humiliation, no heartbreak,
no bitter decline, and wouldn't that have been nice.

Sometimes I think I could live
in the pristine valley
between want and have.

The problem has never been
that I couldn't fall in love with
someone like Florence;

it's that I could.

JUDE
HESITATING, 12:21 A.M.

"Florence—"

"What's up?"

"Nothing."

"You sure?"

"Do you—"

"Do I?"

I pause for a long time.

"Do I what?" she asks again. "You seem like you want to say something."

FLORENCE
UNISON

I touch his shoulder. If I could
do it without breaking
open I'd touch

his face. How do I know
what he's thinking when I hardly
know myself? Our eyes meet,

drop. He laughs a little and
it's almost like something I can
hear, the tightness in my chest

unwinding. My heart like
a metronome, something
I could dance to, something

I could fit words to, something
for Jude, some reassurance. I don't
clamp down. I don't turn

away. It's almost too bright to look at,
this boy in the dark. *You have
me*, I murmur, not even sure

I want him to hear it, *no matter
what*, and when I reach for
the button, he beats me there.

JUDE
BACK ON TRACK, TOWARD MAKING WHAT MIGHT BE A BAD DECISION BUT AT PEACE WITH IT, 12:23 A.M.

We sit side by side in the dark, in the starlight glow of the button panel.

"We're back, Michael Flatley's Ghost," I say. "Come ask us to take vengeance on someone for you or whatever it is you do. What is it he does?"

Florence starts laughing. "I don't know, honestly."

"What, so he just like *appears* and then there's this really awkward moment where you try to have a conversation with a ghost with whom you probably have almost nothing in common? Be like *hey, if you're able to haunt movie theaters, the latest installment in the Marvel Cinematic Universe is supposed to be pretty good. And if it's not, you haven't wasted precious hours of life on it.*"

"I think I'd prefer a vengeful ghost to one who just wants to make small talk," Florence says.

"Same."

"Someday Michael Flatley really will die," Florence says, "and think how anticlimactic it'll be when he comes to haunt this elevator and everyone's like, 'yeah dude, we know. You've been haunting this elevator for like twenty years.'"

"Just absolutely stealing his thunder."

Florence lays her head on my shoulder with no special formality and a lock of her hair falls across my lips, and I think she might be able to hear my rising heartbeat, conducted up through the bones of my chest and shoulders.

"If you ever get a chance to teleport to 4.5 percent of the way across the galaxy, can I come with you?" she murmurs.

"Of course." My voice cracks a little bit and I curse my lack of cool when I most need it.

"Will you take pictures of the pyramids being built?"

"If you're there? All I'll want to do is hang out and talk with you."

JUDE
SEVENTH SENSE

I read somewhere once
that humans might have a sixth
sense, a sense of the spatial
relationship of the body.
This is why you can touch
the tip of your nose
perfectly in the dark.

Maybe there's a seventh
sense, where you can
find someone else's hand
perfectly in a dark elevator,
a hand you very much want
to hold, and you hold it.

FLORENCE
DO-OVERS, 12:25 A.M.

"Florence?"

"What?"

"Nothing."

I can feel his breath in my hair.

"Florence?" he asks again.

"What?"

"I—nothing."

"Nothing?"

"We should take the money," he says, "and go to Europe."

"Yeah?"

"Yeah."

"Okay," I tell him. "Let's go to Europe." I turn my head a little, tuck my nose against his neck. His skin is warm and smells like bonfire and dryer sheets.

"That easy? Kinda thought you were going to get after me for saying 'Europe.' Being so vague. Like, there's a big difference between going to Paris and going to, like . . ." He trails off. "Actually," he says, "I can't think of anyplace I wouldn't want to go with you."

"Even some cannibalistic Scandinavian village?"

"You saw that movie too, huh?"

"Yeah."

"I don't know. I feel like you'd look real pretty in a flower crown."

"And you in a bear suit. But we have to ask ourselves, is that really worth the human sacrifice?"

"Let's go," he says, and pulls away from me a little to look at me. "I'm serious, let's buy our tickets tonight. We'll go before we have to leave for college, we'll see Copenhagen and Barcelona and Athens, we'll buy, like, paper guidebooks and wear ugly American tennis shoes and—"

"Cameras around our necks?"

"Yeah," he says. "I'll make your picture in front of the Spanish Steps."

"Those are in Rome," I say. "Are we going to Rome too?"

"Yes. I'll make your picture in front of the Duomo."

"The Duomo?"

"It's in Florence."

I'm laughing now, helplessly. "I know," I tell him.

"Florence, I—"

FLORENCE
A DECISION

He's looking at my mouth
like I've just bitten into a strawberry.

If you can write down secrets you can't
say out loud, I wonder what you can show someone

in the dark. When he reaches out
for a strand of my hair and turns it a little

in his fingers, I let my eyes go shut.
I let the last three years lean me forward

and there he is, his lips are warm, I let
my arms go around his neck and breathe

him in. Hitch up a little, half-laugh,
is it okay if—and I'm not sure who says it,

him or me, but then I'm on his lap
looking down at him, smiling like I've won

the lottery, or like I've just learned
there's another Sunrise Night in front of us.

All mine, I say to him before I kiss him
again, but what I really mean is *ours.*

JUDE
CECI N'EST PAS UN POÈME

There's really no use
in writing a poem
about something
that's already poetry,
is there.

JUDE
BRIEFLY SURFACING FOR AIR, WHO THE HELL CARES O'CLOCK A.M.

"Hi," I say to Florence.

"Hi," she murmurs back. We're tangled up in each other; she's on my lap. Her hair is tousled like she's been standing in the wind and her lips are swollen. She touches the tip of my nose and goes *beep*.

"Oh shit, I need to—" I pull out my phone. "I gotta go break up with Marley."

"I'm gonna bite you right on the eyeball."

"You can't bite an eyeball. It's like trying to lick your elbow."

"Watch me." She leans forward, mouth wide, and clamps over my eye socket with her teeth. Her breath is hot. "*Rawr!*"

We dissolve into laughter.

"Okay, now try to lick your elbow," I say.

Florence tries. "I think I can—hang on. Still pretty flexible."

"Nope, that doesn't count."

"Hang on—one sec."

"Nope. Here. Allow me." I lick her elbow. "That's the only way your elbow can be licked. By a boy named Jude. You can't lick your own elbow. And if you have no boy named Jude, you're outta luck. No elbow licks for you."

"I wanna lick your elbow now so that we're even."

"You keeping score?"

"Always."

I offer her my elbow. "Go nuts."

She does. "Your elbow feels like a cat tongue," she says.

"Your tongue feels like a cat tongue."

"Are we the two grossest people on earth? Licking each other like cats and biting each other's eyeballs and fully making out in an elevator?"

"In front of Michael Flatley's Ghost no less," I say. "The Lord of the Dance."

"This has been really fun."

"Yeah, this is fun. I like doing this with you."

"I like doing this with *you*." Florence folds her arms and rests them on my chest. Then she rests her chin on her arms, with our noses almost touching.

I gently extend my neck so that our nose tips bump. "*Beep*," I say.

"Why are we here?"

"What do you mean?"

"How did we get here? From a completely random encounter in front of a fire to three years later, sitting in an elevator, having a brief pause in making out."

"Are we gonna make out some more?"

"Unless you have some objection."

"I do not."

"So how did we get here? Like what happened?"

"I honestly don't know. Like somewhere along the way I came down with a bad case of the Florences. It survived the years of silence. It caught fire again every time I saw you."

Florence looks at me for a second and then starts giggling. "Like a cold sore."

"*Florence*. How do you benefit from that comparison?!"

"*Sorry!* I did *not* intend for us to be a gross couple. But here we are."

"We're a couple?"

Florence looks at me and her eyes are soft in the spectral light of the elevator button panel. "Yeah, I think so," she says quietly. "I hope so."

"I think so too." I hope so. I trace the line of her upper lip with my finger.

"Sometimes I think the only things we're put on this earth for are to create art and make connections with the people we're supposed to connect with."

"Only? You say that like those aren't two huge things. Like maybe the two hugest."

"So many people don't believe that," Florence says.

"Yeah."

"The fact you do means we were supposed to connect."

"What do you think would've happened if I hadn't approached you that first night? Where would we be right now? I almost didn't, you know."

"Why?"

"I dunno. Didn't wanna look skeevy."

"I never thought you seemed skeevy. Too awkward."

I laugh. "Thanks?"

"I think if you hadn't approached me, we'd still be together tonight."

"How would that have worked?"

"No clue. But I think it would've. Somehow. Maybe we sit next to each other on a plane. Maybe we're reaching for the same box of cereal at the grocery store and our heads bonk with a comical hollow coconut sound. Who knows? But I think some people are supposed to get together, no matter what happens."

"I like imagining the inevitability of certain good things," I say.

"Especially when bad things seem so inevitable sometimes."

We're quiet for a while.

"While we're in the do-over business tonight, can we have a do-over?" Florence asks. "Of the thing you said earlier?"

"Which thing?"

"About how we ended up here. Because I really liked it and I want a chance to hear it without making a cold sore joke."

"Uh. I don't remember exactly what I said."

"I do. You said, *I came down with a bad case of the Florences.*"

"I came down with a bad case of the Florences."

"*It survived the years of silence.*"

"It survived the years of silence. Should I have my hand on a Bible?"

"Hush. *It caught fire each time I saw you.*"

"It caught fire each time I saw you." I let a moment or two pass for Florence to savor my (her?) do-over. "You have a good memory," I say.

"How do you know if you don't remember what you said?"

"Sounds like what I would have said."

"I have a good memory for things I enjoy hearing. Now ask me how we got here."

"Florence." I pull her closer. "How did we get here?" I kiss my way from the base of her neck to behind her ear.

She sighs. "I came down with a bad case of the Judes."

"And?" I drag my five-o'-clock-shadowed chin slowly down her neck and start over. I see gooseflesh rise on her arms.

"And it survived the years of silence." She sounds out of breath.

"And?" I start over.

"I forget the rest." She grabs my face and pulls my lips to hers and kisses me like there's something inside me she needs to survive.

FLORENCE
POSSIBLY CRIMINALS, ??? A.M.

"Florence?"

"Mmm."

"Florence?"

"Mmm?"

"Florence, honey, I—"

"Did you just call me honey?"

"Is that okay?"

"Yes. Do it again."

Jude laughs. "Honey," he says. "I think something is buzzing in your pocket."

"Oh."

"I think it's been buzzing for, like, ten minutes."

"Why didn't you tell me?" I ask him lazily.

"Because I'm pretty sure neither of us cared. But—"

I kiss him again. He puts his hands up in my hair and pulls me in.

Time passes.

A lot of time passes.

"Honey," he says, muffled. "Your phone."

"My phone. Wait! My phone! That's—"

I pull it out and show him the screen. 3:18 a.m. The alarm says, SECOND CHECK-IN 3AM.

Jude swears. "Nooooo," he says. "No. Uh-uh. Where's my shirt?"

"I'm sitting on it."

"Un-sit on it!"

"Oh God. Do I have, like, knots in my hair?"

"Your hair is pretty much one giant knot. Where is my shirt?"

"I thought I was sitting on it—I wasn't? Did Michael Flatley steal it away?"

Jude Wheeler, shirtless and panicked. I have never loved anything more.

"This is," he says, "not the time to take the name of the Lord of the Dance in vain, okay? We're late."

"We're *seniors*," I tell him. "We're not coming back. Camp ends in two hours. What are they going to do to us?"

He ignores me and turns on his phone flashlight. "There is no shirt in this elevator. Where," he says, "is my shirt."

"Come back and kiss me some more?"

"Oh my God, Florence, where is my shirt?"

"In the elevator shaft? On the moon? Like a flag, waving on the moon—"

"There is no wind on the moon."

I actually don't think that's true."

"What, you're a moon wind truther now? Where is my shirt? They could call our parents! They could dorm us! We could be dormed!"

"Dormed or *doomed?*"

"Do you really want to spend the last two hours we might ever have together in separate rooms while our RAs sit in front of our doors twirling the keys like they're the jailers in some Disney movie from hell?"

I stand up really fast. "Where is your *shirt?*"

3:22 A.M.

"I don't know how it ended up inside your pant leg," he says.

"Run faster!"

"Especially because you were *still wearing your pants.*"

"I'm magic," I say. "Or my pants are a black hole."

"Your pants are a black hole? Do you want to stick with that?"

"Jude—"

"Because there's a lot I could do with that."

"Do nothing. Do nothing but run."

"I don't know if I can. Why aren't you panting? Wait, you're panting!"

"I am not panting. I'm an athlete. Look, we're almost there."

"What are we going to do?" he asks. "They're going to, like, frog-march us away the second we get there."

I pull up short, and Jude does too. Bonfire is glowing, a two-minute desperate sprint away. "I don't know," I tell him. "Can't we just go back to the dance building and hide?"

"No. Remember? They call the cops if you're missing for more than an hour. It's the only way that Sunrise Night works, liability-wise."

"Oh my God, I'm going to have sex hair in my mugshot."

"Is it still sex hair if we didn't have sex?"

"Make-out hair just sounds weird."

"Fair."

"How much time do we have left before sunrise, anyway?" I ask him. "A few hours?"

"Yeah."

"Maybe we should just turn ourselves in."

"*What?*"

"We're going to go to Europe, right? In just a few weeks. And college—"

"You could be going to college in Antarctica for all I know!"

"I mean you could visit. Row a tiny little penguin boat out to see me."

"Not funny."

"A little funny."

"No."

"Jude—"

"No. Uh-uh. I am going to see the sunrise with you, dammit—"

"Jude—"

"*What?*"

"I think your shirt is on inside out."

JUDE
CUE *MISSION: IMPOSSIBLE* THEME, 3:27 A.M.

We arrive back at Bonfire just in time to see the counselor running check-in stuff a sheaf of papers in an NPR tote bag at her feet.

"Okay, okay," I say, running my fingers through my hair, catching my breath. "We need a plan. Gotta just—okay, those papers are probably the check-in list, right?"

"Seems likely."

"What if we were to get our hands on the list? We could throw it in the fire. No. Wait. Can't."

"Why?"

"Because, like, the list *does* serve a legit purpose. What if someone's in a white van somewhere being driven into the wilderness?"

"Good point."

"Think . . . think . . . okay. Here's what we gotta do."

"Tell me." Florence leans in.

"First step, we get our hands on the list. Maybe create a diversion of some kind?"

"I like it."

"Second step, we *replace* it with another bunch of papers while we have the list. If someone just sorta looks out of the corner of their eye, they won't notice it missing."

"Great."

"What step are we on? I'm so tired."

"Three."

"Yeah. Step three, we take the real list and forge the check-in time. How are your forgery skills?"

Florence makes a *so-so* motion with her hand.

"I think I can do it," I say.

"That photographer's eye of yours?"

"It'll work. Okay, step four: we return the real list and take back the decoy list. When they go to check the list an hour from check-in, there we are. Golden."

"I love it. We'll need at least a black pen and a blue pen, to cover our bases."

"Yes. If they use some weird color, we're probably boned."

"Probably."

"We'll have to risk it." I scan the small crowd of HACkers hanging out at Bonfire. "There's Marissa from my photography program. She's one of those people who always has everything in her backpack. I bet she'll have pens."

"Cool. Will she have paper? We need a decoy list."

"She—hey! Boom!" I point over at a campus newspaper dispenser. On top is a stack of flyers. I run over and grab the papers, then come back and hand them to Florence. "Do you think you can handle the diversion and swap?"

"Catlike reflexes, remember? In fact, I might even use a bobcat as a diversion."

"You have access to a bobcat?!"

"Jude, if I had access to a bobcat, do you think I would only now be mentioning it, under circumstances of duress?"

"Good point."

"Fictional bobcat."

"Right. Okay, we gotta make this happen. You good on the steps?"

"Yep. I'm creating a diversion and getting the list and swapping it for a fake list while you're getting pens. We meet back up. You forge the check-ins and we return the list and swap it back for the fake list."

I clap once. "Yes. That's it."

"Wait, am I handling the swap back?"

"I think that would be best."

"Got it."

We start in our different directions. I call back to her. "Florence?"

She turns.

"I believe in you," I say.

She nods firmly and our eyes meet. She raises a fist. We turn.

"Wait! Florence!"

She turns again.

"We didn't discuss the rendezvous point. Meet back at the fire?"

Two thumbs-up from Florence.

I approach Marissa and her friends. Between the three of them I come up with a black Sharpie, a blue gel pen, a black gel pen, and even a red ballpoint. We're going to pull this off. I hurry back to the fire and pace nervously until I see Florence walking briskly toward me, a sheaf of papers held to her chest so they can't be seen from behind. My heart races.

"You did it!" I whisper urgently.

"I sure did," she says.

"I got an assortment of pens," I say, giggling with excitement. "If we can't pull this off, we don't deserve to."

"No we don't."

"Okay, gimme the papers. I'll need a sec to examine the hand-writing."

"Here you go."

Florence hands me the stack of papers. I start leafing through them. "Florence."

"Yep."

"These are the flyers I gave you to use as the decoy list."

"Yep."

"What about the plan?"

"Oh, I just went back to the lady and explained that we were a little late and we were sorry and it was our last night at HAC and we'd deeply appreciate being able to watch the sunrise together because we didn't know when we'd get to see each other again and if we couldn't watch sunrise together we would experience trauma. She said it was cool. It helped that she was able to see you from where she was sitting. I pointed you out and told her you were pacing and hadn't come over to talk because you were so embarrassed and afraid of getting in trouble and you would find it triggering if you had to explain yourself. Do you remember where you got these flyers from, by the way? We should probably put them back, to be nice."

"Florence. You totally played along."

Florence cracks up, until her eyes brim with tears. "I couldn't not. I'm sorry," she tells me as she wipes her face. "You were entirely too cute. You were so excited about your adorable plan."

THOROUGHLY DEFLATED BUT IT'S FINE, BECAUSE WE'RE TOGETHER AND ANY DEFLATION IS MERELY TEMPORARY, 3:48 A.M.

"Hey, I prefer you crying this way on Sunrise Night than any other way," I say.

"Aw, you sweetie," Florence says. She interlaces her fingers with mine.

We're now holding hands as we amble aimlessly around the Quad. "I guess we're HAC official now?"

"HAC official. We'll be the talk of the camp for"—she looks at her phone—"maybe three more hours. Where to next, cowboy?"

"*Cowboy?*"

"Sailor? Flyboy? Tinker Tailor Soldier Spy?"

"I'm still a little sensitive about 'spy.'"

"Understandable. We could go back to the elevator," Florence says with a sly smile.

"We *could*, but we both know what we'd do there."

"I mean *anything* could happen."

"Anything *could*, but anything *won't*. One Very Specific Thing will happen."

Florence shrugs. "What happens, happens."

"Listen, I love the Very Specific Thing. Lord knows. But there's only one thing on this earth I love more, and that's talking with you and time is running out for that."

Florence's smile broadens and her grip on my hand tightens. "Okay, you passed."

"Was that a test?"

"Maybe."

"Because you seemed awfully sincere."

Florence stops us and faces me. "Gimme another taste of the Very Specific Thing."

"If this is a test—"

"It's not."

"Because if it is, I'm about to fail."

"Fail, then."

We do the Very Specific Thing, whispering onlookers be damned.

"Okay," Florence says. "Where to for real?"

I think for a moment. "I got it," I say.

"Yeah?"

"Yeah, but let's get some big beefy rock boys first because I don't have a bellyful of Ravyn's anarchist coffee fueling me this year."

"Big beefy . . ."

"You don't remember? It's what you called Mountain Dews."

"I *did*? I don't remember that. And would it be Mountains Dew?"

"Let's say that it is, just so we can live in a world where it's 'Mountains Dew.'"

We pull dripping Mountain Dews (Mountains Dew?) from a Yeti cooler and crack them open.

I lead us to a spot a little ways from the coolers. "Remember?"

"Was this where we took a nap together on our first Sunrise Night?"

"Nailed it. I watched you sleep that night."

"I watched *you* sleep!"

"What? When?"

"I woke up a couple times and creeped on you. When did you watch me?"

"Right at the beginning, when you first fell asleep, before I did."

I sit cross-legged on the cool grass. Florence sits and then lies back, resting her head in my lap, her blond hair splayed across my thighs. I pull a piece through my fingers, again and again, feeling its satininess on my fingertips.

"It's a good star night," Florence murmurs.

Minutes drip by like warm honey. We talk for a while and then the world becomes very quiet and, catching me very much unaware, a swell of sadness rises in me, too big for me to contain.

"Florence," I say quietly.

"Jude."

"Should this be the last night we talk?"

Florence pauses for a long time as though waiting for me to say something else. "What, like forever?"

"Um. I don't know. Maybe. Yeah."

"What about Europe?"

"Maybe after Europe."

Florence sits up abruptly and turns to face me. She looks at me with hurt-filled eyes. "Why are you saying this?"

"I—I'm really scared."

"If this is a joke it's a really bad one."

"No, it's not."

"If it's—revenge, it's worse."

"It's not!"

"So what are you scared of?"

I hold on to the silence like I'm holding my breath underwater, and I finally have to surface. "Of loving you. You're someone I could love."

I expect Florence to flip out but she doesn't.

"Why would that make you afraid?" she asks quietly. She tugs at a piece of grass.

"Because love doesn't seem to survive around me."

FLORENCE
THE TRUTH, 4:02 A.M.

"Jude."

"No, don't try to convince me, I—I've been the one living my life. You know? I'm the expert on what's happened to me."

"Do you think Marley ever loved you?"

"What?"

"Marley. Did she love you?"

"No. No, I don't think she ever did."

"There you go."

"If you're trying to make a point about my lovability, Florence, I hate to tell you this but—"

"She never *stopped* loving you. She wasn't capable of it in the first place."

"But my parents—"

"Both still love you. A hell of a lot. Even if your dad expresses it by pretending you two are in a Will Ferrell movie or something."

He looks exhausted all of a sudden.

"And then, of course, you aren't counting *me*. Which I'm personally pretty offended by," I say.

"You?" he asks.

"Yeah. Me. Do you realize—I've known you for a handful of nights, this small little collection of hours up here in the northern end of nowhere. These three nights that just . . . rippled outward into everything else. These three nights that, like, flooded me. Took me over. I broke up with my boyfriend. I moved to San Francisco, I was so heartsick over you. Over dance. I started writing *poetry*. One morning this winter in California I woke up from a dream where we were playing chess, in a snowstorm, and then I cried for a solid hour before school."

"This all sounds like stuff I did wrong," he says, quietly.

"How? I was crying because I wanted to be with you, and I wasn't. And it was because I was too proud to get your number and clear up what turned out to be the world's most basic misunderstanding. All I did was think about talking to you. I daydreamed about it like it was a book I could slip into. And then I'd wonder if it was something I'd built up in my head, something impossible to live up to, and now here we are, talking all night, and it's somehow better than the imagining. Tonight I feel like I could pretty much walk across Lake Michigan. I could ride the elevator for another four hours. I could take every single person who made you feel unlovable and tie them together into one giant-like rat king, and let them rat their way together around the darkest pits of hell. You are lovable, Jude Wheeler, and I should know it, because I love you more than I love anything else."

"Oh."

"More than I loved dancing. I love you that much."

"Hey," he says. "Hey, don't cry."

"I'm not."

"You're crying a little bit."

I sniffle. "I'm not crying, *you're* crying."

"I mean I sort of should be. Because I'm scared as hell."

"I'm not that scary. Am I?" I ask.

"The only thing that scares me is that I love you too. And I don't want to lose that, Florence. I think it would break me."

"One: I don't want you to ever think that I would hurt you on purpose, but two: I don't think anything could break you. You see too much beauty in the world to let it take you out. The world is, like, incapable of shaking you down for your lunch money."

"The world's just a big old bully, huh."

"Sometimes it feels like it. When I think about how it's already tomorrow."

His eyes are shining. "And then we have to go back to the in-between," he says. "Those days in-between. I don't want to go back there, without you."

"What about Vienna?"

"That's not just a pipe dream?"

"You have your passport?"

"Yeah. My dad took me trout fishing in Canada a few years ago. You have a passport too?"

"Yup."

"And it's up to date?"

"Yup."

"Oh man," he says. "So . . . Vienna."

"I mean, we can't let Ravyn McHaven down."

"Right."

"That's the most important thing to consider here."

"Florence—"

"I can't let *you* down," I tell him, fiercely. "And I won't. Not ever."

"I know," he says, and we sit there like that for a minute until he tugs me down on the grass. I put my head on his shoulder, and after a minute, he pulls up a flight app on his phone. It takes a little time, because we book the train rides between cities too, but there it is:

Rome, and Vienna, and Paris, and Barcelona.

FLORENCE
REJOICING IN MY FIRST SUCCESSFUL FORAY INTO TRAVEL AGENTDOM, 5:42 A.M.

"I've never spent that much money in my life," I tell him.

"I know. I feel like I'm going to have a nosebleed."

"A nosebleed of *joy*."

"I keep picturing you writing poems over there," he says. "Looking out the window at the Alps, when we're on the train between cities. Even if it's a night train. I bet the Alps are white and snowy enough to see in the dark."

"And you can make pictures. Make a record."

"Some place we can return to."

"A place we've invented. That exists between the two of us."

"Yeah," he says. "Someplace to keep in our heads."

"That's what I want."

He kisses me. "And you said you wanna find hostels to stay at? When we get there?"

"We'll meet people that way, right?" I ask him.

"I don't think we can avoid it. Like sixteen people to a room, in bunk beds. You, like, keep your stuff in a locker."

"Cool."

"Really?"

"Not cool?"

"I don't know. Sometimes I feel like I . . . need to be in control of my space."

"Then we'll get cheap rooms at cheap hotels, so it'll just be us. I mean, I have a few hundred dollars in graduation money from my family, I can make up the difference—what?"

"A week with you, alone, in hotel rooms, in Europe, alone?"

"Yeah?"

"Alone?"

"Say alone again."

"Well, now I'm a different kind of nervous," he says.

"Would it help if we just stayed in elevators instead?"

"Probably. I feel bad about this. I don't wanna have to use your graduation money just because I'm . . . who I am."

"I love who you are. And it's not a big deal. Really. I was planning on stashing it away because I want to study in Italy my junior year at Brown, but now we're basically doing that, so."

"Brown?" Jude asks.

"Crap." I slap my forehead.

"What, are we doing a free association exercise here? Okay, yellow—banana. *Brown?* Brown *University?*"

"Oh crap."

"Florence—"

"Sorry—I didn't mean to blow the big reveal! It just slipped out because I'm so tired. We can go back to pretending we're going to be doing college in a submarine in Lake Superior or something."

"Where is Brown University? That's Ivy League, right? New England? Because—" There's a tremor in Jude's voice.

"It's in Providence."

"Rhode Island? Or heaven?"

"Rhode Island," I tell him, laughing. "You look like a kid from one of those videos where a dad comes home from the army and surprises the kid at his grade school or whatever."

Jude raises his index finger. "Can you pardon me for a sec?" He walks a few steps toward the water, throws back his head, and whoops, the cords on his neck sticking out.

I giggle and join him, whooping also. "Why are we whoopin' and hollerin'?"

Jude turns to me, his eyes ablaze. "My dear Florence. We are whoopin' and hollerin' because of a piece of information that I currently possess but which you do not yet."

"Why are you talking like a magician? Tell me, dork."

"I warn you that coming into possession of this piece of information may move you to spontaneous whoopin' and hollerin', as it did me."

"I already engaged in spontaneous whoopin' and hollerin'. Tell me. Are you drawing this out to make up for my lack of ceremony in revealing where I'm going to school?"

Jude holds both my hands. "I'm going to the Rhode Island School of Design."

I immediately go dizzy with equal parts exhaustion and exhilaration. "That . . . sounds like it's located in Rhode Island."

"It's in Providence."

"Jude."

"Yes."

"Brown is in Providence."

"I recall learning that recently."

"The state of Rhode Island is not large."

"I'm told it's actually the *smallest* state."

"So it stands to reason that Providence is not large."

"That stands to reason."

We pull out our phones with shaking hands.

"We'll be like three blocks apart," Jude says, and he turns to cup my face. "Do you know what this means?"

"What does this mean?" I ask, but I know the answer.

"I get to keep you," he says. "I get to keep you through tomorrow. And the tomorrow after Europe. And the tomorrows after that. If that's what you want."

"I want," I tell him. "I want. Can you excuse me for a second?" I step to the edge of the water, take a deep breath, and raise an ecstatic scream across Lake Michigan. Jude joins me until our throats are raw and our ears ring.

"If I saw a coincidence like this in a movie, I would roll my eyes so hard," I say.

"Same, but in real life I have no objections," Jude says. "Hey, guess what else I realized!"

"What?"

"We haven't made our annual photo of you yet!"

"I don't think I can replicate the dance pose from the first night. Balance's too wonky."

Jude pulls out his phone, opens the camera, and scans around with his eyes. "No worries. Lemme think—"

"I got this," I say. I grab his phone, extend my hand to arm's length, pull him to me, and take a selfie of me kissing him on the cheek, my blond hair windswept across my face. "I'm no award-winning photographer like you, but that should work."

Jude looks at the photo—and the expression of unbridled joy he wears. "Yeah," he murmurs. "That's gonna work."

Then we hug, tight, until I feel Jude looking up over my shoulder.

"Is that the sunrise?" I ask.

"Yeah," he says. "I think it is."

JUDE
ONE MORE FOR THE ROAD

And while your gaze is fixed
on the horizon, you're a silhouette
against the brightening sky, shadowed like you were
before the fire that first night, and once more,
while you're not looking,

I take the picture.

You say you can't dance
like you used to, but everything you do
is a dance to me.

JUDE
SUNRISE NIGHTS

I looked for you three times
in the dark; once without knowing
your name. Now here we are,

watching the sun rise. I'm holding
your hand in the quiet, stretched
like a silk thread before
dawn blooms. You make me believe

the great machinery of days turns
with single purpose
toward our joy. Once

during the silent hours,
when I needed to drown
out the drum of my own
heartbeat, I looked up

the meaning of your name.
Florence, meaning *flourishing*; Florence,
meaning *blossoming*; Florence,
meaning *flowering*. These summer days,

these Sunrise Nights, they hold
a richness: maybe we were born

to this inheritance of chance love. We find
who we can't be without.

FLORENCE
ANSWERS

I'm not good at the present. Tense
or otherwise. I'm always looking for the catch,
the mistake in my past that set me

up for whatever fall I'm about to take.
It's a pattern of thinking, one that's hard
to break. I used to think that growing up

meant a skirt suit, or a mortgage, or a harder
shell between me and the world. That I'd go bulletproof,
that I'd know too much to ever be hurt. Forward

and back. Forward and back. Never the now. Even
now, on the shoreline, the tide tries to tug me away
and I let it, I let myself in to what I'm feeling, I feel

like I'm standing on the edge of something

beautiful. I feel like I might break open
and spill out into stars. I feel like the soft palm
of dawn rising up over the water. I feel Jude

beside me like the end of my next thought,
something I can tell him and so make it whole.
The two of us, a story. Better than any book. I feel like

we should walk around all night and talk about it.

ACKNOWLEDGMENTS

Thanks to Alex Cooper, our brilliant editor, for being a champion of this book. You are the absolute best. Thanks to Allison Weintraub for all her time and care. Thank you to Rosemary Brosnan for believing in this project. Thank you to Shona McCarthy, Mark Rifkin, Laura Mock, and David Curtis; to Lisa Calcasola and Audrey Diestelkamp; and to Patty Rosati and her team. And thanks, too, to Hokyoung Kim for the beautiful cover illustration. Endless thanks to our wonderful agents, Taylor Haggerty and Charlie Olsen. You are the best, for your work on this and all our previous projects.

Thanks to Emily Henry (for everything and also for letting us make you an Easter egg), David Arnold, Margarita Engle, Amber McBride, Jennifer Niven, and Jasmine Warga. Your support means the world. Thank you.

Brittany would like to thank: Emily Temple, Kit Williamson, and Joe Sacksteder; Mackenzi Lee, justin a. reynolds, and Riognach Robinson (sixteen hundred dollars!); my wonderful Interlochen colleagues; and my family, for all their love and care. Thank you to Andrew (and Daisy and Felix and Kitty), endlessly. And thank you to Northwestern CTD, whose sunrise night traditions helped to inspire this book, and to my Interlochen students, who inspire me every day.

Jeff would like to thank: Kerry Kletter, who, as always, keeps me sane while being forever my North Star of brilliant writer and incredible human and BFF.

Thank you to Tennessee Teen Rock Camp and Southern Girls Rock Camp, whose tradition of putting smart, creative kids in contact with each other helped to inspire this book.

Thank you to Greg and Bowie, my dogs, who have taught me that it is enough to pass a quick life as a giver and receiver of love. I try to always remember this when writing stories.

Thank you to everyone who made me believe I could write poetry—especially Ocean Vuong, Ruth Awad, and my coauthor. If you hadn't come up with the idea that we write this together, I would never have presumed to suggest a poetry collaboration with a poet of your caliber.

Finally, thank you to Tennessee Zentner, who offered me, while writing Jude, a live-in model of a brilliant, sensitive, funny, talented, spirited, creative, handsome young man. And thank you to my beautiful Sara. I found who I couldn't be without. Every love story is for you. I couldn't do this job without your love and support. I love you and Tennessee more than words can say, but I'll keep trying.